"I'm not afraid of you!" I said . . .

But my voice was only a croak and my throat was so dry I could hardly swallow. I tried to pull away, but his fingers tightened, only pulling me closer again. His eyes burned into mine.

"Answer me," he said quietly, shaking me slightly as he spoke. "What have you been told to make you so frightened? Have they told you I'm a murderer? A womanizer?" His voice dropped to a soft whisper and his lips had moved closer to my ear. I was shaking, trembling from head to toe as his hands went to my head. His fingers tangled themselves in my hair, and as I looked into his catlike eyes I saw the desire burning there.

I watched, fascinated, as he slowly lowered his head and crushed my mouth with his. I had never been kissed by a man, and the taste and feel of him was shocking. This was not the gentle, innocent love I'd read about in fairy-tales. As he kissed me, I felt his hands leave my hair and move to caress my shoulders and arms. I slowly slid my arms around his waist and moved even closer, reveling in the feel of him and the taste of his mouth against mine.

"I'm not afraid of you," I said again.

"You should be," he said hoarsely. "If you've any sense at all, girl, you will run from me like the very devil!"

ROMANTIC SUSPENSE WITH ZEBRA'S GOTHICS

THE SWIRLING MISTS OF CORNWALL   (2924, $3.95)
by Patricia Werner

Rhionna Fowley ignored her dying father's plea that she never return to his ancestral homeland of Cornwall. Yet as her ship faltered off the rugged Cornish coast, she wondered if her journey would indeed be cursed.

Shipwrecked and delirious, Rhionna found herself in a castle high above the roiling sea — and in thrall to the handsome and mysterious Lord Geoffrey Rhyweth. But fear and suspicion were all around: Geoffrey's midnight prowling, the hushed whispers of the townspeople, women disappearing from the village. She knew she had to flee, for soon it would be too late.

THE STOLEN BRIDE OF GLENGARRA CASTLE   (3125, $3.95)
by Anne Knoll

Returning home after being in care of her aunt, Elly Kincaid found herself a stranger in her own home. Her father was a ghost of himself after the death of Elly's mother, her brother was bitter and violent, her childhood sweetheart suddenly hostile.

Elly agreed to meet the man her brother Hugh wanted her to marry. While drawn to the brooding, intense Gavan Mitchell, Elly was determined to ignore his whispered threats of ghosts and banshees. But she could *not* ignore the wailing sounds from the tower. Someone was trying to terrify her, to sap her strength, to draw her into the strange nightmare.

THE LOST DUCHESS OF GREYDEN CASTLE   (3046, $3.95)
by Nina Coombs Pykare

Vanessa never thought she'd be a duchess; only in her dreams could she be the wife of Richard, Duke of Greyden, the man who married her headstrong sister, Caroline. But one year after Caroline's violent and mysterious death, Richard proposed and took her to his castle in Cornwall.

Her dreams had come true, but they quickly turned to *nightmares*. Why had Richard never told her he had a twin brother who hated him? Why did Richard's sister shun her? Why was she not allowed to go to the North Tower? Soon the truth became clear: everyone there had reason to kill Caroline, and now someone was after *her.* But which one?

CLARA WIMBERLY

THE GHOSTLY SCREAMS OF STORMHAVEN

ZEBRA BOOKS
KENSINGTON PUBLISHING CORP.

"A sister is loved for many things;
For friendship most of all."

To my sister Janice, with whom I've
visited "Stormhaven" many times.

ZEBRA BOOKS

are published by

Kensington Publishing Corp.
475 Park Avenue South
New York, NY 10016

First printing: June, 1992

Printed in the United States of America

No one ever keeps a secret so well as a child.

Victor Hugo, Les Misérables

Chapter One

I shall never forget the day I first saw the beautiful chateau called Stormhaven. It was a perfect spring day in April of 1895, the kind of day that one waits for throughout the long, frigid winters of the Appalachian Mountains.

But that day I hardly noticed the beauty around me, for I was despondent at leaving my family for the first time. Leaving my mother, my two younger brothers, and a younger sister. It was a sad, beautiful day, a day that would lead to events changing my quiet, simple life forever.

Ours was a poor family, sometimes having barely enough money to clothe and feed us all. And had it not been for the generosity of the Blakely family, my mother's employers, I am not sure how we would have survived some of those cold, bitter winters in the mountains of north Georgia.

It had been ten years since Father had abandoned us. I was nine years old then and hardly aware of the problems that sometimes exist between a husband and wife. So I never really knew why he let us believe he was going to his job in the copper mines that day when all along he was planning to leave us forever. Of course mother knew why; she must have. But she never explained, even though I probably asked a hundred times when Daddy was coming home. She seemed more concerned that he had taken the last bit of money she had hidden in the sugar jar in the kitchen cupboard. My mother often said bitterly that the birth of my baby sister a few months earlier was just too much a burden for a man to carry. Four children would be a burden to anyone, she'd say. That was the only explanation she ever offered, and finally I stopped asking.

It was terribly hard those first few months without him. But as soon as Mother was able, she took a job as cook on the large Blakely estate just outside our small town of McCaysville, Georgia.

The Blakelys were wealthy, but they were also kind, Christian people with small children of their own. And they seemed touched by our unfortunate circumstances. So we were treated differently from the other servant families and furnished a small dwelling just down the road from the big house. It did not bother me at all that it was only a tenant's structure.

I can remember, even as a girl, feeling such a rush of relief that we no longer had to worry about being without a home or without enough food for the younger children. I'm not certain why Mother never felt the same gratitude toward the Blakelys that I felt. For even though she was a loyal and dutiful employee, I sensed that she never really liked them, even resented them, in fact, and rarely had a kind word to say about them in the privacy of our home.

Perhaps it was because my mother had grown hard and bitter; even I could see that. Not that she had ever been a loving or affectionate woman to her family. Even when Father was home, she was often cold and distant; her most likely expression was one of anger.

But I learned to live with that somehow. And I think the Blakelys were partly responsible for my acceptance of her coldness as well as the few good things about my young life.

Even though Mother resented it, they insisted that I study with their children and their tutor. And when my

8

two brothers and young sister were old enough, they also were given the same opportunity. But for me, it saved my life . . . gave me something to hope for, to look forward to even when life at home was bleak and lonely.

And the books . . . oh, I shall never forget the books. Hundreds of them just waiting for my eager hands to pull them from the shelves in the library and discover all the wonderful places they would take me. Even if they ruined my eyes, as Mother declared, I could never give up my beloved books. Not even when she complained about the added expense of the reading glasses which I needed as I grew older.

How could I make her understand that I would have risked going blind before I would stop reading? It was the one thing that could make me forget who I was and that all I could ever expect in my future was a sad, poor existence like my mother's.

Suddenly in the autumn I turned nineteen Mother declared it was time for me to be on my own. Where I was to find employment in our small community I had no idea.

When Mrs. Blakely told us about an acquaintance who needed household servants on his large estate in the mountains of North Carolina, I felt a sense of panic. For even as cold and unloving as my mother was, I could not imagine leaving her nor my little brothers Henry and James. And how could I possibly leave my darling little sister Angelina, the brightest and most beautiful of us all? She was almost ten now and I could not bear the thought of her being without me to protect her or to comfort her when Mother was angry and neglectful.

Nevertheless, Mother had insisted, and finally I packed my few meager belongings and sadly boarded the train to North Carolina. I had no idea what position I would be given. Mrs. Blakely hoped that with my education I might be employed as a governess, but that position was already taken. Mother declared that I must accept whatever else was offered.

As I stepped down from the train that spring morning, I must have been very easy to spot in my worn, shabby gray serge suit, for the driver who sat waiting in a fine black carriage stepped down and came directly toward me.

"You be Miss Elizabeth Stevens, a new employee at Stormhaven?" His English accent was very pronounced.

"I . . . I am," I managed.

The man was dressed in the colorful livery of a coachman, something I had never seen except in pictures. Not even the Blakely help wore such bright, elegant clothes. This gentleman's maroon jacket and black pants with a maroon stripe were much finer than anything I'd ever hoped to own.

He was an older man, perhaps fifty, and underneath his cap I could see that his short hair was almost completely gray, as was the large, bushy mustache he wore. His cheeks were round and jolly, a dark, ruddy color, as if he were often in the sun. And he had the fairest blue eyes I thought I'd ever seen. His accent was also something I'd never heard before in our isolated part of the country. I was immediately fascinated by the man.

He took my one worn bag and placed it in the carriage, then turned to help me step up to the back seat.

"I'm sorry we'll have to wait a bit, miss," he said politely. "But there's one other passenger who will be arriving on the westbound train in about fifteen minutes."

"That's fine," I said, settling myself into the soft velvet seat to wait.

The gentleman stood by the open door of the carriage. "She'll be a new employee at Stormhaven, just like you, miss," he said, smiling kindly at me.

"Oh, I see," I said, nodding at him and wondering if she knew any more than I did about what our jobs would be. We probably both would be maids, I expected. Even with my extensive tutoring, I felt I was not qualified for anything else.

I looked around me and breathed deeply of the fresh pine-scented air. It seemed odd there should be a busy train station here among the whispering pines. The city was a small haven tucked in the middle of the surrounding ring of haze-covered mountains.

The few minutes passed quickly as I spent the time gazing about at the people who passed by and those boarding trains. I noted the elegance of their dress and daydreamed about what great adventure they might be beginning. For once I had no one to scold me about my whimsical imagination.

Finally I saw the coachman straighten and peer toward the train and the people who were getting off. A young woman came walking toward us with baggages in both hands that seemed to weigh her down and cause her to walk with an odd straight-legged gait.

The jolly-faced man beside the coach went immediately to her and took the bags, depositing them easily with mine in the back of the coach.

I could hear the girl's chatter before she ever reached us. Her face was bright with a big happy grin. She was plump and round, with a small waist and full hips. Her dress of brown poplin was not much better looking than mine, but it did not seem to bother her at all. She was a pretty girl in a healthy, wholesome-looking way, with auburn hair that curled in wisps about her head and face.

"Hullo!" she said as she gathered her faded brown skirts about her and fairly leapt into the carriage beside me. Her green eyes sparkled at me with genuine friendliness.

The gentleman in the colorful livery seemed taken aback for a moment, as he had been in the process of helping her into the conveyance. Then he shook his head and chuckled softly as he walked to the front to climb into the driver's seat.

"I'm Dorothy Magee," the girl said with a smile. "But everyone calls me Dottie."

"How do you do?" I replied. "My name is Elizabeth Stevens."

"Hello, Lizzie! Are you as excited as me?" she asked, shrugging her shoulders in delight. "I mean, goin' to Master Vanderworth's palace and all?"

"Palace?" I asked, puzzled by her choice of words.

The coach pulled away with a slight jerk and then we settled back for the long ride to the house. "Sure, 'tis monstrous, they say. Big as a palace in England, and more beautiful than any other house in America." Her eyes were shining with anticipation and she could hardly keep herself still. I had to admit her enthusiasm was contagious.

"Well, I . . . I am not familiar with Mr. Vanderworth, nor had I ever heard of Stormhaven until I came here. My employment was arranged by someone else . . . a friend."

"Oh? Well, ye're in for a treat! That ya are, 'Lizabeth. They say there ain't no place you've ever seen like Stormhaven."

Her face was radiant with expectation, and she finally moved back in her seat and turned to look out the window as we drove past houses and a large brownstone church.

I, too, looked about at the city. It was not very big, not much bigger than McCaysville, actually. But there was an energy here, a hustle and bustle that I was not used to at home. And I found myself smiling because I liked it very much.

The large wheels of the carriage rattled heavily across railroad tracks and bricked roadways. Then we slowed as we made a turn. Ahead of us there appeared a line of huge trees where the forest began and the city fell away behind us.

Inside the forest it was quiet and still, all the noises left behind. It was as if we'd entered another world. The trees were so thick and large that they formed a great canopy above us. I imagined our coach must look very small and insignificant as we rode into the darkened, still woods.

"Gor," Dottie whispered. "Ain't it lovely?"

"I've never seen anything quite like it," I admitted, fascinated by every towering tree, every exotic flower, every blade of grass I saw.

And like Dottie, I felt the excitement growing inside me. Nothing in my imagination could have prepared me for this. I grew up in the wilderness, in the rugged, beautiful mountains of Georgia, so I was used to such forested splendor. But I could immediately see the difference here. This whole forest, at least that near the roadside, was cultivated for breathtaking beauty. Rhododendrons and azaleas lit the dark forest with their pink and purple blooms and had been placed at exactly the right spot, it seemed, for the traveler's enjoyment. Small ponds sat still and unrippled, while reflections of azaleas and masses of daffodil were mirrored in their quiet green depths. We crossed small bridges made of brown or gray stone and curved with simple, elegant designs. I wondered if even the songbirds whose voices trilled and echoed about us had been placed here for effect. It was quite the most beautiful, impressive sight I'd ever seen, like the heart-stirring storybook images of a fairy-tale.

Dottie had quieted, her enthusiasm now coming only from her large green eyes and the sigh that fell silently from her round pink lips.

But we soon found that this was no short ride to be seen and quickly done. It went on for several miles, with every foot of the way filled with more breathtaking splendor, until finally I began to grasp the magnitude of Mr. Vanderworth's wealth. And I found myself on the edge of my seat, waiting with bated breath to see this palace called Stormhaven.

Chapter Two

A doe stood at the edge of the forest as we passed. Two small spotted fawns with her lifted their heads and with huge, dark eyes peered at the carriage, but they made no effort to run away.

Dottie squealed quietly and clasped her hands with enchantment as several peacocks paraded across the sandy road in front of us. Their exquisite feathers were fanned proudly behind them as they strutted and preened, displaying iridescent colors of turquoise and blue, brown and gold.

I sensed we were drawing nearer the house. Quickly I unhooked the wire-rimmed glasses from around my ears and took a handkerchief from my pocket. I cleaned the glass lenses carefully before placing them back on. Dottie watched me from the corner of her eye.

"You look mighty young to be wearin' spectacles," she said.

"Oh . . . well, I suppose I am," I said, always self-conscious about my glasses. "But I've always loved to read, and my mother says it has ruined my eyes."

"Readin' sounds horrid to me," she said. "I never learned to read, myself."

"Oh, no," I said quickly. "It isn't horrid or boring. Not at all. Reading can take you away to other countries, exotic places we only dream about. It can even make you believe for a while you are someone else."

14

"Gosh, and why would I be wantin' to do that?" she said with a puzzled look. "I'm perfectly content just bein' who I am."

I smiled at her, for I could see that what she said was true. I suppose I never realized that some people could be so content with themselves, born almost with an innate self-confidence and acceptance that some of us never seem to find.

I turned my attention back to the road as it twisted and turned. Through the trees ahead we began to see a glimpse of open country and azure sky. Then came a flash of white and blue as the big house moved in and out of our vision through the trees.

The carriage slowed as two footmen ahead swung wide a tall, enormously heavy-looking iron gate. It was trimmed with bright spikes that gleamed a bright gold in the mid-morning sun.

Then, as we turned past the line of trees and the gate there, it was before us . . . the most stunning and exciting picture I'd ever seen! Stormhaven, a mastery of architecture, as huge as a castle indeed, and with pinnacled spires and flags and pitched roofs to rival any French chateau. I was speechless.

"Gor," Dottie whispered breathlessly beside me. "Ain't it the grandest place ye've ever seen? And to think we'll be livin' here! Lord, me old Da would be proud to see his little girl in such a fine household."

Only for an instant did I think of my own father, wondering where he was now and if indeed he would be proud of me.

I didn't want to talk, wanted nothing to distract me from the perfect sight before us. The house was set back from the main gate at least two hundred yards with a wide oval green lawn spread before it. The drive made a complete circle around the lawn and was lined by towering hardwoods with limbs that dipped toward the ground and rustled with new green leaves as we passed.

Here in the open, away from the forest, a warm

breeze blew, bringing with it the pungent smell of box-wood and sun-warmed grass. Behind the house, shimmering in the distance, were the blue-green mountains of the Pisgah, a lush paradise of wildlife and flora whose beauty was unequaled anywhere in the world. The picture before us could easily have come from one of the travel books I so often devoured.

I hardly took my eyes from the house as we drove nearer. Then the carriage turned sharply to the right and we were underneath a covered portico that ran from the side of the house to another set of buildings. The driveway here was paved with bricks and beyond it was a brick courtyard surrounded by even more structures and one end of the house.

Immediately two servants came down the wide steps from the house and took our bags, hesitating until we could step down from the carriage and follow them.

Dottie turned to the coachman, who came around to help us down. "Thank you, sir. And that was a mighty fine ride you gave us."

The man laughed and nodded his head, obviously amused with Dottie.

"What's your name, anyhow, sir?" Dottie asked. "After all, we be workin' in the same house now, and I like to get acquainted with everyone."

He laughed even louder at that. "You'll have a time learnin' all the servants who work here, miss," he said good-naturedly. "There be eighty servants in the downstairs part alone."

Dottie drew in her breath in disbelief and her wide eyes turned toward me. "Can ye imagine that?" she whispered. "Eighty servants!"

"And my name is Higgins," the man continued. "Avery Higgins. I take care of the earl's horses and carriages and seein' to the comin's and goin's of his guests. And believe me, at this time of year, that's a mighty big job!"

We followed the two men servants up the steps into a

side door while Mr. Higgins, with a wave of his gloved hand, pulled the carriage through to the open courtyard.

We entered into a wide entry hall with stone walls and marble floors. The air was cold and still. There was a smooth walnut table upon which sat a very large arrangement of lovely fresh flowers, but other than that, the hallway was empty. This was evidently not one of the main entryways.

We followed the silent men ahead of us down a long hallway with high windows along the right filled with brilliant blue sky. There were several doorways on the left. I thought I detected the scent of tobacco smoke somewhere nearby. One of the servants turned and explained.

"This be the bachelors' wing, where the gentlemen gather. This here's the trophy room, and then the smoking room."

Just as we neared the last room on the left, the door suddenly flew open. I was only aware of a blur of color as someone came through the door and turned into the hallway, directly into my path. The collision sent me staggering backward a few steps, but it hardly jolted the man before me. My glasses flew off and the book I was carrying skittered with a swish across the smooth marble floor.

The tall man with whom I'd collided bent to retrieve my glasses at the same time as I. I was on my knees, reaching for the book of poetry, when I looked up with an indrawn breath into the most unusual, most disconcerting eyes I'd ever seen.

It was almost like looking into the eyes of a tiger, for the color was more gold than brown, a strange, smoky amber. There was absolutely no hint of a smile in his dark-lashed eyes nor upon his handsome, aristocratic face.

His hair was straight and full, a rich dark brown color that complemented the healthy, tanned look of his

17

smooth, clean-shaven face. And in our impact, wisps of hair had fallen over his forehead. I was surprised to find my fingers reaching forward to brush it away from his eyes. But I quickly caught myself and moved my hand instead toward the book.

His strong fingers were beneath my elbow, lifting me from my knees as he handed me my glasses with his other hand.

"Sorry, miss," he muttered, placing the glasses in my hand before turning to move on down the hallway.

I stared after him, noting the broad back beneath his tan jacket and the long stride of his legs as his booted heels struck the marble floor.

"Gosh," Dottie finally said, as if she'd been holding her breath. "And who the devil might he be?"

One of the servants who stood waiting patiently with our bags finally spoke. "That's his lordship Mr. Derek Vanderworth, the Earl of Chesham. He's the bloke what owns this bloomin' palace." The young man was grinning broadly, and there was a certain amount of pride in his voice. I noted that like Mr. Higgins, he had an English accent, and I wondered if he had come all the way here from England with Mr. Vanderworth.

"Are you all right, 'Lizabeth?" Dottie said.

"Oh, yes," I assured her, brushing the dust from my skirt and placing my glasses back on. "I'm not hurt at all."

We turned to a small stone stairway and made our way carefully downstairs around the turns of the narrow shaft.

Here in the confines of the stairway, the two young men seemed more friendly and not quite so formal. They turned frequently and looked up at us with smiles as they cautioned us to watch our step.

"Are you from England?" I asked them.

"I am, miss," said the one who had spoken earlier. "But Johnny here, he's a Yank, born and bred. Comes from right here in the North Carolina mountains."

There was a teasing quality in his voice as he jostled the other young man with his elbow.

I noticed Dottie's glare at the young Englishman. "Ain't nothin' wrong with bein' a Yank. Me Da's an Irishman, first generation here in America. But I am the first Magee born in this country and proud of it!" she declared huffily.

"He was only joshin'," the American boy replied shyly as he looked up at Dottie with eyes as blue as the summer sky.

"Well, joshin' or not, I ain't callin' nobody his lordship!" she said. "We don't hold with titles and fancy royal ways in this country!"

Both the boys laughed and poked each other in the ribs. But I could see that Dottie was dead serious. And I thought with a smile that I liked that about her. In fact, I was beginning to like the vivacious Irish girl more and more.

As we reached the bottom floor, we could hear the clank of pots and pans and smell the delicious aromas from the kitchen. The neat, bright room was abuzz with activity. It was a large room, big enough for the chef and his eight or ten cooks besides the servants, who moved about quickly as they prepared glass-topped serving carts and silver trays of food. I was impressed with the room because of the modern equipment I saw there. And even though the electric lights were small and dim, I thought it an amazing sight. There were ice-boxes and dozens of huge copper pots and kettles that hung from a rack above the work area.

The room was awash with light from several large windows that faced the mountains, and I found myself hoping I would be working in this room.

A large gray-haired woman stepped forward to us and wiped her hands on the apron that tied around her ample waist. A gold watch pendant was pinned to the bosom of her dark blue print dress, and at her waist was a metal ring containing what I thought

19

must be a hundred or more keys.

"I'm Mrs. Pennebaker," she said, looking us both over from head to toe. "I work directly for the housekeeper and help supervise the kitchen staff." Her voice was curt and impersonal, although her round face seemed open and friendly enough. I supposed she was just very busy.

She looked at Dottie. "What's your name, girl?"

"Dottie, ma'am," she said with a little curtsy. "Dottie Magee."

"Well, Dottie, you look like a good strong lass. I think you'll do fine workin' for the laundress." She pointed toward the door. "Down the hallway to your right. Someone will tell you where to put your things."

With a smile and small wave of her plump hand, Dottie turned to leave. "See you later," she mouthed silently.

The stout woman looked at me for a moment. "And I suppose you are Elizabeth."

"Yes, ma'am," I said.

"You're a wee little thing, aren't you?" she mused. For a moment I felt my heart skip a beat, afraid she would turn me away. And now that I was here in this magnificent place, I found I did not want to leave so soon.

"Yes, ma'am," I replied. "But I'm quite strong and used to working."

"You speak well for a servant girl," she said bluntly. "Are you educated?"

"I . . . well, yes, ma'am. A bit. I can read and write."

"Good," she declared, turning to the young Englishman who still held my bag. "Frederick, show Miss Stevens to the maid's room on the third floor. She'll be close enough to Mrs. Vanderworth's room there."

To me she said, "Our upstairs girls need something between their ears," she tapped a finger to her head. "You'll be looking after noblemen from all over the world and wives of heads of state. I think you'll do quite well, my girl."

"Thank you, ma'am."

"The housekeeper is Mrs. Hunt. She's busy at the

moment with last-minute details for tonight's dinner party. So after you've found your room, you may feel free to look around a bit, if you like. Don't venture below the second floor, though mind you and don't go into any of the bedrooms. Is that clear?"

I nodded my head in agreement.

She looked at my worn gray dress and with a slight lift of her brows, she said, "You'll be given a proper maid's uniform to wear, so there's no need to worry about your clothes." Then she reached for my arm to turn me about. "Perhaps after you're here awhile, the seamstress can make you a new gown, hum?"

"Yes, ma'am," I said, smiling at her gratefully. "Thank you."

"Good. Run along now, Elizabeth. I've work to do." With that she promptly turned and began hovering over the trays and silver dishes of food that lined the long tiled cabinets.

I followed Frederick down hallways and corners and up more stairs until I was so confused I wondered if I would ever be able to find my way around in the large maze.

But it was exciting and new . . . giving me for the first time a feeling of hope that I would not find working here so unpleasant after all. But more than that thought was another that wandered around inside my head.

Mrs. Pennebaker had said I was to be near Mrs. Vanderworth's suite. That meant the handsome amber-eyed man had a wife, and I could not understand why the thought of that disturbed me so. After all, who could be more out of my reach than this man . . . this strange, enigmatic man whom the servants called Master and his Lordship, the Earl of Chesham and owner of Stormhaven?

Chapter Three

Frederick was breathing heavily by the time we reached the corridor of the third floor. The hallways near the stairwell were so narrow and dark that the tiny electric lights hardly made a difference. The sounds of the house had fallen away from us and there was nothing to greet us here except silence.

Frederick moved ahead of me to lead the way. As we passed a large grilled ironwork structure he hitched his thumb toward it and turned to glance back at me.

"Even got us an elevator," he said proudly.

"An elevator?" I whispered. I'd never seen an elevator and I paused to peek between the patterned ironwork. I gasped and stepped back quickly as I saw the long, empty shaft that dropped frightfully away.

Frederick laughed. "If ye're scared of heights, you might not be overly fond of your room, lass."

"Why?" I asked.

"You'll see," was all he would say.

We moved to a wider, more pleasant hallway now, and there were windows to the left of us. I stopped to gaze out, seeing the long green lawn in front of the house. Far away, past the entrance gates, was a small hill striped with white walkways and benches and I thought it would be the perfect place from which to survey the house.

"That's the arboretum," Frederick said, waiting for me.

From here on the third floor I could see the rooftops of part of the house below us. I saw that the color of the rooftops and spires that I'd noticed on the approach to the house was copper. It had weathered into a beautiful verdant shade. Directly below was the rooftop of an octagonal room. Spread out below the first roof was one of paneled glass, also trimmed with the blue-green copper stripping.

"What's that?" I asked Frederick, pointing down to the octagonal structure.

Frederick stepped to the windows and peered downward. "It's called the winter garden; even in the winter there's always plants there and blooming flowers. There's even a fountain. If you'd like to see it, you can go down early some morning, before anyone's up and about."

He paused at a short hallway to the right. "Your room is right this way."

I followed him into the small cubicle where he sat my bag and moved to open a door on the other side of the room. "In here's the sewing room, and there are other maids' rooms in this part of the house as well. You have a nice sitting room just down the hallway."

"Thank you, Frederick. You've been very helpful."

"Oh, think nothing of it, miss. I think you'll like it here if you work hard and mind your manners," he teased boldly. "And you seem like a girl what's easy to get along with."

"Yes," I smiled, pleased by his attention. "I suppose I am."

"You must pay no mind to the gossip you hear or the ones trying to frighten you."

"Frighten me? What do you mean?" I asked.

"Well, some say as how the house is haunted . . . the top floor, that is." He pointed toward the ceiling. "But there's not much up there now except unused furniture and a few storage rooms. Even when the house is filled to overflowing with guests, they never put anyone up there. So there'll be no need for you to go there at all."

"Oh, I see," I said, glancing upward with curiosity.

"And there's the wind at night. It always blows here and the house sits so tall, why naturally it makes noises as it whistles around us. It storms a great deal here, bein' so near the mountains. They say that's why old man Vanderworth, the earl's grandfather, named the place Stormhaven. Sometimes the wind is so fierce it sounds like a thousand voices cryin' in the night. That's the Stormhaven wind, the one they say foretells a tragedy in the house."

I nodded. "Well, that's very interesting. But I assure you I am not in the least afraid of storms or wind and I'm hardly a superstitious girl."

"Yes, ma'am," he replied with a grin. "Then you'll get on well here, I suppose."

"I hope so," I answered. He seemed to hesitate for a moment. "Was there something else, Frederick?" I asked.

"Just that we have a jolly time of it here sometimes. We have our own dining room downstairs and a large parlor . . . what they call the servants' hall. There's a phonograph and card tables, and I was hopin' you might join us there tonight after supper."

"Why, of course," I said, happy to be included. "I'll look forward to it. I can see Dottie again and meet the rest of the household help."

He smiled and nodded and left me alone to unpack and survey my small room. It was a tiny room, probably smaller than some of the closets at Stormhaven, I thought with amusement.

But I felt an unreasoning joy rising within me as I glanced around. My very own room, privacy where I could read to my heart's content! I clasped my hands to my breast and surveyed the tiny room. I could hardly believe my luck.

I'm sure that to anyone else the room might have looked small and shabby, but to me it was heaven, albeit a plain and simple one. The floor, though well worn, was oak, laid in patterned squares, and in the middle was a round, faded blue-and-white rug. Against one wall was a small maid's bed covered with a worn blue coverlet. Nearby was a washstand upon which sat a gold-rimmed pitcher and bowl marked with a gold letter V. Behind it was a small oval mirror. The only other piece in the room was a large oak chiffarobe which occupied most of the opposite wall.

But the thing about the room that fascinated me most was the view. There was only one window, about waist high, and it stood open now as the wind blew the white curtains billowing out into the room. From here I could see the mountains and I imagined that lying in bed I'd even be able to see the stars at night. It was like being on some great mountaintop. The room was at the very back of the house. Unlike the front, it dropped precipitously far below into a grassy glen that stretched away from the house. I stepped to the window and breathed in the sweetly scented breeze as I studied the scene below the house.

Past the glen lay lush, rolling hills and beyond that I could see the silver-blue course of a river. I thought it the most perfect sight I'd ever seen, but then I smiled, for I'd thought that everything on the estate today was perfect.

I moved my eyes directly to the ground far below and felt a quick lurch in the pit of my stomach. I'd never liked heights, although here, for some reason, I felt fairly safe, with the screen upon the window and the windowsill at my waist. Still, I would not like to be on a ledge suspended from this height.

Finally I turned and unpacked the few things in my bag, humming as I worked. I was eager to explore the rest of the house before Mrs. Hunt came to explain my duties.

Once I'd finished, I nibbled on some cheese and bread that I'd packed for my trip. No one had mentioned lunch, and I wasn't sure how long it might be until supper. Once I finished eating I was ready to explore.

I had not noticed as we came in that across the small hallway from my room was a closed door. I knocked timidly on the wood. Hearing no answer, I turned the knob.

"A bathroom," I whispered as I surveyed the gleaming white room. I could hardly believe the luxury.

I proceeded out into the main hallway and glanced with pleasure across the lawn and across to the arboretum. Then my attention was drawn to the many portraits and prints of French and English nobility that lined the hall. There were also glass cases of figurines, some of them strange and grotesque and others that were quite beautiful. I wondered who had chosen these pieces, for there must be hundreds of them in this part of the large house alone. I could not say that I liked them very well.

As Mrs. Pennebaker warned, I did not attempt to open any of the doors along the hallway, but if there were guests in them, I did not hear any sounds from within.

The hallway finally opened into an enormous room right in the middle of the house. The hallways from both ends of the house led into this one room and I supposed it was some sort of sitting hall for the guests and residents of the third floor. There was a gigantic fireplace and several sofas and chairs covered in dark prints scattered about the room. Here again the room was filled with a unique and probably very expensive collection of statues, vases, and clocks. I was sure I could spend the afternoon and never see everything in this one huge room.

I noticed a wide railed stairway across the room and walked quietly over to it. The chandelier that hung in the middle of the circular stairway was breathtaking, if only for its immense proportions alone. It hung from a giant chain from the fourth floor above me all the way to the main level. There were lights at each floor, each larger than the last, until finally it burst into an extravaganza of heavy scrollwork and candelabra at the bottom. Looking down through the circular pit created by the stairs made me dizzy and for a moment I stepped away and removed my glasses to clear my vision.

Deciding to venture down to the second floor, I placed my hand on the smooth curved banister and tried to keep my footsteps quiet on the stone stairway. At the second level I found another huge sitting room like the one above. It was different from the first; the decor was not so dark and somber, but there were still influences of medieval and gothic in the collection. Along the north wall were lifesize paintings, and as I stepped closer I could make out the artist's signature: "John Singer Sargent."

I continued leisurely through the sitting hall, stopping when I head a noise coming from one of the rooms down the hallway. I listened. I was certain it sounded like someone crying. It was a sad, forlorn sound, as if the person's heart were breaking.

I stepped across the sitting room and looked down the long, dark hallway behind the great stairwell. I heard the sound again and moved slowly toward it.

I stopped in front of a closed door and listened, certain that the sounds came from inside this room.

"Hello," I called softly.

The crying stopped, then moments later, began again.

"Hello, is something wrong?" I called, a bit louder this time.

I heard nothing else from inside the room. Finally I rapped lightly upon the door, afraid that one of the guests might be ill and in need of help.

"May I come in?" I asked.

Still no reply.

I turned the knob and found the door unlocked. Pushing the heavy oak door open, I peered inside, unable to see through the gloom of the heavily curtained bedroom.

"Hello?" I called again.

This time I heard a sniffling sound from the canopied bed. I walked quickly to the windows and threw open the curtains, letting in the bright spring light and banishing the gloomy shadows from the room.

When I turned to the bed I held my breath, suspended by surprise. There, seated in the midst of numerous lacy pillows and a fluffy down comforter, was a little girl. Soft blond ringlets curled about her face and her luminous tear-filled eyes. She did not appear to be more than four years old, and she was so small she was almost lost in the large bed and mound of cover. Down her pale round cheeks ran a steady stream of tears.

"Here, here," I said, going immediately to her. I did not even think who the child might be or that I was intruding where I did not belong. All I knew was that the child was frightened and alone in this huge house and she was in need of comfort.

But the little girl moved away from me and pulled the covers tightly about her chin. Her bright eyes were large with fright, and her tiny chin quivered uncontrollably. My heart seemed to turn over just looking at her sad, lovely little face.

"Don't be afraid," I whispered. "I only came to see if I might help you. Are you sick? Did you have a bad dream?"

Still she did not speak, but only looked at me with fright-filled eyes as she continued to sob quietly. Her whole body shook, and I had no idea what to do to help her.

I glanced quickly about the room, which was filled with numerous expensive dolls and toys that any little girl would adore. The blond child followed my look and her arms moved from beneath the covers.

With both chubby hands raised, she motioned toward a tall piece of furniture across the room, making little grabbing movements with her fingers.

"What is it?" I asked. "Something in there you want?"

Her eyes pleaded with me, and she continued to reach toward the tallboy. I walked to it.

"This?" I asked.

Her movements became even more frantic and at last her tears stopped. I opened the doors of the cabinet and saw sitting there on a high shelf a scruffy little bear with button eyes and a silly turned-up grin that had been sewn with red thread.

I looked at the little girl again. With all her expensive toys she preferred one that appeared to have been made by hand, and rather primitively at that.

"The bear?" I asked. "You want the bear?"

The child lowered her arms and looked anxiously at me, the sparkle in her eyes giving the answer to my question. I took the bear and carried it to the waiting child, who took it from my hand and hugged it tightly against her chest.

I sat down slowly on the bed, careful not to alarm her any further. She did not smile, but when she looked up at me the light from the windows reflected upon her face and I found myself gazing into uniquely colored amber eyes . . . eyes that I had seen only once before.

"What's going on here?" The deep, cultured voice that sounded from the doorway was stern and angry and I jumped.

I turned and gazed into the eyes I had just envisioned. Derek Vanderworth stood, a silhouette in the doorway. His tall form was imposing and authoritative, and he was just as unsmiling and stern as he had been downstairs earlier.

"I . . . I'm sorry," I stammered. "But I heard the child crying, and . . ."

"It will not hurt her to cry," he declared coldly.

29

"Surely you cannot be serious," I said, forgetting who he was and that I was only an employee in his household.

His hard eyes flashed with anger as he walked toward me. I was aware that the little girl beside me cowered away as he came nearer. Instinctively I reached and placed a reassuring hand upon her chubby arm.

"I assure you, miss, I am most serious. Who the devil are you, anyway, and why are you here in my daughter's room?"

"I . . . I'm Elizabeth Stevens. I just arrived today and have been assigned as upstairs maid . . ."

"Yes," he said quickly halting my words. "I know who you are now." He walked to stand beside me and with one slender finger reached out to flick disdainfully at the corner of my glasses. "You're the girl with the glasses, the one in the hallway downstairs." His darkly lashed eyes lifted languidly, and I thought his look was as cool and emotionless as any I'd ever seen.

"Yes," I replied, moved now by sheer stubbornness not to call him sir.

"I'm sure you will understand, Miss Stevens, when I tell you that my daughter is not allowed visitors. Her governess has just put her down for a nap."

"But she's so small to be left up here alone. And she was crying, Mr. Vanderworth . . . as if her dear little heart would break. I could not bear to . . ."

"It is not your responsibility to bear *anything* here, miss," he said curtly.

"But I was just trying to help. If you will only ask her, she can . . ."

"My daughter can not speak, Miss Stevens!" he snapped before turning from us to pace to the windows.

I glanced quickly with disbelief toward the beautiful child in the bed. She sat watching her father with round, questioning eyes.

There was something in his voice that belied the anger and arrogance of his manner. There was pain and frustration, and I thought he'd turned away so that I could not see it in his eyes. And as sympathetic as I was to his revelation about the child, I wondered why it caused him such unreasonable anguish.

"I'm . . . I'm sorry. I did not know."

"No, of course you didn't," he said as he gazed out the windows, his hands clasped behind his back. "But from now on, Miss Stevens, you are to stay where you belong. And you are not to approach my daughter again."

He turned then, and the light behind him made his face shadowed and dark, his eyes unreadable as he stared at me.

"Is that clear?" he asked.

I stood up from the bed and held myself straight with my shoulders back. I lifted my chin and looked straight into his eyes.

"Yes, Mr. Vanderworth. You've made yourself quite clear."

With a sad glance toward the little girl, I turned and left the room as the man at the windows continued to stare after me.

As I walked toward the great stairway to proceed back to my third-floor room, I found my legs trembling so badly I could hardly climb. My face was flushed with humiliation, and my pulse beat rapidly at my throat. And I was not at all sure whether these physical reactions were caused by anger or by the mere presence of the cold, sardonic master of Stormhaven.

Chapter Four

I was preoccupied as I entered the third level of the house and walked through the huge sitting room. The masculine voice that halted me was decidedly British, much more so than that of Derek Vanderworth, who had the slow, drawling inflection of the North Carolinian.

"Well, well, what have we here?" the man said.

I turned to see someone sitting in one of the large wing-backed chairs. He seemed to blend into the brown material of the upholstery with his tan suit and sandy-colored hair. In fact, all I could see for a moment in the dimness of the room were his pale face and ash-colored eyes.

As I stared at him he stood up, his movements slow and easy, unlike the clipped words he'd just spoken. He was tall and slender, the jacket he wore hanging loosely upon his lean frame.

"I . . . I'm no one," I said with a slight curtsy. "Only a housemaid."

"Aha," he said with a glint of amusement in his gray eyes. "Only a housemaid. Well, young lady, allow me to introduce myself. I am only a houseguest." He bowed in an exaggerated manner.

I could not decide if he was being genuinely friendly or simply having a bit of fun at my expense. But I could not resist smiling at him. He was so different from

Derek Vanderworth, so much more open, that I felt an immediate warmth in his presence.

"I'm Elizabeth," I said.

He stepped closer and took my hand in his own. "And I, sweet Elizabeth, am Charles Simmons." He bent to place a cool kiss upon my hand.

As I felt my face growing warm, I withdrew my hand, still unsure of his true intentions.

"You're new here," he said, smiling down at me.

"Yes. I only arrived today."

"And what do you think of my dear cousin's ostentatious manor? Quite impressive, hum?"

"Cousin? You're Mr. Vanderworth's cousin?" I asked, my eyes scanning his face for any signs of similarity.

He laughed, a rather bitter sound, I thought. "Oh, yes. Indeed I am. A poor relative, you might say, often dependent upon my cousin's kind generosity."

His thin lips curled into an unpleasant sneer as he gazed at me in an almost challenging manner.

"Oh . . . I see," I said quietly, hardly knowing what else to say.

"Oh, dear," he said, the sneer immediately gone. "I did not mean to make you feel uncomfortable. I suppose if I were as well bred as my family wished, I would not speak of such matters in the presence of a stranger."

"It's all right," I assured him, feeling an immediate sympathy "I promise you no one will ever know you spoke to me."

He laughed. "You are quite refreshing, do you know that? And quite pretty."

I blushed again and lowered my eyes from his gray gaze. "I really should go," I said. "I'm to meet Mrs. Hunt, I believe, to learn about my new duties."

"The dragon lady," he said with a derisive laugh. "Don't let her fool you. She isn't quite as ferocious as she seems."

I looked at him for a moment, wondering at his outspoken manner concerning the household.

"In any event," he continued in his cool, curt accent. "It's a pity. For I would truly enjoy talking to you further."

I smiled and turned to leave the sitting room.

"Do you think we might?" he said. "Talk, that is. Or perhaps take a walk later in the gardens."

"Oh, I don't . . . I'm not sure if . . ."

"If you're worried about my dear cousin Derek, don't. He is too preoccupied with his parties and the accumulation of all these . . . things." He waved his hand about the art-filled room. "He would hardly notice."

I detected that little sting of bitterness in his voice again. I was certain I should not become involved with this man. For I was not at all sure his cousin was as unconcerned with the behavior of his household staff as he would have me believe.

"It's not that," I said. "I'm not sure it would be proper. Besides . . ."

"Proper?" he shouted, throwing his head back with a hoot of laughter. "I had no idea young American women were so concerned with being proper. I supposed that was an entirely British tradition."

"Besides," I continued, ignoring his amused words. "I'm sure there are many young ladies here . . . houseguests, who would be a more suitable companion."

He quirked an eyebrow at me and grew quiet and more serious. "I am not a snob, sweet Elizabeth. Your position means nothing to me. As I said before, if it were not for the hospitality of my cousin, I would more than likely hold the same occupation as you."

I sighed. He simply was not going to take no for an answer.

"Please," I said, deciding to be totally honest. "It's my first day. I have no idea what proprieties are expected of me. But if you will give me a few days to familiarize myself with the routine and to find out what is expected of me, then I think I should like very much to get to know you better."

"Splendid." He grinned, the reaction making him look young and carefree. "You are a straight talker. I like that, Elizabeth . . . what was your last name?"

"Stevens," I said, smiling at his enthusiasm.

"Well, Elizabeth Stevens. My room is just down the hall." He pointed past the grand staircase in the opposite direction from the maids' quarters. "And I'm usually here in the sitting room in the afternoon before dinner. I hope your familiarity with the routine here comes quickly so we might begin our acquaintance."

I smiled and walked away, aware that he stood watching me as I turned down the hallway toward my room.

My first day was turning out to be one of strange meetings; for as soon as I turned the corner I saw a woman standing in the hallway, looking straight at me, as if she were waiting for me.

She looked to be in her thirties and was a striking-looking woman with dark hair that curled about her olive skinned face. Her dark eyes slanted at the corners, giving her an exotic, foreign look. But when she spoke I noted the local accent, although it was certainly more cultured and refined than the usual resident's might be.

I could hardly miss the glint of anger in her eyes or the way she stood with fists curled at her hips, waiting for me. I realized she was Mrs. Hunt and again my heart sank, for I had obviously displeased her already.

"You would be wise, Miss Stevens, to stay away from Mr. Vanderworth's houseguests. Most especially his cousin Charles."

I wondered how much she had heard.

"You're Mrs. Hunt?" I asked as I stopped in front of her.

She nodded as her slanting eyes looked disdainfully up and down my figure. It was obvious she saw no reason for Mr. Simmons' interest, but she said nothing.

"I'm sorry," I began. "I was only walking through the . . ."

She held up her hand to stop my words. She pursed

35

her lips and looked at me with dark, cold eyes. "There will be nothing more said about it. But Mr. Simmons is a frivolous man and a troublemaker. Anything he can do to irritate Mr. Vanderworth seems to bring him the greatest of pleasures. So do not feel yourself flattered by his attention, miss."

"I . . . No, I don't."

I felt very foolish as I stammered and stumbled over my words. I could hardly believe that within the span of an hour I had been chastised by my employer, flattered by his cousin, and now upbraided by his housekeeper. It was very disconcerting, to say the least.

"I have very little time to waste before the dinner party, so let us begin," she said coldly.

I followed her as she took me from room to room, showing me the guests' quarters. They were the ones nearest my room. The hallway where Mr. Simmons had pointed out his room was reserved for himself and other family members. Mrs. Hunt's room was also in that section of the house, and I was surprised when she opened her door to reveal a warm, elegant room of maroon and gold decor. If her room was any indication, then Mrs. Hunt held a most prestigious position indeed.

"It's lovely," I murmured from the doorway.

Her eyes grew a bit warmer as they gazed with pleasure over her possessions. "Yes, it is. I enjoy it very much."

It was obviously a completely feminine room and one occupied only by her. But I was curious about her status, knowing everyone called her Mrs. Hunt.

"Does your husband work here as well?" I asked.

"My husband is dead, Miss Stevens," she said, her eyes turning cold once more.

She turned abruptly and I followed her silently back through the now empty sitting room toward the maids' quarters. She efficiently went about showing me the various rooms which we were permitted to use for our private pleasure. All the cleaning items were located here as well as stacks of pristine linens and various quilts and coverlets. One closet held glasswares, water pitchers, and washbowls with the elegant gold lettered V.

"Each day you will straighten the rooms, make the beds, and change the linens. When a new guest arrives, I will assign them a room and tell you myself if special arrangements need to be made. Mr. Vanderworth is a very indulgent host and nothing is spared to make his guests comfortable. Do you understand?"

"Yes, ma'am," I said.

"Your duties will begin first thing tomorrow morning. Of course, some of the guests wish to sleep late, so it could be well into the afternoon before you'll be able to clean all the rooms. It is a custom here for our guests to leave their doors open when they go downstairs. If you find a door closed, do not disturb its occupant."

"Yes, ma'am."

"You are welcome to eat either downstairs in the servants' hall or here in the maid's sitting room. The kitchen staff will send up tea on the dumbwaiter there at the end of the hall if you wish, and they can send up any other meal you prefer to eat here."

I nodded. "Thank you. I've already been invited to join the others in the servants' hall tonight," I said.

She looked at me sharply, furrowing her brow. "Oh? I was not aware you knew anyone else here yet."

"Oh, yes," I said quickly, aware of her irritation with me. "There was another girl who came on the coach with me today. And then Frederick, who carried my . . ."

"Well," she said with a quiet huff. "For a plain-looking girl you certainly manage to attract your share of men, don't you?"

Once again her eyes assessed me as a look of mockery crossed her face. I said nothing, though my face burned with humiliation. Why this woman had taken such an instant dislike to me I could not imagine. I was certainly in no way a threat to her.

"As I said before, Miss Stevens, it would be best if you stayed away from Charles Simmons. He is an aristocrat and far too sophisticated for a mere girl like you. And as for Frederick, well . . . you'd be wise to take care around him." Her words of caution were said with a knowing sneer. "I doubt Mr. Vanderworth would take kindly to one of his servants delivering a child within nine months of her employment."

I almost gasped at the ugliness of her warning. But I said nothing. I wondered why she was so bitter and if she spoke to all the servants at Stormhaven in such a crude manner.

"In any case," she continued breezily. "Don't try to become familiar with any of the guests. Remember, you are only a servant here; try to comport yourself as one. And I'd advise you to rid yourself of that affected accent of education. It is not at all becoming in a servant girl."

My mouth flew open at her words, but before I could reply, she had turned sharply and was gone. I stood in the hallway outside my room, shaking my head in confusion. It was true I was inexperienced in dealing with a job. And I did try to speak properly, as I'd been taught. But was that any reason to be treated so rudely by this woman? With a shrug of my shoulders I went to my room, vowing to forget Mrs. Hunt's hatefulness and hoping I would not need to be in her presence often.

It was growing late, near dinnertime, I suspected. I walked across to the bathroom and peeked longingly in the door. The cool-looking white tiles and deep, footed tub looked so inviting. I wondered for a moment if I dared to use it. It was not something Mrs. Hunt had mentioned, and I did not want to risk annoying her again.

I tiptoed across the floor and turned the water tap above the tub. Immediately there was a clang and a spurt of water from the pipe. I jumped, wondering if the

38

noise had been heard and if someone would come and scold me for my boldness. But no one came.

While the water filled the tub I went across to get clean clothes, looking forward to the luxurious pleasure of a real bath for a change. Only for a moment did I feel a tug of homesickness, thinking of the old galvanized tub that we used for our bathing and of the many times I'd given little Angelina her bath in it. But as soon as I was in the tub, the warmth of the water and the lovely scent of soap chased away all those sad feelings and I gave in to the new pleasure of a long, leisurely bath.

Later, as I made my way down the twisting stairway, I noted the quiet of the house. I still had not met any of the others who would be working on the third floor.

The sun was lying in a golden cloud just above the darkening peaks of the Pisgah Mountains. As I passed various windows I could see the long shadows of the house across the lush front lawn. The arboretum across the way was awash in the golden light of dusk, and I stopped for a moment to marvel at the sight.

There was so much to see here. So many new things to discover that I found myself anxious for each new hour to come. And more than that was the mystery that seemed to surround the Vanderworth family. I found myself very curious about the sad, angelic little girl I'd met today, not to mention Charles Simmons and his seeming bitterness toward his cousin. And I wondered how Mrs. Hunt fit into the family's life. She certainly appeared to be treated as an equal.

Yes, this house held many secrets, I felt; many hidden emotions beneath its fashionable, sophisticated facade. And I could not deny that I was more than curious about the ones that involved Derek Vanderworth.

Chapter Five

As I entered the downstairs area my ears were assailed by the rattle of dishes and the quick voices of those working in the kitchen. I peeked in the door long enough to find directions to the servants' dining room, then continued down the narrow corridor. I was impressed by the number of rooms along the way, each used for a different purpose. There was a room filled with fresh vegetables, one stacked with canned stock, and another with shelves of extra teapots, dishes, and oil lamps. I also passed the laundry room, where floor-to-ceiling drying racks held freshly washed sheets, and I wondered what duty Dottie had been given there.

I heard the low hum of conversation from the servants' sitting room before I arrived and stopped momentarily at the door. Several of the people inside glanced at me and smiled. Then I heard Dottie's familiar brogue as she motioned to me from the rear of the room. She was with Frederick and Johnny, and they all smiled in greeting. Frederick moved close to me in a slightly possessive gesture, and put his hand at the small of my back to escort me into the room.

It felt good to see someone I knew, especially after Mrs. Hunt's patronizing manner toward me. The other servants in the room were very cordial as Frederick introduced me to each one. As we moved among the people I noted the small, homey atmosphere of the room and wondered if the Vanderworths had provided the furnishings or if they belonged to the servants themselves. There were several rocking chairs and tables which contained checker and chess sets. On one table in the corner was a large phonograph which even now carried the sounds of a waltz into the room. It was a cozy, pleasant room, and it was evident that the servants were very proud of it.

When a bell rang across the hall, we all filed into the dining hall, where a long, narrow table was spread with a plain but sparkling white linen tablecloth. The china was also white porcelain but was rimmed with gold and in the middle of each plate was the elegantly lettered V I'd seen elsewhere in the house.

As we ate our meal of mutton and freshly cooked vegetables I noted the free and spirited conversation about the table. Here, I supposed, in these two rooms, the servants could be completely themselves, not having to restrain themselves in any way, as they did during the course of the day. And it was in these two rooms that I was to learn more about the brooding man who owned this vast estate called Stormhaven.

It was a leisurely meal, and conversation was relaxed. I suppose it is only natural for servants to find pleasure in the life of their employers. After all, it seems so much more interesting and exciting than the simple day-to-day tasks they perform.

Frederick and Johnny joined in the good-natured talk although I, being new, sat listening instead, speaking only when given a direct question.

I was certain some of the people present felt the need to bring Dottie and myself up to date, so to speak, on the gossip of the Vanderworth family.

"So, you're on the third floor, eh?" one of the women asked me. "Ruthie down there at the end of the table is assigned duties there as well." The woman pointed to a small blond-haired girl who I'd noticed giggling during the meal. As I looked at her, she grinned and waved a hand at me in acknowledgment.

"And Miss Olivia has a room there as well. She's our seamstress and worked for the Vanderworth family in England for many years before coming here." The woman she pointed out as Miss Olivia was an older lady with lovely silver hair. She sat straight and slim in her chair and looked dignified enough to be a member of the wealthy family about whom we'd been speaking. She nodded to me gracefully, her pale blue eyes not quite meeting mine, then picked up her teacup and continued with her meal.

"Has anyone told you about the ghost, Elizabeth?" one of the men asked with a touch of mischief in his eyes.

Most of the people at the table laughed, especially Frederick and Johnny. But I noticed that some of the others glanced about at each other with decided looks of unease on their faces.

"Well," I said. "Frederick might have spoken briefly about it, but . . ."

"She's being kind," Frederick said with a laugh. "I told her not to listen to you old biddies and your tales of ghostly wanderings on the fourth floor."

The woman who had been speaking earlier said with a touch of irritation, "Well, for your information, Frederick, I've been upstairs more than you. And I say there *is* a ghost. I've seen it!"

There were quiet murmurs about the room and a few rumbles of laughter. Whatever the truth was, it certainly seemed to make for a controversial evening of entertainment.

"What about you, Miss Olivia? You ever seen the ghost?" Johnny asked the elegant seamstress.

I was surprised at the look that crossed her face. She turned directly to me, and there was a definite warning in her blue eyes.

"Perhaps that's a subject best left alone," she said.

I did not really intend to become involved in the speculation. I was not sure I believed in such things as ghosts. And even if I did, it was not a subject that frightened me overmuch. But now as the woman looked at me so seriously, I wondered.

"You might as well know," Ruthie said, her eyes wide with apprehension. " 'Tis said it's the ghost of Mrs. Vanderworth what walks the halls at night. I keep my doors locked at night. Miss Olivia does too; she just don't want to admit it." She looked at the older woman with an apologetic glance.

"Mrs. Vanderworth?" I asked, wondering if they meant Derek Vanderworth's mother.

"Aye," Ruthie said quietly, her bright eyes almost bulging with excitement. "The young master's wife. She threw herself off the upper-story balcony last year during the spring ball. It was a horrible night, it was, all dark and stormy. The poor thing fell way to the bottom of the grounds below and wasn't found 'til the next mornin'."

I shivered remembering the frighteningly steep drop from my window. Without realizing it, my hand was clutching the bodice of my dress. Derek Vanderworth's *wife?* Dead by suicide? I could hardly believe what I was hearing, and I looked blankly at Frederick.

He was watching my every expression and seemed very amused by the horror on my face. "Don't let 'em josh you, love," he said blithely.

I turned and looked at the others gathered there. Was it a terrible joke they were playing on us because we were new?

"Now Freddie, you know it's the truth!" Ruthie snapped. "The poor thing flung herself off the balcony . . . kilt herself, she did. You can't deny that!"

With a sigh of exasperation, Frederick turned to me. He drank lazily from his cup before he spoke. "That part's true enough. Although it could have been an accident. No one had any reason to think she would try to kill herself. I mean, why should she? She had everything any young woman could want, didn't she?"

"Oh, that's hogwash, Freddie, and you know it!" Ruthie continued. "What was she doing on the fourth floor at that time of night, anyhow? And while the ball was going on downstairs! I suppose she just staggered out onto the balcony, unlocking the big glass door first mind you, and then *accidentally* fell over the balcony? Now, that would be a real chore, since she would have had to climb up to get over it."

For the first time Frederick quieted. He shrugged his shoulders. "Well, I don't know about that part."

"No, you don't," she snapped. "Just as you don't know about a lot of things that happened in this house."

Everyone looked at her, causing her to blush and lower her eyes as if she'd said too much.

"Whatever do you mean by that?" Miss Olivia asked sharply, frowning at the young girl.

"Nothing," Ruthie said quickly. "I don't mean nothing at all."

But her comments certainly seemed to put a damper on the jovial atmosphere that had prevailed around the table. Everyone grew quiet, some rising from the table to go stealthily back across to the servants' hall.

Miss Olivia stood and smoothed the material of her black uniform. "If you'll excuse me, I believe I'll retire for the evening. I hope, Miss Stevens, that you won't let Ruthie frighten you. Stormhaven really is a lovely place to work, and Mr. Vanderworth is a very compassionate employer."

"No," I muttered. "I won't."

Ruthie could hardly wait until the older woman was out of the room before turning to me once again. "Beware of the stormy nights, Elizabeth, when the Stormhaven winds blow. That's when the mistress walks the halls. And hers is not a happy spirit, either. It's been almost a year since the ball, and who knows what will happen on the anniversary night." Her whispered words sounded ominous in the long, quiet dining hall. Then she too rose and went across to the room where the music had once again begun to play.

I wondered if her words were to be taken seriously or if she only intended to frighten Dottie and me . . . two new recruits to the servants' hall.

There were only myself and Dottie, Frederick and Johnny left at the long, empty table.

Dottie laughed uneasily, and for once she seemed to have little to say. Johnny slipped an arm slyly behind her waist and grinned at her impishly. "Don't worry, Dottie," he said. "I'll keep you safe from the ghosties."

"Oh, you," she said, laughing as she took a light swipe at his arm.

"It's true then?" I asked. "Mr. Vanderworth, the one we saw in the hallway today . . . it was his wife who committed suicide?"

"Aye," Frederick said. "And a mighty shame it was, too. She was a real looker, all right. Blond hair, big blue eyes. And I never believed for a minute all the things they said about her."

I envisioned the little blond-haired girl, this woman's daughter. She must look very much like her mother.

"What . . . what did they say?" I asked, finding myself more interested than I had any right to be.

"They say she was a nobody . . . a saloon girl, some say, who charmed Mr. Vanderworth with her looks. And that she only married him for money. She wasn't a bookish sort, I'll admit. But she always seemed like a nice, friendly sort of person to me," Frederick said.

Johnny nodded. "Yeah, real nice. Though some said she might be a bit *too* friendly, if you know what I mean. But I never seen her with Mr. Simmons, like some of the others said. Besides, Charles Simmons is family. Why shouldn't she talk to him if she wanted to?"

Charles Simmons again. Was this the reason Mrs. Hunt had told me to avoid him? And the reason he seemed so bitter toward his cousin?

45

"Oh, ho," Dottie whispered, interested now that a romantic triangle seemed to be revealed. "The young, beautiful wife was playing around, was she?"

"It's not so funny at that," Johnny said. "There must have been something to the rumors. After all, Mr. Vanderworth was under suspicion for several weeks after his wife died. A jealous quarrel the night of the ball, some said. But nothing was ever proven. Finally they decided it had to be suicide. But they's some even now what don't believe he didn't have something to do with her falling off that balcony."

I shivered, recalling the hard, cold eyes of Derek Vanderworth.

Frederick snorted disdainfully. "Well, I never believed it. Never met a finer man than Derek Vanderworth. Grew up with him, played with him when we were boys. He don't put on airs like some of the royals in England. Why, I'll wager he wouldn't hurt a fly, let alone a beautiful woman like Desiree Vanderworth. He was in love with her, for God's sake!"

I looked at Frederick. He was loyal to his employer and obviously believed what he had just said about the man. But I wondered. I had found Derek Vanderworth to be cold and arrogant, hardly the man my new friend had just described.

We all sat silently for a few moments before Dottie yawned. "Well, ghosts or not, I've got to get some sleep," she said. "It's been a long, hard day."

I felt a bit guilty, for in all the talk about ghosts and love scandals, I had not even asked about her new duties. As I told her goodnight, I resolved to spend more time with her soon.

"I'd better go up too," I said. "From what Mrs. Hunt said, I'll have a long day tomorrow."

"Would you like me to walk up with you?" Frederick offered, a light blush upon his fair cheeks.

I smiled. "There's no need," I said firmly. "I told you I don't believe in ghosts."

But as we said our goodnights and parted, with promises of seeing each other the next night at dinner, I was not so confident as my words sounded. The conversation had made me uneasy. I just wanted to be alone for a while in the quiet of my new room. And besides, I had developed a splitting headache, as often happened when I wore my glasses for long periods of time.

The dinner party was apparently still going on, for as I passed the kitchen, they seemed every bit as busy as before. But as I left that area and walked toward the narrow stairway that led upstairs, I found the rest of the house eerily quiet.

Any other time I would have been fascinated by the delicate electric lights that dimly lit the hallway. But that night I felt uneasy and restless and passed by them with hardly a glance.

A draft whispered down the long, narrow corridors, making a low moaning noise. I shivered and walked quickly up to the first level. I could hear the music and the sound of laughter from there, even though the main party was far away in another part of the house. I saw no one and continued up to the third floor. The lights here were even smaller and dimmer than those downstairs, and I wished I had left a lamp burning in my cozy little room.

Once I was inside, I found the small electric lamp by the bedside table. I turned the delicate ornate switch, allowing the light through its frosty glass globe to illuminate the room. I felt immediately better and would have felt infinitely secure if only there had been a key to the lock on my door and the one to the sewing room.

But I did not intend to let anything spoil the joy I'd felt this afternoon on discovering my own private room. I turned then to the small window to gaze out at the moonlit-covered land surrounding the great mansion. The green rolling meadows were now silver, the night blurring the edges of everything until it was almost impossible to find any landmarks. I could barely distinguish the peaks of the mountains far away in the distance. The air that wafted through the open window felt cool and fresh, causing me to wonder if I'd ever get enough of the scents and sights of the place. It was a wonderland to me and one I longed to see more of during the hours I was not working.

With that more positive thought in mind, I readied myself for bed. I took off my glasses with great relief and rubbed my tired eyes.

It was my habit to read before sleeping, but that night my head ached so that I decided I would not. I turned out the light instead, probably a mistake. For now, in the darkness, I saw visions before my eyes and heard the questions that whispered inside my head.

I was aware of the image of amber eyes, hard and cold, and a deep voice warning me to stay away from the beautiful little girl. Poor baby, I thought. To have lost her mother at such an early age. Even more reason, I would think, for her father to treat her with special kindness. But why didn't he?

I knew I did not want to believe the handsome man could be so cold and sinister, so uncaring of his own daughter. And yet what was I to believe after all I had heard about him tonight?

My first night at Stormhaven turned out to be restless and wearying. And as I finally drifted off to sleep, I thought I heard the strains of music drifting up from the open windows of the ballroom far below.

And I dreamed of a lovely blond-haired woman in yards of filmy white material, dancing, dancing with a handsome amber-eyed man. They spun about in a whirl of mist as lightning flashed and thunder rumbled in the distance around them. I could feel myself watching them, and there was such a depth of feeling within me I thought I would die from its bittersweet pleasure. It was something I had never felt before and could not identify. I was not certain if it was fear or longing that I felt.

Somehow, then, in my dream, the tall, arrogant man's arms were about *me,* and *I* became the girl in the exquisite filmy white gown, dancing gaily through a strange, storm-enshrouded night.

Chapter Six

The morning came on with a gray light, darkening the house and bringing a cool dampness to everything I touched. Glancing out my tiny window, I could see the angry black clouds that hid the peaks of the mountains and threatened everything in their path.

The stormy weather was no doubt the reason for my strange dreams. But it was not something I wanted to dwell upon. I was too eager to begin my new duties and to see the beautiful rooms that were hidden behind all those doors.

Ruthie and I divided the rooms between us. Miss Olivia, she said, was already in the sewing room and had a lot of work to do. I took that to mean that Ruthie and I would do the rest of the work on the third floor.

I was surprised to find the large number of empty rooms at such an early hour. But Ruthie informed me there was an early morning hunt, even more reason for us to finish our chores quickly, before the party of guests returned for lunch.

It was well past mid-morning and I had worked my way to the rooms near the huge sitting room, or living hall, as it was called. I had finished dusting, a lengthy chore in itself, and took the bucket of freshly cut flowers that the gardener had sent up. I had no idea about arranging flowers, except for what I'd read in books. Still, it was pleasantly distracting work, and I did not hear the footsteps upon the stairs until someone spoke behind me.

"That looks lovely, my dear," the feminine voice said.

I turned to see an older lady step from the stairs and stand watching me from the end of the room. I could not decide in the shadowy light if the hair that was swept up on the top of her head was silver or a very pale blond. As she came nearer, I noted the lines upon her face did not seem quiet compatible with her trim figure or the lightness of her step. But when she spoke I could hear the age in her quiet voice.

"You seem to have a knack for working with flowers," she said.

I smiled at her. She seemed very kind and friendly and I wondered who she was. "Oh, I'm not sure," I said. "I've never done this before, but I have read a few books on the subject."

She turned her head and smiled broadly, lifting one eyebrow as she did so in a strangely familiar manner.

"You like to read," she said, as if she found that interesting.

"Oh, yes," I said. "I can't think of anything I'd rather do than read." I continued placing the fragrant flowers in the large, colorful vase.

"A splendid pastime," she agreed. "And one I enjoy as well. I shall have to speak with my grandson about allowing you to use the library downstairs. Have you seen it?"

Her grandson? Derek Vanderworth was her grandson? That would explain my misunderstanding about the room assignments when I first came. She was the Mrs. Vanderworth to whom they had referred.

"No," I said. "I have not been past the second floor. Yesterday was my first day here and Mrs. Hunt told me I might look about as long as I did not go down to the main floor."

"Oh, yes," she said with a twinkle in her eyes. "Sometimes I think the staff is more particular about such things than those of us who live here," she laughed.

I smiled. Even if she was the arrogant Earl's grand-mother, I found myself liking her very much. She had the look of a grand dame and her speech was beautifully correct but without the slight English accent of her grandson. She sounded like an American.

"In any case," she continued, "if you are interested in books, flowers, the gardens . . . then I'm certain Mrs. Hunt would not mind your seeing all those things on your off-hours. I'm certain my grandson would not object. I commend you for your love of reading."

I looked away from her when she mentioned her grandson, for I was not so sure he would have no objections. But I dared not be so forward as to tell her what he had said to me yesterday about remaining in my place.

"What is your name, my dear?" she asked.

"Elizabeth, ma'am. Elizabeth Stevens."

"Well, Elizabeth, I am Maude Vanderworth. My room is right here at the head of the stairs." She pointed to a room that I had not yet entered. Then she laughed quietly. "Derek insists that I should take a room down-stairs . . . that I should not have to climb the stairs each day. I suppose I could take the elevator, but I do not in-tend to sit down and grow old . . . not yet, anyway. I believe exercise is good for us."

"Yes, ma'am," I said. "I agree."

She smiled sweetly. "I have a feeling we probably agree on many other things. In fact, we're probably more alike than you might think. So . . . if you'd like, I will speak to my grandson about your taking any books you want from the library."

"Oh, ma'am . . . that would be wonderful!"

I was almost speechless at her friendliness and gener-osity. I could not believe my luck. In only two short days there was already the possibility of a wealth of new books at my disposal; I could hardly wait to see the li-brary.

52

Mrs. Vanderworth left. I'd just finished with the flowers when Ruthie came looking for me.

"Ooh," she said, pointing to the flowers I placed on a large table near the fireplace. "Lovely," she said. "It's beginning to rain, which means the hunting party will be back soon. You ready for a bit of lunch, 'Lizabeth?"

"Yes," I said, feeling surprised that noon had come so quickly. "I am rather hungry."

"Me and Miss Olivia, we usually have our lunch up here in the sitting room. I've already asked Cook to send up something. So, if you're ready . . ."

I followed her down the hall, watching the flutter of her hands and the way her blond curls bounced. She chatted as we walked, and I wondered with a smile if she was ever quiet.

Miss Olivia was already in the sitting room and busied herself placing our lunch upon a small round table that was covered with a white crocheted cloth.

"Hello, Elizabeth," she said with a wide smile. "I hope your first day has been a pleasant one."

"Yes," I said, glancing briefly about the room. "It has been."

This room was near the north end of the house. One large window at the end of the room stood open, letting the sound of rain into the small, cozy room. I walked curiously across to look out. From here we could see the cobblestone courtyard and the stables beyond. I wondered about Mr. Higgins, the coachman who'd been so kind to Dottie and me. But he was nowhere in sight. The only people I saw were the guests riding in from the hunt. They were laughing and talking and did not seem to mind the rain that pelted down upon them.

Ruthie came to stand beside me, curious as usual about what was going on.

"Do you see that handsome devil Charles Simmons?" she asked with a sly whisper.

I laughed at her, but said nothing. I did not see Charles, for my vision and my imagination were captured by the man who had just ridden into the courtyard.

There was no mistaking Derek Vanderworth's imposing arrogance. He sat tall and straight upon a prancing jet-black horse. His hands held the reins casually.

The horse wheeled and strutted, still fresh and spirited even after the hunt. Its coat shimmered like silver in the misting rain. But the man astride the big black horse held it in a fluid, seemingly effortless manner.

The horse and rider arrested my attention so completely that I had hardly noticed the woman riding beside them.

She seemed very small, riding a little chestnut mare beside the man and his massive ebony horse. Pale blond hair peeked from beneath her stylish riding hat.

I continued to stare at the couple as the woman moved nearer the man. She leaned toward him and placed a small gloved hand upon his arm. My breath caught in my throat as he leaned closer to catch her softly spoken words. There was no denying the intimacy of their actions. I found myself strangely curious about who the petite blond woman was.

"Oh, oh," Ruthie whispered with a giggle. "Looks like his lordship's not spending too many lonely nights these days."

"Ruthie," Olivia said sharply. "Come away from that window. It is not seemly for you to be gossiping about the earl and his family this way."

"I'm not gossiping," she answered just as sharply. "I'm only observin'. I ain't blind; can't just turn my head every time some pretty woman makes eyes at Mr. Derek. If I did I'd wear my neck right off its hinges!" She laughed at her own silly words.

"Who is she?" I asked, risking Miss Olivia's censure.

"That's Miss Diana Gresham, his dead wife's sister." She spoke in a low, conspiratorial whisper.

"Ruthie," Olivia warned again from the table.

"All right, all right," Ruthie said. "We're coming!"

54

She pulled at the sleeve of the heavy corded material of my black uniform as I glanced back toward the window. But the couple was no longer there in the courtyard.

I was distracted as we took our places at the table. Even the tempting soup and fragrant buttered bread could not hold my attention for long. But I did not want to be accused of gossiping. Besides, I knew if I waited long enough Ruthie would probably tell me everything I wanted to know. She could hardly contain herself; it was in every twist of her body, every flash of her eye as she glanced at me slyly.

But we let Miss Olivia dictate the conversation and I tried to answer each of her questions politely. We were so engrossed in conversation that the sudden light tap at the door took us all by surprise.

"Come in," Olivia called, looking over her shoulder toward the doorway.

I smiled as the elderly lady came into the room. Mrs. Vanderworth's manner was neighborly, not at all the haughty lady-of-the-manor one would have supposed. Across one arm she held a dress, one with yards of shimmering pale blue satin material. It was so lovely I could hardly take my eyes from it.

"Oh, I'm sorry," she said. "I didn't think I might be disturbing your lunch."

"Nonsense. Come in, Maude," Olivia said, rising to take the dress from the woman's arm.

I looked at the seamstress with a bit of surprise. She had called the woman by her first name.

"You are not disturbing us in the least. Would you like some tea?"

"Well, yes, I would," Mrs. Vanderworth said. "Lunch seems to be late today. I suppose they're waiting on Derek and his guests to change from their wet clothes before they begin serving. But I admit, I'm quite famished."

"Then sit right down this instant. I'll have the kitchen

send up some more soup," Miss Olivia insisted.

"Oh, no," Mrs. Vanderworth said. "Tea will be fine. And I would love a slice of that delicious-smelling bread." She turned to me as she settled herself. "Hello, Elizabeth. It's nice to see you again. Are Ruthie and Olivia taking good care of you?"

"Oh, yes, ma'am," I said, smiling at her.

"Good, good," she said. "As you might have guessed, Olivia and I are old friends. Several years ago when I visited my grandson in England, she fashioned some of the most splendid dresses I ever owned. And I'm very pleased that she decided to come and stay here permanently at Stormhaven. That way I get to see her whenever I wish."

The two women smiled companionably at one another while Ruthie and I sat and watched.

The rain continued to fall heavily, at times causing such a loud noise that it muffled our conversation. I thought I had never spent a more pleasant hour in my life. There was something about being a part of this household and in the presence of such gracious women. Whether it was the quiet way they spoke or the elegant way they conducted themselves I was not sure. I only knew that they made me feel secure and content. Perhaps it was because I had never been subjected to it in my own home, had never witnessed this gentility in my own mother. And I think it was on that day, in that secluded little sitting room, with the sound of the rain outside, that I absorbed what the term *lady* really meant. And I knew immediately it was what I wanted for my own life. And I was so young and naive that I saw absolutely no reason why I could not attain it.

Chapter Seven

Mrs. Vanderworth turned to me. "Did you leave a family to come here, Elizabeth?" she asked politely.

I told her briefly about my mother and young brothers. And I suppose I was unable to disguise the homesickness I felt for my little sister as I spoke of her.

"I hated to leave Angelina. She's only ten."

"You seem to love children," she said quietly. "Many girls your age would not be so reluctant to leave the responsibility of caring for younger children and embark on a new life."

I looked across at her. She was looking at me with only the kindest, gentlest of smiles.

"Yes," I said, probably realizing for the first time that I did have a certain way with children. "I do like children . . . very much."

"Then you must meet Amy, Derek's little daughter. She is delightful . . . a most precious child with blond hair and . . ."

She stopped, seeing on my face the chagrin I had not been able to hide.

"Oh," she said as if remembering something. "Derek told me about one of the servants . . . a new girl, he said. Seems she came to Amy's aid yesterday. Would that by any chance have been you?"

"Yes, ma'am," I said with a flush. "I'm afraid it was.

I did not mean to pry, Mrs. Vanderworth, honestly I didn't, but . . ."

"You don't have to explain a thing to me. I would have done exactly the same had I heard a child crying. And I told that stiff-necked grandson of mine so, too."

"You . . . you did?"

"I certainly did!" She stopped for a moment and took a deep breath. There was the wrinkle of a frown between her eyes. "But . . . so much has happened in his life. Please don't judge him by his behavior just now, Elizabeth. He's been hurt and, well, I suppose I should not be discussing his personal problems this way. He certainly would not thank me for it. He's as stubborn as he is moody, I'm afraid. So much like his grandfather." She seemed to become lost in her thoughts, and I could see she was remembering her husband.

Miss Olivia and Ruthie had been sitting quietly, listening to our conversation. Ruthie turned her head back and forth between us as if watching a children's game while Miss Olivia sat with her eyes decorously lowered as she sipped her tea. But now the seamstress sat forward in her chair.

"Now, Maude," she said. "What exactly shall I do with this lovely blue gown you've brought me?"

"Oh," the woman replied, obviously jolted back from her daydreams. "I'm sorry, must be getting old," she laughed.

The two of them took the dress to the corner of the room, where the light was better. Between them they came to an agreement about the alterations.

Before Mrs. Vanderworth left she turned back to me. "Oh, Elizabeth . . . if you will come to my room this evening after dinner, I will bring some books from the library for you."

"Thank you, Mrs. Vanderworth, I'll do that," I said, feeling a surge of joy within me. The books I had brought with me had been read and reread so many times that the pages were ragged, the words practically worn from the paper. It would be wonderful to find new ones for my quiet evenings in the small, cozy room.

"Well," Ruthie said after Mrs. Vanderworth had gone. "She certainly took a shine to you!"

"Now, Ruthie," Miss Olivia chided. "You know Mrs. Vanderworth is kind to everyone here."

"Oh, she's kind, all right. I ain't denyin' that. But she never offered to bring me books, or even asked about my family for that matter." Ruthie sniffed her nose loudly as if her feelings had been hurt.

"I'm sure she only feels sorry for me," I said, not knowing what else to offer.

Ruthie looked at me and instantly her blue eyes cleared and a bright smile lit her pretty little face. She nodded. "That's probably it," she said. "After all, your glasses do make you look sad. And that black uniform on your slender little body just makes you look like a tiny, sorrowful blackbird."

"Ruthie!" Olivia said, shaking her head at the girl.

I knew Ruthie did not mean it to sound so cold and insulting. I could see regret cloud her clear blue eyes immediately, and I smiled at her.

"It's all right, Miss Olivia," I said with a laugh. "I understand what she means. I suppose I do look a bit sad in black. I must look as dull as dirt with my plain brown hair and white skin."

"Nonsense," she said. "You are a lovely girl. Your skin is lovely and clear, and your hair has sparkling golden highlights. There's nothing dull about that. But you should wear rose, the deep color of the azalea in spring. And the clear dark green of the emerald." She came to stand near me, turning me about as she gazed up and down my figure.

"I shall make you a new gown soon, one that will bring out all your lovely features. How would that be?"

"Oh, Miss Olivia, you don't have to do that."

"I know I don't," she said with a haughty lift of her brows. "But I want to and so that's that."

I'd never had anyone pay such attention to me before and it made me feel quite giddy.

"In that case then, Miss Olivia, I think it would be heavenly to have a new dress."

She turned to Ruthie, who stood watching anxiously. "And for you, Ruthie. I'll make one for you as well."

"What color should I wear, Miss Olivia?" Ruthie asked with a wistful little sigh in her voice.

"Pale yellow and green," the seamstress declared. "You shall look like a lovely little buttercup, bouncing in the wind."

Ruthie clapped her hands together in delight and fairly danced as we went out the door and back to our duties. I thought I'd never felt so happy as we walked down the hallway from the sitting room.

I began to believe that day, really believe, that coming to Stormhaven was my blessing in disguise. I had been here only two short days and already I had experienced more kindness than I'd ever dreamed of. And I believed I was on my way to gaining real friends in Miss Olivia and Ruthie, as well as Dottie, Frederick, and Johnny. And yes, even with the difference in our ages, I felt a kindred spirit with Mrs. Vanderworth, and in my naiveté I saw no reason why we should not be friends as well.

That evening after dinner I hurried back upstairs, anxious to see Mrs. Vanderworth and discover what books she had brought me. I had stayed longer in the servants' hall than I had expected, having such funny and pleasant conversation that I was afraid I might be too late.

But when Mrs. Vanderworth opened her door, she was still dressed and her pale eyes shone brightly as if she were not tired at all, but truly happy to see me.

"Come in, come in," she said as she motioned me into her lovely room.

I thought how suited it was to the lady of the house. And like her, it was stately and elegant. I had been awed by all the rooms I'd seen, but with an indrawn breath I gazed about me, thinking I'd never seen such splendor.

Seeing my look she only smiled. "You like it?" she asked quietly.

"Oh, Mrs. Vanderworth," I whispered. "I've never seen anything like it."

The room was decorated in Louis XV style, which was very feminine. The furniture and the paneling were full of graceful curves and rococo scrollwork. The walls were covered in a soft yellow silk material while the upholstery was purple and gold velvet.

"Look around," she offered. She watched me carefully as if she enjoyed my astonishment.

I walked across the soft Savonnerie rug and reached out to lightly touch the various priceless items, the Spode porcelain. I stopped at a grouping of pictures on the wall and gazed at engravings by Wille and Bervic and another lovely detailed one by Drevet.

"I love the French artists," I said, almost to myself.

"You are familiar with these artists?" she asked. She was not able to keep the surprise from her voice.

When I turned to her, she was gazing open-mouthed at me, much as one might upon finding that an animal could talk. I could not quell the laughter within me.

"Books," I explained. "As I said before, I read everything. I did not mean to sound pretentious . . ."

"Nonsense, child," she said, waving her hand in the air. She composed herself further and said, "I find that very admirable, my dear. Very admirable indeed. Don't ever apologize for your knowledge. It is a precious, precious thing.

"And speaking of books," she continued. "I did manage to find Derek alone after dinner long enough to talk to him about your using the library."

I wondered what he thought and if he remembered me. But of course, I chided myself silently. I had interfered with his daughter, and insulted him. How could he not remember me? I found I was holding my breath, waiting for her to tell me that her grandson would not allow me in his library, nor indeed anywhere else in his house.

"That's all right . . ." I began in anticipation of her words.

"He was delighted," she said.

"Delighted? He . . . he was?"

"Well, as delighted as could be expected," she said with a wry grin. "He is becoming entirely too serious for his own good, I'm afraid. But yes . . . he has no objections. In fact, he made a suggestion that I found very interesting."

Now it was my turn to stand open-mouthed. For I could not imagine what suggestion Derek Vanderworth might have that concerned me.

"As you will see, the main library here is quite extensive . . . over twenty thousand volumes, and that does not include the smaller groupings of books in other rooms. Why, the one in the bachelors' wing is as large as one might normally expect to find in a household."

"Twenty thousand . . . books?" My mind was in a spin. Never in my wildest dreams would I have imagined a house with so many books.

She laughed aloud at my expression.

"Yes," she said, still smiling. "Derek had begun cataloging all the books when . . . when Desiree died. Since then I suppose he has not had the heart. He asked if I thought you might be interested in continuing with the cataloging."

"Me? Oh, I don't know." Suddenly I was overwhelmed by the possibility of such a job. "I know nothing of cataloging . . . there . . . there might be things I would not understand, books I could not even read, or—"

I did not want to risk making a fool of myself. Why had I even told her about my love of books? Now I did not know what to do and I did not want to risk insulting her after all the trouble she'd gone to for me.

"Oh ho," she laughed. "Indeed there *will* be books you cannot read, nor can I, for that matter. But unlike me, my grandson speaks several languages. So don't trouble yourself with that. It is not necessary that you do. There are many things you will be able to achieve; I'm certain of it. Trust me, I'm an excellent judge of character."

I took a deep breath, not quite so certain as she seemed to be. "Do you really think I can? Does he . . . your grandson know that it's me who will be working in his library?"

She laughed aloud at that. "My dear, I made it perfectly clear who you were. And he definitely remembers you."

I blushed just thinking about our confrontation.

"My education is not extensive and I'm hardly qualified. After all, I'm only a . . ."

"A very bright, perceptive girl," she finished. "And one who is willing to try, and sometimes, my dear, I think that's the most important characteristic of all, don't you?"

What could I say when this woman who hardly knew me seemed to have more confidence in me than I had myself? Certainly more than even my own mother ever had.

I smiled at her and nodded. "Yes, I suppose. And I do want to try. I want to learn."

"I know you do," she said. "I can see it in your eyes. And you shall. You may begin with one day a week for now. Wednesdays, I think. I shall speak to Mrs.

Hunt myself first thing tomorrow. You may continue to live here on the third floor and continue your duties on the other days. That should pacify our Mrs. Hunt, don't you think?"

"Yes, ma'am," I said, still in a daze. "I hope so."

As I left she was still assuring me that I would do fine and that her grandson would not be disappointed with me either. My head was in a whirl. I could hardly believe how quickly all this had happened, and I could believe even less that Derek Vanderworth would allow me to remain in his house to work, much less perform such an important task as cataloging his books.

I hardly was aware of walking along the hallway toward my room. I was much too preoccupied with trying to remember each word Mrs. Vanderworth had said — especially anything that pertained to her grandson Derek. And I found myself trembling at seeing him face to face again.

I felt exhilarated later as I got into bed. The only thing missing was the sharing of my good news with someone. Perhaps tomorrow I would write Mother and tell her. I had no illusions that she would be pleased for me . . . she rarely expressed pleasure about anything I did. But at least I could tell myself she was happy for me, since I would not be able to see her face or the sneer of dismissal when she read my words.

My sleep that night was one of complete contentment. So much so that when a sound woke me in the night I thought nothing of it and turned over to go back to sleep. But suddenly I realized someone was crying, and from the sound of it, they were very near to my room.

I sat up in bed, not bothering to turn on the lamp. I turned my head to listen, wondering if I'd only dreamed the noise. Then I heard it again, a soft moaning cry . . . not the sound of someone in pain, but rather like the low cry of someone who grieved. I reached out to turn on the lamp, feeling a relief at the small glow of light.

I listened for a while, not knowing if I should get up and see what was wrong. I thought of little Amy and how I had angered her father with my interference.

But this was not a child's voice I heard. No, I was certain it was a woman. I remembered the stories I'd heard about Desiree's spirit and could not suppress a shiver as I wondered if it were possible.

But I did not believe in ghosts, I reminded myself. And I would not let myself be frightened by such morbid thoughts. Still, the muffled sobs that echoed through the hallway outside my room were disturbing, and suddenly I felt terribly alone and very vulnerable there in my tiny room.

Just as suddenly as the weeping started, it stopped. I heard the quiet thud of a closing door, and once again the house was silent.

Without a second thought I sprang from bed and tiptoed to the hallway. But I saw nothing, no one. Then I saw the door to Miss Olivia's room open slowly and the glow of a light spread out into the hallway as someone moved forward carrying a small oil lamp before them.

I was hardly aware of my gasp as the woman in white moved and her long, flowing white robe spread out behind her . . . like the wings of a pale butterfly.

She heard my gasp and turned sharply to me. I breathed a heavy sigh of relief as the light reflected upon Miss Olivia's frightened face. I realized I had probably frightened her as much as she had me.

"What are you doing out here?" she asked sharply, frowning at me. She was not at all the kind-voiced woman I was just beginning to know.

"Why, I . . . I heard the crying," I replied, stunned by her accusing tone of voice.

"You must have been dreaming. There was no crying," she said curtly with a lift of her brow.

"But there was. I'm . . . I'm certain of it. You must have heard it, too. Isn't that why you're here?"

She stared at me for a long moment and there was a look of disapproval on her usually serene face. Then she sighed and her shoulders dropped slightly.

"Elizabeth, my dear, I know you mean well. But I think you're mistaken." Her voice was cool now, but not unkind. "That is not why I'm here. Now perhaps you should go back to bed. It's going on toward dawn and not long 'til your duties begin. I suggest you get as much rest as possible." Then she turned to go down the hall. She seemed anxious and in a hurry to be away from me.

"But . . . but Miss Olivia . . ." I began, wondering at her strange reaction toward me.

She turned, all patience with me gone. "Please, Elizabeth! Just do as I ask. I'd have thought you much too intelligent a girl to be taken in by all this silly talk of ghosts and spirits. If you heard anything at all, I'm sure it was only in your imagination. Now goodnight."

She waited, staring at me as if she would tolerate no more arguments. I shook my head slightly, perplexed by her sudden change of manner. But it was not worth arguing about, so I turned obediently back toward my room.

She continued standing there until I had turned into the small, short hallway outside my room. Then I saw the shadow of the light moving down the hallway toward the landing of the back stairwell.

I slid quietly along the wall toward the hallway where I'd last seen her. I could not resist watching to see where she went. And I wondered as I saw the wavering light move onto the stairway and up toward the darkened fourth floor. Why on earth was Miss Olivia going up there at this hour of the night? And why wasn't she as terrified as I was?

After returning to my room, I sat in bed for a long

while, wondering about the cries I'd heard. I think something in me was waiting for them to begin again. But they did not. And I wondered about Miss Olivia and her curt dismissal. It was as if she was trying to hide something. But what?

I was still awake when the night sky outside my window began to lighten and turn a velvety blue. I heard a rooster crow somewhere far in the distance and felt the early morning breeze begin to stir its cool breath into the room.

"Well, Elizabeth Stevens," I whispered as I clutched the sheet tightly in my fists, "what strange place is this you've come to, and what have you gotten yourself into now?"

Chapter Eight

It was a tradition at Stormhaven that every servant should have Sundays off. Of course, the kitchen help still had duties, but they were limited ones and were done on a strictly voluntary basis. Ruthie said that most of the cooking was done on Saturday. Since the house was equipped with amazing appliances, including immense, closet-like refrigerators that were cooled by ammonia gas and brine water solution, the food could be kept safely until the next day.

Ruthie and I were up early on Sunday and carried towels and other necessities to the rooms. But we finished early, since it was also a tradition that any servant who wished could attend the family's Sunday morning church service.

It was the first time I'd walked all the way down the grand staircase to the first level of the house. As we went, I asked Ruthie about the crying I'd heard the night before.

" 'Twas the ghostie!" she declared. "I knew I heard it, but Miss Olivia declares she heard nothing. But then," she lowered her voice conspiratorially, "she's the sort won't admit it 'til she sees it with her own eyes."

"Have you ever seen this . . . this ghost?" I asked.

"Oh, yes!" she chimed. "Right there in the hallway one night. She walked silently, sort of flowin'-like, as if she wasn't touchin' the floor. Went right past your room there. She was dressed in white, like a long robe, and it fluttered back behind her like wings that almost reached from one side of the hall to the other."

Ruthie's account was too detailed, I thought, to have been made up. But what or whom had she really seen? I did not for a moment believe the specter in white was the ghost of Desiree Vanderworth. Miss Olivia had told both of us that she'd heard nothing. But I was more positive now than ever that she was there in the hallway because of the crying sounds.

But we had reached the main floor of the house and thoughts of the ghostie, as Ruthie called it, vanished. There was simply too much to see and do.

The church service, it seemed, was to be held in and around the winter garden, or the Palm Court, as others called it. This was the section of the house I'd looked down upon from the third-floor hallway, the part with the domed glass-paneled roof. But I hardly had time to look at the rest of the house here for the service was about to begin and we had to hurry to take our seats.

The Palm Court was near the center of the house just off the entrance hall. It was an octagonal room of pale marble. Large, open archways all around the court allowed a view of the fountain and greenery from every angle of the house. It was like a peaceful, green oasis. A wide marble hallway surrounded the Palm Court with access to other rooms.

As we walked around the court I caught a glimpse of the people seated in the circular gardenlike room. Derek Vanderworth sat in the front row. His bearing was as usual, solemn and rather unreadable. But as Ruthie and I walked through one of the archways and made our way down the short flight of steps, his tawny eyes moved, seeming to follow our every step.

Mrs. Vanderworth sat beside him. She looked even more regal than usual in her plum-colored dress with a ruffled fall of lace at her throat. She smiled sweetly and dipped her silvery head gracefully toward us. Beside her was the blond-haired young woman I'd seen in the courtyard after the hunt. She hardly gave us a glance.

I saw little Amy Vanderworth at almost the exact moment she saw me. She was partially hidden on the other side of her father. As her lovely little face turned toward me I saw a quick but unmistakable smile of recognition wash across her features.

Like a flash she scooted from her chair, and before either her father or grandmother could react, she ran toward us. I hesitated, uncertain for a moment where she was going.

But without a qualm she ran to me, clasping both chubby arms about my knees. I was totally unprepared for her impulsive welcome, and I laughed aloud with delight as I bent to hug her.

There were at least thirty servants seated in the row of seats behind the Vanderworth family. Now there was a murmur of laughter among them and smiling nods of enjoyment as they watched the little girl. I could imagine this delightful child was the pride of a household that could sometimes be staid and formal.

So I was not prepared for the cold, resentful look I saw in the eyes of my employer when I glanced up toward him.

"Amy!" he said quietly, his voice controlled and yet unmistakably annoyed. "Please return to your seat." He did not make a move to go to his daughter, but rather waited, his amber eyes demanding as he gazed at her.

She clung even tighter to my skirts, and as she did, she shook her head no, rubbing her face against the material of my dress. I glanced at her father, meeting his eyes as he glared at me. That look angered me. I could see no reason for his being so strict and controlling in this situation. The child's actions had been perfectly normal. After all, what child ever did the predictable on all occasions?

Mrs. Vanderworth rose and came toward us. "Come, Amy," she said with a smile. "It's time for the service to begin."

But again the child shook her head, still hiding her face in my skirts. I sank to my knees beside her and took her gently by the shoulders. The glimmer of tears in her eyes made my heart melt, and I knew without a doubt that I should not become involved with her. I had already angered her father once on that account.

But I could not abandon her, could not be harsh with this beautiful child who did not speak and yet whose eyes said everything.

I had not noticed Mrs. Hunt's presence in the room until she rose and came to me. Her slanting eyes held a flash of fire as she trained them on me.

"Miss Stevens," she hissed, just barely loud enough for me to hear. I got the impression she would do almost anything to avoid a scene, even be civil to me.

"Get up immediately!" she snapped.

"Amy," I whispered quickly. "I'm so happy to see you again. But you must go sit with your father now. Perhaps after the services . . ."

As I knelt at Amy's level, I heard Derek Vanderworth's deep, authoritative voice rumble above us.

"It's all right, Mrs. Hunt," he said. "Perhaps to avoid further delay, Amy would prefer to sit with Miss Stevens. That is, if she has no objections."

I looked up into his eyes and those of Mrs. Hunt beside him. I could see the displeasure on their faces, but it seemed Mr. Vanderworth was willing to allow this small indulgence. I took a deep breath and stood up, taking the little girl's tiny, plump hand in mine.

"I would be delighted," I said, meeting his steady gaze with a forced smile.

I was certain Mrs. Hunt would truly have loved to strangle me then, her look was so vicious. But she whirled and went back to her seat.

Some of the servants moved over so that Ruthie and Amy and I could sit behind Amy's family. As we took our seats, I glanced about, hoping to find a friendly glance from Charles Simmons. But he was not present.

Diana Gresham twisted all the way around in her chair to look with disapproval at us. Her look was

71

haughty as a sneer curled her full red lips.

Ruthie nudged me as she saw the woman's look, but I did not turn to her, but busied myself with the hymnals that someone handed down the row. For the first time I noticed the ornately carved piano that was partially hidden by several tall green palms. The woman seated there began to play a soft, peaceful selection from Bach.

The room grew quiet, the only sound that of the piano and the trickle of water from the lovely fountain statue.

I took advantage of the quiet moment to gaze about the room, beginning first with the fountain. The bronzed figure of a young boy rose from the water and at his feet were swans, their wings outstretched. Above us, from the lovely oak arched framework of the glass dome, there hung heavy, ornate iron lanterns. It was a room of extreme peacefulness, a quiet small haven in the middle of the house's vast maze of rooms and hallways.

Amy wiggled in her seat beside me, nudging herself closer to me until I placed an arm around her. I didn't know why she had taken such an interest in me when there were so many others in the house who were more than willing to give her love and attention. But perhaps her father kept her from them as he had tried to keep her from me.

I allowed my eyes to wander now to the man in my thoughts. He sat very near to me, near enough that I could see the curve of dark brown hair that curled over the back of his collar. I looked at the slant of his jaw and his sculpted chin, which he held proudly upward. I could even see the flicker of his dark lashes as his gaze drifted about the room. My eyes moved to his lips, which were well shaped and soft, even sensitive. Strange, but they did not seem to fit with the cold, hard image of him that was slowly developing in my mind.

I suppose I was daydreaming a bit, for he turned his head slightly and caught me unawares as I studied him. For a heart-stopping moment I was caught, ensnared by the gleam of his amber gaze as he looked at me from the corner of his eyes. Quickly I looked away, lowering my eyes and hiding them behind my glasses. I did not look at him again and only hoped he looked away before he saw the slow blush of color that I could feel upon my face.

During the service Amy snuggled up against me, finally laying her head on my lap and closing her eyes. As she slept I could not resist letting my fingers smooth the rumpled, feathery curls of her blond hair. When the pastor had finished speaking and the last prayer was said, I sat quietly as most of the others stood up to leave. I did not want to disturb the sleeping angel upon my lap.

Mrs. Hunt, as I expected, came immediately to me, her exotic eyes still blazing. Her voice was a mere whisper as she spoke to me. "How dare you make such a scene, Miss Stevens! Mr. Vanderworth does not wish his child to be unduly spoiled and indulged. I cannot believe you took it upon yourself to encourage the child to defy her father!"

"But I . . . I didn't," I stammered, shaken and embarrassed by her harsh reprimand. "The child came to me . . . she . . ."

"That will be enough," she said angrily, glancing about her. "We will speak about this later . . . in private!" She whirled about and in her brisk, efficient manner, turned to go. I saw her nod curtly toward Derek Vanderworth, who stood quietly nearby. He had been watching us, and I was sure he had heard Mrs. Hunt's angry accusations.

My face burned with embarrassment, and I could feel a layer of perspiration at the back of my neck. I pulled at the tight collar of my dress, which suddenly seemed too hot and uncomfortable.

I looked up into Derek's eyes, expecting to see a smug look of satisfaction. But even though his look was just as cold and unemotional as usual, I saw no satisfaction. There was no triumph, no censure, and certainly no sympathy. His look was totally empty, and I wondered how anyone could become this way.

Mrs. Vanderworth came to me, smiling tenderly at her

great granddaughter. By then Derek Vanderworth was distracted by the lovely blond Diana. She seemed agitated by something and was gesturing almost wildly at him as she spoke.

"Amy's governess will be here directly," Mrs. Vanderworth said. "This poor little dear is resting so well, I hate to disturb her."

I, too, hated to disturb Amy. It broke my heart to think that the child might be sleepy because she spent lonely nights crying in her room.

I saw Diana turn to leave the room. She did not glance our way again. Derek moved immediately toward us then, and I was certain that now he would discipline me too. But his quiet voice and easy manner took me by surprise.

"I'll take her," he said to his grandmother.

He bent low toward me as he reached for his daughter. I could feel his soft breath upon my cheek and smell the tangy citrus and spice scent of his shaving lotion as he bent near me. For a moment I felt strangely disoriented.

Quickly I placed my arms beneath Amy and moved to place her in her father's arms. For a moment she made a sleepy protest and twisted toward me, then immediately was asleep again. Her movement caused my hand to become captured between her body and Derek Vanderworth's hard, muscular arm.

Instinctively I looked up at him, directly into his face, just as his dark lashes flickered open. My breath caught in my throat. His eyes were no longer blank and emotionless. There was something there in their depths, some hidden stirring I could not quite decipher. For a moment I thought it was fear. Then it was gone, hidden by the shuttered lowering of his lashes as he lifted the small, warm bundle into his arms.

As he looked down at his daughter, I saw a noticeable softening of his features, a warming of the cold facade I'd seen before. But without a word to me or his grandmother he turned and carried Amy up the stairs from the

Palm Court and away from my curious eyes.

The older woman turned to me. "Pay no mind to him, dear," she said. "I'm afraid he's distracted lately by . . . many things." She picked up the skirt of her plum gown and moved toward the steps. "Oh, and Elizabeth, don't forget Wednesday is your day in the library. I've already spoken to Mrs. Hunt about it."

Ruthie had been quietly listening during this time and now I found her standing practically on top of me. "Day in the library? What does she mean, day in the library?" she asked.

I explained briefly what I'd been asked to do, trying not to make a big issue of it.

"Well!" she sniffed. "I suppose they think the rest of us ain't smart enough to do such work. I, for one, have never been asked to help below stairs!"

"It's only because I like to read, Ruthie. I'm certain they would never have asked otherwise." The last thing I needed was for Ruthie to turn against me.

"Well . . . that could be true. I don't care for readin'. Still, I'd watch my step if I was you. Everybody knows that Diana Gresham is aimin' to take her sister's place here. You start gettin' too cozy with Mr. Vanderworth and she will have you workin' in the kitchen, scrubbin' pots and pans!"

"I have no intention of getting cozy, as you say, with Mr. Vanderworth, or anyone else here, Ruthie." She was beginning to irritate me. If I had learned one thing since coming to Stormhaven, it was that everyone seemed determined to run everyone else's business. And it was something I found hard to tolerate, having always been a private person.

Ruthie at least looked a bit sheepish, realizing, I'm sure, how overbearing she sounded. "Well, you're a very nice girl," she said. "I just don't want to see you get hurt."

"I won't," I declared, as much to myself as to her. "I promise I won't be."

"Well, if you expect any attention from the earl, you're

75

only foolin' yourself. He's not for the likes of you and me." Then, with a sudden grin, she changed the subject. "Well, I have a date with that nice new boy in the stables. So if you'll excuse me, love." Then she was gone, swinging her skirts and walking with a saucy gait toward the entranceway.

The pastor, whom I had hardly noticed until now, was still standing at the small oak podium. He watched Ruthie as she left and then, with a smile, came toward me. I was certain he had been listening to our conversation all along.

"Good morning," he said. "You're new here, aren't you?"

"Yes," I said. "This is my first week."

"I'm sure you'll find the Vanderworths fine people to work for." Then he bowed slightly. "I'm James Webster, pastor of the St. Andrews Presbyterian Church."

I had been so distracted during the services that I had paid little attention to him. Now I saw that he was young, quite young, it seemed, to be the pastor of a church.

He was tall, though perhaps not as tall as Derek Vanderworth. His hair, already thinning on top, was light brown, almost the same color as his eyes. He wore a very short, neat beard. His face was kind and open, but something about him did not fit the picture most people might have of a minister.

"I'm Elizabeth Stevens," I said.

"I could not help noticing, Elizabeth, how taken little Amy is with you."

"Yes," I said. "She seems like such a sweet child, and so affectionate that I can hardly resist her."

"She's a great deal like her mother," he said almost distractedly.

"Is she?" I answered politely. I had many questions about Desiree Vanderworth. But I wasn't sure this man was the one I should ask.

"Well, in looks, anyway. Desiree was a spirited woman, full of fun and mischief. But I believe little Amy's personality is turned a bit more inward, like her father's."

I watched his eyes as he spoke. There was something deep within them when he spoke of Desiree, and I wondered if, like Johnny and Frederick, he too had been a little bewitched by her.

"Has Amy been mute since birth?" I asked.

His eyes swung back to my face and there was a look of surprise in them. "Why, no. Didn't anyone tell you? But then, no, I suppose they would not."

Something in the tone of his voice made me shiver with an intuitive feeling of apprehension.

"What?" I asked.

"Little Amy stopped speaking the night her mother died. The doctors have found no reason for it. One would not expect to find such an expression of grief in a child so young. But that seems to be the only explanation . . . shock and grief." He shook his head as he spoke.

"How terribly sad," I muttered. His words made me feel sick inside.

"Yes, well, it's been extremely hard for the family. And now that the anniversary is approaching, even doubly so. Perhaps once that milestone is passed, things will appear brighter. And now that Derek is no longer a suspect . . ." He stopped suddenly, aware that he was discussing the most intimate of details with a servant girl.

"I'm sorry," he said quickly. "What must you think of me, a man of God, gossiping this way?"

He looked so embarrassed that I felt an immediate sympathy for him.

"You've said nothing out of the way, Reverend Webster," I assured him. "And you need not worry. I won't repeat anything we've discussed."

"Thank you, Elizabeth," he said with a deep warm voice. "You have a kind heart, I think. I thought the moment I saw you that you had such an open, sweet face."

He did not mean his compliment to be anything other than friendly, and that's exactly the way I took it. I thanked him and we parted with polite words of promise to talk again at the next Sunday service.

I had been so eager to see this part of the house. It had stopped raining and the sun now cast long, brilliant beams of light from the different rooms out into the hallway. The Palm Court came alive as the sun rippled down through the glass dome.

But my mind was not on the house or seeing the magnificent and priceless pieces of art. I walked up the grand staircase, seeing only the vision of little Amy Vanderworth and wondering what terrible memories she must have of that night . . . the night her mother fell from a balcony on the upper floor.

There had been talk among the servants that Desiree's death was not a suicide. Were there some who still believed it was murder? And since Derek Vanderworth had been a suspect, as the Reverend Webster mentioned, did that mean he was capable of murder? Evidently someone thought so.

I shivered as I walked up the winding marble stairway. As I recalled the cold glitter of those amber eyes it was not hard to imagine them turning deadly. And yet something inside me would not let me believe he was some monstrous murderer. And I think on that beautiful Sunday morning, against all my better judgment, I became fascinated by Derek Vanderworth, and more curious than I should have been about finding out the truth of his wife's death.

Chapter Nine

When I next saw Miss Olivia, she seemed to have totally dismissed her rather harsh words to me of the previous night. She seemed the same kind person as before.

After a pleasant Sunday afternoon lunch with her, I spent a few hours in my room, reading and napping. And although I was very eager to go outdoors and see the grounds of the beautiful chateau, I learned that more guests were expected in the evening and that my services were needed.

Ruthie still had not returned from her meeting with the stableboy, and so it was left for me to do. The lovely rooms on our floor were ready, but there were several details that needed to be attended to.

We remained busy the following day, and I had little time to dwell on the problems surrounding the Vanderworth family. And fortunately, little time to worry about my new library duties on Wednesday.

Late on Tuesday afternoon I was in the living hall finishing up the last of the chores. My eyes were burning and I'd just taken off my glasses when I heard footsteps coming up the grand stairway and turned to see who it was.

When Charles Simmons' sandy head appeared, I smiled. I had not seen him since our first meeting. And there was something about him and his manner that made me feel as if I were seeing an old friend.

"Well, if it isn't our beautiful Elizabeth," he said with a grin as he moved toward me.

He carried a small canvas bag which he sat on the floor at the top of the stairway.

"You've been on a trip," I said, glancing toward the bag.

"Yes," he said with a wave of his hand. "Business. A boring subject. I'd much rather talk about you and learn what you've been doing while I was away."

I swung my hand good-naturedly toward the living hall. "Cleaning," I said with a smile. "It's my job, you know."

"Ah, yes," he said. "Sometimes I forget that you're not one of the grand ladies guesting here for the summer."

I knew he was teasing me, but it did not matter. There was something in his look and the twinkle of his eye that let me know his joshing was done with affection.

"What's happened to your glasses?" he asked.

As I held them up in my hand for him to see, he frowned.

"Oh," he said. "I hoped you had thrown the nasty things away."

I blushed then, for the glasses were perhaps the one thing I was extremely self-conscious about.

He saw the blush and was immediately contrite. "I am sorry," he said, moving toward me. "It's just that your gray eyes are so lovely. Almost like silver. I don't think I've ever seen eyes quite likes yours, and it's a shame to hide them behind glasses."

"But I can't read without them," I said, placing the wires back behind my ears. "I only took them off for a moment because I've developed a headache."

"Then I'm doubly sorry," he said gallantly with a little nod toward me.

I smiled at him just at the moment Derek Vanderworth came up the last step of the grand stairway. He stopped quietly and stood watching Charles and me together in the dimly lit living hall. But Charles's back was to the stairway and he did not see his cousin, nor apparently had he heard his quiet footsteps.

I don't know why, but something told me that Derek Vanderworth would not approve of his cousin speaking so intimately with one of his servants. I tried to warn Charles with a look, but he had glanced away, looking down at a black lacquered table between us as he ran his fingers across its shiny surface.

"Now that I'm back," Charles said. "I hope you will consider what I asked you before. I would be honored if you would walk in the gardens with me one evening."

I was trapped, embarrassed that Derek Vanderworth heard Charles's softly spoken words. I looked across Charles's shoulders straight into Derek's disconcerting tigerlike eyes. There was no doubt he had heard the proposition, and he looked at me with a taunting smile.

"I'm sure Miss Stevens is much too busy to entertain you, Charles," he drawled.

Charles spun about on his heel, obviously startled by the voice behind him. I could see the side of his face and the clenching of his jaw as he confronted his cousin.

"And I, cousin, am certain that Elizabeth is old enough to make up her own mind. That is, unless you, as her employer, would forbid it?" His words carried a sneering challenge, and a definite resentment.

Derek came slowly across the room toward us. One hand was in his trouser pocket, and he looked for all the world like a man of position, one who had everything and knew it. When he reached us, he smiled, but his amber eyes were still as cold and hard as a statue's.

"Of course I do not forbid it. But neither do I want

you to use your standing here to coerce anyone into doing as you wish." He glanced at me with a questioning lift of his brows.

Something about that look infuriated me. He was discussing me as if I were not even present, or worse, as if I were merely another collected possession in his magnificent home.

Charles thrust his chin forward. "Now look here . . ."

"If you both would allow it, I am perfectly capable of speaking for myself!" I said, my voice sounding loud in the quiet room.

Now both of them looked at me with slight surprise. It was as if they had forgotten I was present.

"Of course you may," Derek said, his voice clipped and even more impersonal than before. I could see my words had hit a nerve. "You are hardly a prisoner here, Miss Stevens."

I lifted my chin and looked at both of them through my thick glasses. "Mr. Simmons has not coerced me in any way. He has conducted himself always as a perfect gentleman."

Charles straightened his shoulders and could not hide the confident smile that played upon his face as he glanced at his cousin. At that moment I could not decide which of the two was the more arrogant.

I continued. "But as I told Mr. Simmons, I did not want to do anything that would be inappropriate to my position here."

Derek's lips curled ever so slightly at one corner as he looked at me. I suppose I was quite a humorous sight, standing there stiffly in my housemaid's uniform, so angry that I dared to speak boldly to "his lordship," as some called him.

"Then let me put your mind to rest, Miss Stevens. There is no caste system in my household. You may see whomever you please, whenever you please . . . it is certainly nothing to me." With that, he turned to leave us. "Excuse me," he murmured as he proceeded past us and down the hallway toward the sewing room.

I watched him, speechless with anger and frustration. He was so changeable and such a hard man to understand.

"Well," Charles said with a self-conscious little laugh. "I suppose that should answer all your questions."

But now I felt irritated, not only by Derek Vanderworth, but also by his cousin Charles. He seemed so smug and sure of himself, as if he had won a great victory. And I did not miss the fact that I was only a pawn in their game of wills. I did not like it. I did not like it at all.

I turned to Charles, intending to set him straight. But the look of happy anticipation in his gentle eyes and the boyish smile on his face took my words directly away. I did not want to hurt him. Besides, it was hardly his fault that I found his cousin so bewildering.

"It does indeed answer all my questions," I said. "And I suppose there's no reason why I should not walk with you in the garden sometime."

"Today?" he asked.

I laughed, my anger disappearing almost completely. "Yes, today would be fine."

"Then I shall meet you right here before dinner," he said, obviously pleased. "Around five o'clock."

I had just turned to go when I saw that Mrs. Hunt had stepped into the room. She was practically glaring at Charles.

"Mr. Simmons," she snapped. "I greatly dislike your making plans with one of the help when she hasn't been properly dismissed for the day."

Charles turned. His eyes widened and a big grin moved across his face. Slowly and deliberately, I thought, he let his eyes wander down Mrs. Hunt's trim figure and back again to her angry face.

"Why, Mrs. Hunt. As always, such a pleasant surprise to see you. You're looking lovely as ever."

"Don't try your charming ways on me, sir," she said angrily.

"Oh, I wouldn't think of trying such an obvious ploy with you," he said with amused sarcasm. "I'm sure you're much too clever for that."

Mrs. Hunt turned to me. Her disapproval was clear, and I wondered if I would ever be able to do anything to please her.

"You're to clean the silver in the back closet, scrub the floors at the stair landing, dust all the pictures along the hallways, and . . ."

"Miss Hunt . . ." Charles interrupted with an exaggerated sigh. "What is this all about? Surely you don't expect the girl to work all night." I detected a firmer note in his voice now and I wondered if Mrs. Hunt was aware of the change in him.

"I don't believe, Mr. Simmons, it is your place to question my authority. And if I say . . ."

"Oh, but I assure you it *is* my place." Charles's smoky eyes sparkled like crystal, and the lazy drawl had left his voice. "And as for your authority, it goes only as far as the Vanderworth family wishes it to go. Perhaps you've forgotten that my mother was a Vanderworth, and therefore, you are working for me as well as for Derek."

I could hardly believe the change in him, the spark in his eye as he dared her to disagree. There was certainly nothing of the frivolous nature in him now.

Small spots of color appeared beneath the smooth olive skin of Mrs. Hunt's cheeks. Her lips quivered slightly as she stood stiff-backed and glared at him.

"I was only attempting to do my job," she said quietly as she lowered her eyes.

"I understand that," he said softly. "And I would not wish to interfere. But this matter has already been discussed with my cousin. He has agreed that there is to be no difference made in this house according to the status of its occupants. I'm certain that you would agree." There was again the note of sarcasm in his voice.

I wondered if he and Mrs. Hunt had had differences before. For somehow their conversation made me feel as if I were eavesdropping, as if what they were saying to each other was quite personal.

Mrs. Hunt took a long breath of air and lifted her chin defiantly, looking straight into Charles's eyes.

"Yes, Mr. Simmons, I do agree." But the rebellion was still in her eyes.

"Good," he said, his lips quirking into a slight smile. Then he turned to me, leaving her standing behind him fuming silently.

"Then I shall see you at five, Elizabeth, just as we planned."

I'm certain he recognized my look of exasperation and uncertainty, but he only smiled. I could understand why everyone talked of his charm. He did have a way about him, and I had to admit that his anger had only made him more appealing. I laughed even as Mrs. Hunt glared at us.

"All right," I agreed. "Five o'clock it is."

Mrs. Hunt and I watched as he picked up his bag and walked around the balustrade and down the hallway to his room. Then I hurriedly finished replacing the items I'd taken from the tables while dusting. I did not glance at Mrs. Hunt, even though I knew she still watched me.

My behavior was as much for her as for my own embarrassment. I knew she must be terribly humiliated to be treated in such a way before one of her employees.

"Don't think to fool me with your quiet, meek ways, Miss Stevens. I'm sure you'll be gloating soon enough with the other servants." Her voice was cold, but there was a glint of moisture in her exotic eyes.

"Believe me, Mrs. Hunt, I'm not gloating."

"Well . . ." she tossed her head and turned to go. Slowly she turned back to face me, and this time there was a strange look of sympathy on her attractive face.

"You're very young, Elizabeth. Charles Simmons is a very attractive man, but I'd hate to see you taken in by him, that's all." She sounded sad and defeated as she walked swiftly from the room.

I finished my chores and went to the end of the hallway near the maids' quarters to put away my work supplies. From the narrow stairway just beyond I heard the sound of voices that raised and lowered as if in a heated discussion.

I walked to the doorway and looked toward the stairs, but there was no one on our level of the house. The voices came from directly above me, from the fourth floor, where I'd been warned never to venture.

I heard the slam of a door and then footsteps coming nearer. As the sounds moved to the staircase I stepped instinctively out of sight beneath the overhang of the steps. It was not that I meant to hide or to spy. I just was not sure who it was, and I suppose I was a bit frightened. Besides, the last thing I needed was to get myself in trouble again.

As the footsteps and the voices came closer, I could clearly distinguish that there was a man and a woman. I flattened my body back against the wall as far as I could, holding my breath as they came nearer and moved onto the third floor. From my shadowed vantage point I peered out at the couple before me.

Derek Vanderworth and his sister-in-law Diana stood for a moment. There was obviously a great deal of tension between them.

"You should not have gone up there alone," Derek said firmly to the young woman.

"Why? Are you afraid of Desiree's ghost as everyone else in this house seems to be?" Her question carried an annoying, derisive tone.

"I would not expect you, her own sister, to speak so blithely about the matter," Derek replied in that cool manner I'd heard so often before.

"And why not? Simply because she was my sister? I can't believe that you, of all people, have made a saint of her since she died."

I was hardly breathing. This conversation was much too personal for me to hear, and I knew if I was discovered it would be terribly embarrassing for all of us. And a part of me did not want to chance the wrath of Derek Vanderworth. He seemed a very volatile and unpredictable man. And I was beginning to realize more and more that his cool demeanor only masked a hidden rage.

His voice was deceptively calm. "I'm sure you know, Diana, that I never regarded your sister as a saint. Her death has not changed that."

"Then am I to assume you no longer loved her? No longer lusted after her, as all the rest of the men in her life did?" Her voice was defensive and bitter, and I thought there was also a great deal of jealousy there as well.

Derek raked his hand impatiently through his hair and took a long, slow breath.

"Don't do this, Diana," he said.

"Why? Why shouldn't I? You never want to talk about it. Everything has to be on your terms. Well, I'm sick of it, do you hear? I want to know how you felt about Desiree!"

He did not answer, but placed his hand at her elbow. As he did, she leaned toward him, as if she could not help herself. The look on her face was pleading and there was no longer any anger there. His touch, it seemed, had erased all her indignation.

"Diana," he said. "This is not something I am going to discuss with you. I've told you that before."

His voice was the kindest I'd ever heard from him. I sensed he did not want to hurt her. As he spoke, he moved toward the doorway, urging her along with him.

I might have been naive, but I recognized the look on her beautiful face; it was one of complete adoration. I was not surprised. He was certainly an appealing man, in many ways. I could understand any woman falling under the spell of those tawny eyes, being fascinated by the quiet smile on his sensuous lips.

Diana pouted prettily, but she seemed to know it was no use arguing any longer. She went with him, then, with only a frustrated little flounce but with no further protests.

As they moved away I heard the low rumble of his voice, and the words he spoke were mysterious ones. "I don't want you to go up there alone anymore. Do you understand me? The situation is too unpredictable. From now on, I will take care of everything."

After they were gone, I was left in the shadows of the narrow stairwell, wondering what he meant. As I eased quietly from beneath my hiding place, I glanced up toward the top of the stairs of the forbidden floor. A shadow darted swiftly away from the upper landing. There was someone there! Someone else had overheard the conversation between Derek and Diana . . . someone who stood silently on the stairs above them.

I shivered, suddenly feeling uneasy and uncertain about what lay above us on the next floor. But certainly I did not believe in ghosts, I told myself. What a ridiculous notion. But if no one ever went up there, then who, or what, had I seen?

I hurried back to the security of the maids' quarters and finished putting the work closet in order.

Hadn't Frederick told me there were items stored on the top floor? Yes, I told myself, I was certain he had. That would explain the shadows I'd seen. It was probably only one of the servants working up there today, perhaps bringing something down to the main level of the house.

I breathed a sigh of relief at my conclusion and hurried to my own room. Suddenly I needed to be outside in the sweet, gentle breeze that spring generates. I needed to talk to another human being and walk leisurely through the fragrant flowers that filled the gardens. Perhaps I'd only been stuck inside the house too long and listened too often to Ruthie's whimsical ideas about ghosts and spirits.

Those thoughts reassured me, and I allowed them to ease the frightening feelings of intuition that had begun to plague me. Feelings that were somehow tied up in a tumultuous bow that connected the death of Desiree Vanderworth with the conversation I'd just heard between her husband and her sister.

Chapter Ten

I did feel better once I'd bathed and pulled the long strands of my hair back with a bright green ribbon. I had only one other dress to wear beside my old gray suit.

The dress was no more stylish, but at least it was a bit more feminine. And although it was well worn and the material thin from so many washings, the white color seemed to make its age less noticeable. I wore no bustle; I did not even own one. Mother often said that our money was to be spent on much more important things than fashion.

But the white muslin material of the dress skirt was pulled back at the hips and gathered into a softly ruffled flounce that I hoped was flattering. I then took a long green ribbon that matched the one in my hair and tied it about my waist. I was not so naive as to think I could ever be considered *en vogue,* but I certainly did feel better than when I wore the somber maid's uniform.

I made my way to the sitting hall just as the clocks chimed five. Charles was already there and turned to greet me as he heard me approach.

He walked to me and extended his bent arm, looking down into my face. He smiled and a glow of pleasure lit his clear eyes.

"I do like a lady who is prompt," he said breezily as he

escorted me through the sitting room and toward the stairs.

It felt odd walking with Charles down the great marble stairway into the cavernous entrance hall. I glanced toward the Palm Court, which the afternoon sun had turned into a glowing splash of gold. The varied green plants there looked cool and inviting.

We exited the house through massive double doors and walked out to a sidewalk which flanked both sides of the house. Here sat great stone lions with sharp fangs bared as if to guard the doorway.

Charles steered me to the right and as we walked past the front of the house and turned the corner I could see the blue-green mountains that rose in the distance, the same mountains I could see from my upstairs window.

"I hope the dragon lady wasn't too nasty to you after I left," Charles said rather quietly.

"If you mean Mrs. Hunt, no, she wasn't," I said glancing up into his face.

He pursed his lips thoughtfully and with his head lowered, seemed to be concentrating on the pebbles that he kicked with the toe of his shoe.

"She's a very attractive lady," I said. "It's so sad that she's become a widow at such a young age."

He looked at me from the corners of his eyes and smiled teasingly. "Are you trying to tell me something?"

"No," I said slowly. "There just seem to be some . . . some unseen emotions between the two of you."

He laughed and shook his head. "You're a very observant girl," he said with a grin. "The emotion I believe, is hatred . . . at least, on Mrs. Hunt's part."

"Oh, I don't believe she hates you for a moment," I said.

He ran a long, slender finger over his chin. "Well, she dislikes me greatly. I'm not sure if it is because of who I am or what she thinks I am."

"Now, what do you mean by that?" I asked lightly, not sure if I should.

"Why, haven't you noticed? I have Vanderworth blood, although I'm not as socially acceptable, it seems, because my father was poor. He never fit in, either, never wanted to, I guess. And of course, there is the talk of my scandalous reputation . . . which you would do well to heed, my girl." He shook his finger at me in a mock warning.

"So I gather," I said with a smile. Somehow I did not believe all the rumors I'd heard about this man. He was too kind and gentle to treat a lady in any kind of scandalous manner.

"Oh, so Mrs. Hunt *has* warned you away from me?"

"As a matter of fact, she did. She said you were very attractive, but I was too young to be taken in by a man like you."

He stopped and looked at me for a second with a puzzled expression on his face. Then he threw his head back and laughed with delight. He shook his head as he grinned at me. "As I said, you are refreshingly direct. But she's right, you know. You shouldn't become involved with me."

"Oh, I don't believe that for a moment. I think you're a very nice man."

His eyelids lowered, shutting away his eyes from me. I wasn't sure he liked being told what a nice man he was.

"And do you know what else I think?" I asked, feeling bolder.

"I'm sure you'll tell me," he replied in a droll voice.

"I think Mrs. Hunt's behavior has to do with her feelings for you."

"What? What on earth do you mean by that?" he asked with a hoot of laughter.

"I think she likes you." I turned then and walked on along the path we had chosen.

Soon Charles caught up with me. I could see as I glanced sideways at him that he was pleased, but he tried hard not to show it.

"Do you mean *likes,* as in a man/woman kind of way?"

"That's exactly what I mean," I said, enjoying seeing his shyness.

"No," he said, shaking his head.

"Oh, yes. Those sparks between you have to come from somewhere, you know," I said.

"Why, Miss Stevens, what kind of thing is *that* for a young, innocent girl like yourself to say?" But he laughed, and I could see how much he enjoyed sparring with me.

As we walked on I said no more on the subject. But Charles was unusually quiet and I thought perhaps he was as interested in Mrs. Hunt as she was in him.

Charles changed the subject by pointing toward the end of the house. "The library is here, in this end of the mansion. And this is called the library terrace."

The terrace was shady and cool, covered by overhead trellises of wisteria and trumpet creeper. The gardens beyond took my breath away with their size and elegant formality.

"This is the Italian garden," Charles said as we stepped down to walk toward three large pools.

The garden was walled on the west, the side that faced the mountains. This was also the side where the land dropped off steeply to the lush green meadows below. On the opposite side were huge boxwoods, taller than a man's head.

We walked quietly along the graveled pathway beside the wall. Charles seemed to enjoy showing me each small detail of the garden. And no matter how he had protested before about being dependent upon his cousin, I could see the glow of pride in his eyes as he spoke about the estate.

"This design dates back to the sixteenth century. I daresay there isn't another like it in all of America." He motioned to the three pools, symmetrically designed.

"This pool contains the sacred lotus of Egypt," he said with a certain air of accomplishment.

We walked past the second pool, which contained a statue and a bubbling fountain. "And this one, as you see, has exotic species of water lilies. The English ivy you see growing along the stonework there came from cuttings brought from the Vanderworth Castle in England."

"I've never seen anything like this place," I said. "But then I've been amazed by all the splendor at Stormhaven."

He placed his hand on mine where it rested in the crook of his arm. "Yes, well, cousin Derek certainly has an eye for the best things in life." A muscle moved spasmodically along his jawline.

"What was his wife like?"

He stopped for a moment as if surprised by my question. I looked up into his face just as he moved forward again. I was certain then that there had definitely been some feeling in him for Desiree Vanderworth. Of course, I could not say what, I could only surmise. But if the look on his face was any indication, I wondered if it was not love he'd felt for his cousin's wife.

"Desiree was . . ." He stopped and pulled away from me. His eyes looked wistfully far away into the distance as if he saw her face there in the mountains. "She was the most beautiful woman I ever knew. She was everything I was not . . . strong-willed, courageous, full of fun and energy. She had a tremendous zest for living . . ." He stopped and looked at me self-consciously. This time his eyes were filled with pain so real that he could not hide it.

"Charles," I said, stepping beside him and placing my hand on the sleeve of his jacket. "I'm sorry. I did not mean to bring back painful memories."

He was trying to compose himself and the effort had left him unable to speak. He simply clasped my hand and squeezed it as he continued to look toward the mountains.

I heard footsteps in the loose gravel of the pathway.

94

As I looked toward the house I saw Mrs. Vanderworth strolling casually toward us. Her hand was tucked securely about her tall, handsome grandson's arm.

Even from this distance I could see the stormy look on Derek Vanderworth's face as he saw us. I removed my hand from Charles's and stepped away, then was immediately angry with myself for doing so.

I had nothing to prove to this man, absolutely nothing. And I was ashamed that I'd allowed his presence to interfere with my showing simple friendship to Charles.

"Elizabeth . . . Charles," Mrs. Vanderworth said as they approached us. "Isn't it a lovely afternoon for a stroll?"

"Yes, grandmother, it certainly is," Charles said, wiping the sadness from his face. He walked to her and bent to place a light kiss upon her cheek. "I was just showing Elizabeth the gardens before dinner."

"Good," she said smiling at me. "You look lovely, dear."

If anyone else had spoken those words to me, I would have doubted their sincerity. But her kindness only made me feel grateful and perhaps a bit more secure with myself.

I did not glance up into the smoldering eyes of her other grandson, even though I knew his gaze was upon me. I could not understand him, or myself. He had not shown me anything other than cool disdain since our first meeting. And yet I found myself wondering if he also thought I looked well. Or did he simply find my attempts humorous . . . the pitiful machinations of a maid who longed to look like one of his fashionable guests? Suddenly I could not wait to be away from him and his studied looks, his cool, unreadable expressions.

I placed my arm back in Charles's and gave him an unnoticeable tug. With hardly a glance at me, he took the hint and moved us away in the opposite direction.

"I'll see you at dinner Grandmother . . . Derek," he said with a polite nod.

"Oh, Miss Stevens," Derek called. The sound of his deep voice calling my name halted me where I stood, and I felt a warm flush move from my throat to my cheeks.

"Don't forget, we have a long day together tomorrow. Don't let Charles keep you out too late." There was no mistaking the mockery in his voice.

I turned sharply toward him, my eyes hot with anger. And even though he was already turning away, I did not miss the smile that tugged at the corner of his mouth, nor the way his grandmother was glaring at him.

"Oh!" I said beneath my breath as I whirled back around.

"Don't let him annoy you," Charles said. "It's exactly what he wants."

"I know that," I said sharply. "But why?"

"Who knows?" he said with a shrug.

I watched the play of emotion across his face. He could not fool me. Suddenly I knew exactly the game these two were playing with each other. It was male pride, plain and simple. But I could hardly believe that I, a plain little nobody, was the object of such blatant preening.

"It's because of me, isn't it?" I said, angry now with both of them. "And is that the only reason you asked me to walk with you, Charles? To defy and annoy your cousin?"

He stopped, staring down at me in disbelief. But he could not hide the flicker of truth I saw in his gray eyes.

"Why, no. Of course not. Whatever gave you such an idea? I . . ."

I pulled away from him then. "Don't deny it!" I said. "I can see it in your eyes. The antagonism between the two of you is as plain as day when you're together. And I suppose you think it's very funny and clever using a poor, dumb little housemaid to further this silly game between you!"

He was now staring at me open-mouthed. And he

could have been no more surprised at my display than I was myself. But I was angry, more angry than I'd ever been in my life. And I was hurt. At that moment I didn't care if they sent me packing for my impudence. I could not seem to stop.

"Elizabeth . . ." he began.

"Let me tell you something, Mr. Charles Simmons. I'm neither poor nor dumb. And neither am I a fool! Did you really think I couldn't see the rivalry between you every time you're together? And I'm intelligent enough to know it has little to do with me! But it has *everything* to do with Desiree Vanderworth, doesn't it?"

I stopped, horrified at the accusations that tumbled from my lips. What on earth must he think of me? I turned toward the house, running now from his look of astonishment. What a fool I had made of myself! And for what? Because they had used me? Yes, that was the reason, a voice whispered inside my head. And I simply refused to listen to any other voices that scratched at my subconscious. It hurt much less that way.

I did not stop until I was in my room where I flung myself upon the small, narrow bed and let the tears come. I had fooled myself into believing that someone might actually be interested in talking to me, might actually enjoy being with me. But I should have known that a man like Charles Simmons could never want a girl like me for a friend. And certainly neither would a man like Derek Vanderworth.

When Ruthie peeked inside my room a few minutes later, I turned my back to her as if I were sleeping.

" 'Lizabeth?" she asked quietly. "We're goin' down to dinner now. You comin'?"

"No," I muttered against the pillow. "I have a headache . . . and I'm not hungry."

"Oh, another headache," she cooed. Her voice was so filled with sympathy that I was immediately filled with regret about lying.

"I'll bring you something back for later, then," she

said, backing out of the room and closing the door softly behind her.

It was not like me to give in to my emotions that way. I knew I should get up and follow Ruthie down to supper, stop feeling sorry for myself. But for some reason I simply could not. Finally I slept, drifting into a deep, dreamless sleep.

I woke to the sound of someone knocking. As I opened my eyes to the darkness of the room, I was confused and disoriented and could not understand where the tapping sound came from. Finally I realized there was someone at my door. Probably Ruthie, I thought as I pushed my hair back and brushed at my wrinkled dress.

When I opened the door and saw Charles there in the dim light of the hallway, I took a step backward. My hand flew out to push the door shut, but he was quicker.

But it was not his physical strength that kept me from closing the door. It was the pleading tone of his voice and the solemn look of remorse in his ash-colored eyes.

"Elizabeth . . . please," he said quietly, his hand still upon the door. "Won't you allow me to explain?"

I looked at him for a long moment, then, with a deep breath, stepped out into the hallway beside him. "We can talk in the sitting room," I said, motioning toward the end of the hall.

The lamps in the room were lit, casting a pleasant glow upon the worn but comfortable furniture. I sat on the couch while Charles took a seat across from me.

He leaned forward, placing his forearms on his knees as he clasped his hands loosely together. With an indrawn breath he looked at me and began to speak.

"I'm sorry if I hurt you," he said simply. "And I wanted to tell you straightaway that you were wrong if you thought I wanted to spend time with you only to spite my cousin. I genuinely like you and enjoy talking to you. It's as simple as that." He looked into my eyes as if for permission to continue.

98

"Go on," I said, waiting.

"But your observation about Derek and me is very perceptive . . . too perceptive for my own comfort. This is something I have discussed with no one except Pastor Webster, and even now I do so only to convince you that I'm sincere." Again he glanced into my eyes.

I nodded but said nothing.

"You were right about Desiree. I was in love with her . . . had been for a long while. But it was only last year when I came here that I learned she returned my feelings. We . . . we had an affair. It isn't something I'm proud of. But she was planning to tell Derek . . . to . . . to ask him for a divorce. She said he had stopped loving her long ago. Still, she said he was so jealous, so possessive . . . the way he is with anything that belongs to him." His eyes were glazed now and hardened with regret as he relived that time.

"She said he refused to let her go, threatened her even if she went through with it. He said he would ruin her and take Amy from her forever if she continued to see me." Charles stood restlessly, and his lanky form cast shadows against the sitting room wall as he paced before me.

"And did you? Stop seeing her, I mean?" I asked.

"Yes," he said, running his fingers through his fine brown hair. "Although it was not what I wanted. I begged her to come away with me. We could have gone to England, escaped the scandal that he threatened, but she was too afraid. God, if only I had made her listen to me, made her leave here!" His voice was filled with agony, and I sensed the remorse he was feeling.

"What happened then?" I asked quietly.

"She killed herself, that's what! She could not face life here with him any longer and she jumped to her death! And I must share a part of that responsibility for the rest of my life!" He moved to the windows and stood with his back to me.

"Charles," I said, rising and going to stand behind

99

him. "I'm so sorry. The last thing I wanted was to dredge up all these painful memories."

"No," he said, turning to me. "It's all right. I needed to talk about it. I have spoken of it to no one since the day of her death."

"Someone knew about the two of you before she died?"

"Only because I was in danger of losing my mind," he said. "The afternoon of the ball, I went to Pastor Webster and confessed. I told him I was in love with Desiree. Oh, I knew he would condemn me, tell me to repent my sinfulness. But I had to tell someone!"

"Yes," I said. "I understand that."

He took my hands in his and looked at me tenderly. "I know you do. I suppose that was what drew me to you the first day we met. You have such a sweet, understanding face. I knew I could talk to you, trust you. And now I've hurt you too."

"No," I said. "You haven't, now that I understand."

"The rivalry you sensed between Derek and me is real. I won't deny that," he said sincerely. "But as much as I despise him, I can tell you that my cousin is no snob in regard to your position here. And I swear to you, it was not my intention to use you in any way to badger or annoy him. My wish to be friends with you is an honest one. I hope you will believe that."

I did believe him. Here, now, in the quiet of the sitting room, I felt none of the anger and confusion I'd felt in the gardens earlier. I needed a friend as much as Charles and I hoped tonight would be the beginning of that friendship.

"I do believe you," I told him. "I'm glad, though, that you came and explained."

"So am I," he said with a gentle smile. "Will I see you again soon?"

"Yes," I said. "I'd like that very much."

I felt much better after he'd gone; my old optimism returned. And when Ruthie and Miss Olivia came into the sitting room moments later, I ate the sandwich they'd brought as we sat and chatted.

It was only later, in the silence of my room, that I began to wonder again about Charles and Desiree, about Derek Vanderworth and what Charles called his possessiveness. Yes, I could imagine that fierce pride of his would never allow him to lose at anything. But could that same fierceness have caused the death of his beautiful wife? It was something I dared not mention to Charles, no matter how very curious I was to know his opinion. He knew his cousin probably better than anyone, and something inside me did not want to hear what he might have to tell me.

I went to the window and looked out over the breathtaking moon-washed glen and the soft light upon the spreading tree branches. The wind had begun to blow, moaning about the huge house like a lost animal crying for its mother.

The wind continued throughout the night, whispering and crying out to me even through my sleep until I would waken with a start and look around the darkened room. It was a long, wearying night which little prepared me for my meeting the next morning with Derek Vanderworth.

Chapter Eleven

I was ready early the next morning, long before the appointed time for me to arrive in the library. I paced the floor and looked out the window as the sun began to spread long streaks of honey gold across the meadows.

Finally I walked leisurely down the hallway, pausing from time to time to look across the front lawn toward the arboretum. But I could wait no longer. Nothing could hold my interest except the vision in my mind of what the library must be like.

No one was about this early, and on impulse I ran like a child down the steps of the grand stairway, letting my hand slide along the smooth rail as I went. The freedom I felt was exhilarating, and I laughed aloud as I turned the corner of the second floor.

I fairly jumped from the last step onto the wide landing. And there, watching me with an air of amusement, stood Derek Vanderworth.

I stopped, immediately embarrassed at being caught in such childish behavior.

"Good morning," he said with the slightest whisper of a smile upon his lips. As I nodded a silent greeting, he fell into step beside me.

I was very careful that the steps I took down the rest of the stairway were reserved and more decorous.

He said nothing about our previous meetings, and

neither did I. In fact, I felt quite awkward in his presence that morning.

I glanced from the corner of my eye at him, at the silky white shirt that billowed softly as he moved. He looked younger with the neck of his shirt unbuttoned casually. I thought to myself that his air of cool restraint and conservatism made him seem older than he really was. Looking at him now, I realized he probably was not yet thirty.

Had he always been so coldly formal? I wondered. And if so, surely he had not treated his wife in such a way. And yet Charles's words about him were hardly flattering.

Once we reached the main floor, he directed me to a long gallery at the back of the house. Great tall glass doors to the right gave glimpses of a long balcony and a splendid view of the mountains. The gallery itself was breathtaking, with three great tapestries hanging upon the wall. Between the tapestries were giant fireplaces painted from mantel to ceiling with pictures that matched the tapestries. I leaned my head back and looked up at the stenciled ceiling.

"It's so beautiful," I said almost to myself.

He lifted one dark eyebrow and stopped, staring down at me. "I'm very happy you appreciate it," he said. "I suppose I've grown used to it."

I frowned at him. "Used to it?" I asked with disbelief. "I don't think I would ever become accustomed to living in a place like this . . . especially if I knew it was mine."

He looked at me with an odd expression. "I might have thought that too once . . . a long time ago, it seems now."

There was a wide doorway at the end of the gallery and on each side of the door were two life-size paintings. As we came nearer, I saw the one on the right was a portrait of Derek Vanderworth. It was very life-

103

like, and the artist had captured the rather serious, arrogant look of him. In the painting he looked every bit the man behind his reserved English title.

I glanced toward the other picture and my breath caught in my throat. From the description others had given, I knew immediately it was Desiree Vanderworth. And where her husband's picture was dark and somber, hers was filled with light. There was a feeling of spirited fun about the painting and in the look of the beautiful blond-haired woman who graced it.

"This was . . . was your wife?" I asked shyly, not knowing how he would react.

"Yes," he said as he gazed up at the picture. "The beautiful Desiree." His voice sounded husky, almost a whisper, and his amber eyes had grown dark and clouded. But almost immediately he turned away, standing aside as he motioned me into the next room.

If I live forever I shall never forget seeing that room for the first time. Loving books as I did, I was overcome by a feeling that I can only describe as a deep, primitive longing. It struck me in the heart with such a force that I took a step backward and my mouth flew open as I gazed in silence about me.

The man beside me laughed quietly. It was odd, hearing him laugh, for I think I had convinced myself that he did not ever feel pleasure. But I did not turn to look at him. I could not take my eyes from the rows and shelves of books that surrounded us in his magnificent library.

"You're impressed," he said softly.

"Impressed," I sighed. "I'm not sure the word does it justice." My arms flew out as if by their own accord to encompass everything I saw. "Awed, astonished . . . overwhelmed! Even more . . ." I actually felt close to tears by the passion I felt and even the man's presence could not make me hold it all in.

When I finally looked around at him, he was watching me carefully, his eyes narrowed. There was a puzzled, whimsical look on his handsome face.

"I think you're the first woman I ever met who's been more impressed with my library than by the rest of the house."

"Oh." Had I insulted him? "Your house is wonderful, as are all your treasures. But this . . . this just takes my breath away."

He was smiling at me again with that odd little look on his face. I looked away, embarrassed now by the way I had let my emotions run away with me.

"I . . . I'm sorry," I said, not knowing what else to say.

He frowned at me then and shook his head. "You don't have to be sorry, for God's sake. Actually, it's quite refreshing to meet someone who cares more for books than money." His voice held a sarcastic tone as he walked away from me.

I did not follow him but stood instead looking at every detail of the room. It was filled with the glow of rich polished wood and gleaming brass. And although it would be considered a huge room in comparison to those in a normal house, it had a smaller, cozier look than any of the other rooms I'd seen at Stormhaven.

Derek stood before the large fireplace and motioned for me to join him. "Would you like me to tell you something about the room before we begin work?" he asked.

"Oh yes," I said, going immediately to stand beside him.

He pointed toward the elaborately carved black marble mantel. Above it was a richly grained panel of wood, arched at the top and filled with baroque detailing. A small tapestry hung in the middle of the panel and it was flanked by life-size wood carvings of two beautiful robed women.

"The carving was done by Karl Bitter," he explained. "One is Hestia, goddess of the hearth, and the other is Demeter, goddess of the earth." He pointed to the ceiling, which alone was enough to make the room memorable. But in my earlier enthusiasm I had hardly noticed it.

It was covered by a painting, filled with clouds and angels and what I thought the Sistine Chapel must be like.

"I brought it here from a palace in Venice."

I looked sharply at him, unable to believe how casual his tone was as he spoke of all his unbelievable possessions.

"You make it sound so . . . so ordinary, as if all this was accomplished so easily."

"It is easy," he said. "When you have money, accomplishment and objects are nothing."

In a corner near the fireplace was another elaborately carved structure. It was a small semicircle of arches and columns that reminded me of an outdoor gazebo. But this was made of the same rich, dark wood and inside it was a circular iron staircase leading up to the next level of bookshelves. There was an iron rail all the way around the top part of the room. The entire room was used for books, from the floor to the magnificent painted ceiling.

"I'm afraid I won't be able to work in here," I said with a whisper of awe.

"Why?" he asked with a worried frown.

I clasped my hands together and turned about to take in every inch of the room. "I will be too busy admiring everything."

His grunt of laughter was spontaneous and the look I saw in his eyes was kind, surprisingly so.

"I'm pleased you approve. This is my sanctuary." His voice was soft as he followed my gaze around the room. "There was not even one nail hammered in this

106

room that I did not supervise."

I watched him for a moment. I felt such conflicting emotions where this man was concerned. Today he was even different than before. I'd heard so many opinions about him. And now I found it hard to believe anything except what his own comments told me. I wondered how anyone who carefully built such a room and who loved books so could be as cold and devious as I'd been told.

"Well," he said with a shrug of his broad shoulders. "Perhaps I should explain what I'd like you to do."

He led me to the back of the room where a long table sat beneath the overhang of the railed walkway. On the table were several leatherbound books.

He explained to me how he would like the books arranged on the shelves, then cataloged into the large books. It would be a slow, tedious process, for I would have to take each section apart, arranging and rearranging until every book here could be placed in its proper niche. Then it would be entered in the books so it could be easily found afterward.

I could hardly wait to start and I glanced up to look at the shelves of books around us.

"I'm afraid my grandmother has found a rather boring task for you, suggesting this job." He was watching me with wary eyes, ready, I supposed at any resistance, to have me go back to my duties of dusting and cleaning.

"Oh, no!" I cried. "I would never find it boring working here. Books . . ." I glanced around the room. "Books were often all I had. I sometimes felt they kept me alive." Quickly I clamped my lips together. What must he think of me, telling him such personal things about myself?

He drew himself up from the table. The look on his face was one almost of kinship, certainly recognition of what I meant.

107

"Yes," he said quietly. "I certainly understand that."

I looked at him then with a different eye. He sounded so sad, so unhappy. Was it possible for a man like him, who seemed to have everything in life to feel the same loneliness? And to lose himself in books?

But I could never see into his tawny eyes and I suppose that's as he wanted it. He left then, making some excuse about seeing to a guest, speaking as if he had nothing better he cared to do. Once again he was the distant, cool, and rather arrogant Earl of Chesham. The man Charles said cared for nothing except his precious possessions.

The day passed so quickly I could hardly believe it. I would have forgotten to eat had it not been for Mrs. Vanderworth. She undoubtedly was curious about me and how I liked the work, but I thought she also came because of her kind, friendly nature. When she discovered I had not eaten, she went right away to tell someone to bring tea to the library.

She returned later, fluttering her hands as she moved toward me. The servant behind her who carried a large silver tray smiled at me. I could not recall his name, but I'd met him before in the servants' hall.

"Hello," I said, nodding to him as he placed the tray on the long table where I worked. I felt a little uncomfortable having one of my fellow workers wait on me this way.

He bowed and smiled again, then backed from the room in a funny, polite little way.

Mrs. Vanderworth was chattering away as she poured the tea and placed a delicate gold-trimmed plate before me.

"I did not intend that your work for my grandson should cause you to starve to death," she said wryly.

"Oh, but he's been very kind," I said. "I just became so lost in what I was doing that I forgot the time."

She placed several small sandwiches on my plate,

then took a cube of sugar between the small silver tongs and held it above my teacup. "Sugar?" she asked.

She dropped it in almost before I could nod my head yes. I smiled; I'd never met anyone like this elderly woman. She was so full of life and I imagined she would be a joy to have as a grandmother.

"Why are you smiling?" she asked pertly.

I hesitated, wondering if I should speak to her so informally. But working in the magnificent room, sharing tea with her, gave me a confidence I probably would not normally have had.

"I'm smiling at you," I said. "I was thinking what a good grandmother you must be."

She lifted her delicate eyebrows and smiled warmly into my eyes. "Well, thank you, dear," she said. "And I suppose you were also thinking how very nice I am for such a wealthy lady."

Now it was my turn to look surprised. I laughed aloud. "As a matter of fact, yes, I was," I admitted.

"Well, Elizabeth, you might be surprised to know that my background is not much different from yours."

"Mine?" I asked, wondering at her words.

"Oh, yes," she said, sipping her tea. "I was not born into money, you know. I grew up in the mountains not far from here, those very mountains you can see in the distance from the west side of the house. Yes . . ." Her eyes became slightly glazed as she delved into her memories.

"Derek's grandfather came here as a young man, looking for land. It was his first visit here from England, and he fell in love with our wild, rugged countryside. My father owned a small acreage in the mountains where he barely managed to eke out a living for our family. But he was a proud man and determined to hold onto what was his."

I listened carefully, curious now to know what had

happened and how she had fallen in love with the young man from England who had come to buy her father's land.

"I didn't like him, and he didn't like me," she said with a laugh. "He thought I was entirely too independent, and a wild little mountain ragamuffin to boot!"

"And what about you?" I asked. "What did you think of him?"

"Why, I thought he was the most handsome man I'd ever seen. He came riding into our yard on a fine black stallion, looking for all the world as if he were a prince. And I was horrified later when I thought of how I ran out and faced him, demanded that he leave our property." She laughed. "Oh, I was every bit the little rebel he accused me of being."

"But how did you . . . ? I mean, you two must have been so different."

She looked at me and smiled. "Love is the perfect leveler, my dear," she said. "It cares not one whit for one's station in life."

We were silent for a while as I thought about what she said. The vision of her young man danced in my mind's eye. A proud, handsome prince of a man, confident as he rode the black stallion. And the face I saw before me was Derek Vanderworth's. I shook my head slightly, silently chiding myself for my romantic notions. The effects of too many fairy-tales, I told myself.

When Mrs. Vanderworth left, I thanked her for bringing tea and for thinking of me. "I always enjoy talking to you," I said.

"And I you, dear," she replied with a wave of her hand.

Fortified by the light but tasty meal, I could hardly wait to get back to work. In fact I probably would have worked far into the night had it not been for my employer's appearance.

I heard his footsteps across the oak floor. Then he stopped. "Why are you still here?" he demanded with a note of surprise.

I glanced up, realizing for the first time that someone had lit the lamps and that the light from outside was now a dusty, gray color.

I stood up and took my glasses off. My eyes were burning, and without being aware of it, I discovered my neck and shoulders had grown stiff and sore.

"I . . . I didn't realize it was so late," I said.

He walked to me and took the glasses from my numb fingers. "You should not have worked so long," he scolded. "I never intended for you to wear yourself out the first day."

"I'm not tired," I lied.

"Your eyes are red; they look tired," he said. Then he held my glasses up between his fingers. "Wherever did you get these?"

"I . . . my mother got them . . . from a traveling salesman, I believe."

He frowned and handed them back to me. "You should see a doctor, get yourself some proper glasses."

I felt myself blushing. It always embarrassed me when someone took note of my glasses and it was worse coming from this serious, handsome man.

"Yes," I whispered. "I will."

Suddenly I felt the touch of his fingers as he reached out and placed them beneath my chin. An odd feeling ran through me, one of shock, as if someone had hit me in the chest. It was surprise, I told myself. Surprise at his familiarity. But then I looked up into his amber eyes and I saw surprise reflected there as well.

"Your eyes are much too lovely to be ruined by overwork," he said, his voice only a husky whisper in the still room.

He had not said that my glasses were ugly or that

they made me ugly. His only concern seemed to be that I was tired.

I don't know what I said then, or what I did. My heart was pounding so that I felt a bit dizzy and out of touch with reality. I only recall his eyes, those tawny, compelling eyes as they gazed down into mine and would not let me think.

He took a deep breath and stepped away from me.

"Perhaps you'd better go to bed now, Miss Stevens," he murmured. "You've had a very long day."

"It was the most wonderful day I've ever spent," I said foolishly. As soon as the words fell from my lips, I wished I could take them back. I sounded like a breathless, gushing schoolgirl.

He laughed. His eyelids lowered, shutting his beautiful eyes away from me. And when they opened again, I was amazed at how clear they were and how warm as he studied me so seriously.

"Goodnight, Miss Stevens," he said abruptly before turning to leave.

"Goodnight," I whispered to the empty room.

Chapter Twelve

I thought the week would never pass until the next Wednesday. I thought often of the work I was doing there and how I could make it better or more efficient. But I had brought several books with me to read during the week, and that pastime in itself was a joy.

It was a busy time. The house was again filled with guests. Miss Olivia insisted on beginning a new dress for me. The summer material of lawn was lovely and cool, more beautiful than anything I'd ever owned. And I hoped the mauve color would be as flattering to me as Miss Olivia declared it would be.

The weather had grown quite hot, and Charles and I took our walks in the garden later in the afternoon. Sometimes we waited until after dinner, just before the faraway sun fell behind the shimmering mountains.

I learned more about the estate and all the exotic flowers and plants. Derek Vanderworth, it seemed, was as knowledgeable about gardening as he was about books.

But in that week Charles hardly mentioned his cousin's name. He did speak of Desiree; now that I knew his secret, I suppose he felt at ease talking about it. And I sensed his need to speak of her, to perhaps help him banish the grief and guilt he still felt about her death.

Sunday was the only day I saw Derek, and he

hardly acknowledged my presence. But at the services that day, it seemed assumed that Amy would sit with me. She came to me as sweetly and spontaneously as she had that first day in the Palm Court. And she sat beside me, kicking her tiny feet and looking curiously about the room. She was so spirited that I found it hard to believe she could not speak.

After the service she went reluctantly with her father and Diana. And I was alone and feeling angry at myself because I had somehow expected more.

Afterward, when the Reverend Webster approached to speak to me, Charles joined us as well. We stood talking for quite a while, and I learned that the pastor was staying for Sunday luncheon.

He seemed a very nice man, one who was solicitous of the Vanderworth family, although not overly so. But I sensed a certain coolness when he spoke to Charles, and I wondered why. Was it because he knew about and disapproved of Charles and Desiree's relationship? But surely a righteous man would not hold the sins of one of his flock against him. Would he?

Finally the day I'd waited for arrived, my day to return to the library. Miss Olivia had finished my dress only the night before, and I reluctantly decided to wear it that day. I was certain Mrs. Hunt would not approve if she saw me, but still I could not resist.

The dress made me feel special, with its tightly fitted waist and bustled train that dipped fashionably in the back. The bodice was cut low, exposing more of my skin than I was used to. But somehow even that did not deter me, but made me feel feminine and excited. I did not let myself think why I wished to look feminine and pretty that day.

I spent the entire morning in anticipation and I could not deny the reason. But as lunchtime came and

Derek still had not appeared, I began to feel almost ill with disappointment.

Again Mrs. Vanderworth bustled in and we ate lunch together. She told me more about herself and her husband, how she had gone to England with him for two years and then come back to the mountains to begin building this magnificent chateau. She said Derek had always loved Stormhaven and had practically grown up here. Thus the reason for his English accent being not quite so pronounced as Charles's. She mentioned only briefly how Charles's parents had never been as close to the Vanderworths.

"After Charles's parents died, Derek invited Charles here. I'm not as close to my other grandson as I am to Derek. But I hope that will change. Charles seems to hold some resentments against us all, and I'm not certain he is quite ready to let us fully into his life."

I sensed she did not wish to discuss it further, and I wondered if she, too, suspected the relationship that had existed between Charles and Desiree.

"Your grandson Derek met his wife here, in this country?" I hoped my change of subject would brush away the worried look I saw in her pale eyes.

"Yes, when he was very young. She was married to a very abusive husband, and . . ."

I knew my face reflected my astonishment, but I could not help it. "Married?"

From the twist of her lips I knew she had not approved. "Yes," she said in a clipped voice. "Derek was very protective of women, still is. And he could not bear seeing this poor, beautiful young woman treated so horribly. There was a violent fight and Derek gave the man a terrible beating. He almost died. I never thought my grandson capable of such savagery." She looked at me sadly. "I told him it was something he would have to live with for the rest of his life. And for what? A woman who was not even his to fight for!"

Her voice was angry now, and I could hear her bitterness at Derek's brutal defense of the woman he would marry.

"What happened?" I asked.

"The man went away, swearing to someday avenge what had happened. Then we received news that he died a few months later. Not from the wounds of the fight, thank goodness. But needless to say, Derek's subsequent marriage to her caused quite a scandal among our friends, although I must say just as many flocked to Desiree's defense, more from curiosity than anything, I always said. Then it seemed to be the thing . . . to be a confidante of Desiree Vanderworth, the beautiful woman whose husband had fought for her and almost killed for her."

I said nothing, and the pain that had been gathering about my heart now felt heavy and endless. Derek was much too proud a man to have something like this scandal happen to him, to have people discussing his private life. I wondered how he had stood it.

"She never loved him," Mrs. Vanderworth said with a little sniff. "But I would have given anything if she had, if only to spare Derek the pain of finding out." Suddenly she placed the tip of her fingers against her mouth. "I've said too much. I should not have burdened you with all this, my dear. Derek would be furious if he knew."

"He will never know that you've told me," I swore.

"You are a very sweet girl, Elizabeth. I'm so happy you've come to Stormhaven."

"So am I," I told her as she rose to go.

The afternoon passed, and although I enjoyed the work, there was a quiet disappointment within me. And I knew it was because Derek had not come.

What did I expect? Had I honestly thought that a wealthy, sophisticated man like the Earl of Chesham would be interested in spending a summer afternoon with one of his maids?

The late-afternoon sun blazed through the long French doors at the back of the library, and the room had grown very warm. Impulsively I walked to the heavy doors and turned the brass handles, intending to step outside for a breath of fresh air.

The sight that greeted me was like a nightmare, one where you try to run but cannot. Past the library terrace in the Italian garden, I caught the glimpse of color at the first pool. By the time I realized that the flash of yellow was little Amy's dress, she had already tumbled head-first into the water. I saw her governess raise her hands to her mouth even before I heard the scream.

The paralysis that held me there on the terrace seemed to last forever before my legs finally began to move. I was hardly aware of lifting my bundlesome dress to run or of losing the glasses from my nose. All my attention was focused on the thrash of water in the pool and then, with heartstopping terror, the sight of smooth, clear water as Amy ceased to struggle.

The governess was petrified with fear and could only stand there screaming. "Help!" she cried. "I can't swim! I can't swim!"

Without thinking I jumped into the pool and came up gasping for air. The thick clumps of lotus grabbed at my legs even as the water penetrated the material of my dress and threatened to pull me to the bottom.

"Amy," I gasped. *"Where are you, Amy?"*

It was almost impossible to see through the thick green plants and the murky water. "Get help!" I screamed at the governess as I dived beneath the surface of the water.

I could see only shadowy outlines as I turned my head from side to side beneath the water. Panic filled me with such desperation that I could hear the pounding of my heart through the murky darkness. Just

117

when I thought I would die without another breath of air, I saw it!

There, not three feet away, was the faint glimmer of yellow, the flash of color I'd seen just before Amy fell into the water.

I dared not risk surfacing for air, even though I thought my lungs would burst. I was too frightened that I would never find her again.

Finally I had the limp yellow material clutched in my fist and I pulled her tightly against me. Then, with one desperate kick, I thrust my way to the top of the pool.

I heard the sound of running feet as I pulled myself and Amy to the side of the pool. My wet skirts were so heavy that I felt as if a lead weight was attached to my legs. I managed to drag myself awkwardly up onto the edge of the pool. Then I pulled Amy's small, limp body across my lap, holding her about her waist as I bent her head forward. She was not breathing.

As I stood up, pulling the child with me, I heard voices and more people running toward me. I was so frantic that I barely glanced their way. But it was long enough for me to see the stunned expression on Derek Vanderworth's face. He had lost his wife, and I could see the fear that now he might lose his daughter as well.

I had no idea what to do. I suppose it was pure instinct that made me hold the tiny little girl upside down. At the same time I held one hand across her chest while with the other I pressed against her back. Within seconds, Amy began to cough and choke as water came gushing from her mouth.

"That's it," I said shakily. "That's it, little one. Spit it all out."

Finally she began to cry, and I did not even stop to think that it was strange to hear the unusual sound of her voice. The sound was so heavenly that I did not think of anything. I only felt . . . a relief that left me trembling so badly that I doubted my legs would hold me much longer.

When Derek took his little girl from my arms, I sank slowly to the ground, where I sat gasping for breath. Now that it was over, I felt myself growing weak and faint.

I was not aware of those around me. The sound of their cries of relief seemed far away and unreal. And when someone picked me up in his arms, I simply closed my eyes and gave in to the numbing fatigue that swept over my body.

I was placed on the long sofa that sat before the library's fireplace. When I opened my eyes I tried to hide my surprise as I gazed into the concerned gray gaze of Charles Simmons.

He covered me with a colorful Turkish shawl that lay across the back of the sofa. Then he knelt beside me and took my hand in his.

"Are you all right?" he asked.

"Yes," I said, my head becoming clearer. It had only been fright, I realized, that had made me so weak. It had all happened so fast.

"Are you sure? I'm going to bring you something warm to drink. But I don't want to leave you if . . ."

"I'm fine, honestly. Just a little frightened."

After Charles had gone, I sat up, testing myself to see if I was injured anywhere. But I was not, and the only thing I could think of was Amy. It seemed a miracle that she had begun to breathe again, and I was afraid that I had only imagined it.

Just then the large French doors opened and an entourage of chattering people moved into the library. Derek was carrying his small daughter, who was clinging to him with both arms. Her face was buried against his neck.

There were people all around him, the governess,

119

Mrs. Vanderworth, and a few of the house servants. But I had eyes only for the little girl, and the man who carried her.

When he saw me he stopped. Then he kissed Amy and murmured something into her ear as he handed her to his grandmother. Mrs. Vanderworth looked across the room at me with such gratitude as she murmured her thank you.

"We're so grateful," she said, her voice so quiet, I could hardly hear her.

I nodded and smiled. My heart melted as Amy looked up at me from her grandmother's shoulder and waved her small fingers toward me. It was such a relief knowing she would be all right.

After they'd all left the room, Derek came to me. I was aware of my hair hanging limply about my shoulders and plastered against my head. I ran my fingers through it self-consciously and glanced down at my beautiful new dress, which was now ruined.

He sat on the couch with me and I drew my legs in closer to my body so that we would not touch. He looked worried as his eyes took in my wet, shivering figure.

"How are you?" he asked.

I could only nod my head; the words I tried to say would not come past my chattering teeth. And yet I didn't feel cold.

"How can I ever thank you . . . for saving my little girl?"

This humbled man was not the cold Derek Vanderworth I'd come to know. And yet that fierce pride was still there. I could see it in the way he held his jaws so tightly, in the way his white teeth clamped upon his lower lip. Why, he was as frightened as I was!

"There's no need to thank me," I said. I found myself wanting to touch his hand, to reassure him, somehow. Seeing him in such obvious pain was not something I enjoyed. In fact, I could not really understand what I felt at the moment.

He looked at me strangely, as if he did not believe me. "But surely there must be something I can do, something I can give you." He waved his hand about, indicating all the treasures of his home. "Just name it."

I only looked at him, stunned by his words. Surely he did not think to *pay* me for pulling Amy from the pool? Perhaps he was like Charles had said . . . a man concerned only with the gaining of more and more possessions. Was that all he thought life was about?

"You can't be serious," I said, sitting straighter, with my back against the arm of the sofa. "Do you think I would actually accept your money or . . . or any of these . . . things you've accumulated, for helping that beautiful little girl?"

He frowned, his amber eyes puzzled. I could see the frustration on his face as he struggled to understand me.

"Then what . . . ?" he asked.

"Nothing!" I said angrily, throwing the shawl from my legs and coming quickly to my feet.

Only for a moment did I feel a wave of dizziness. I put my fingers to my head and clutched at the sofa with my hand. Derek was immediately at my side, placing one strong arm about my waist and easing me back down to the sofa.

"Take it easy, will you?" he snapped.

It was then, with Derek's hands still at my waist and his dark head bent close to mine, that Charles came back into the room.

He looked at us with surprise, one golden eyebrow arched pointedly as he set a tray on a nearby table.

"What's wrong?" he asked, seeing our strained looks. "Are you all right, Elizabeth?"

"Yes, I'm all right," I said more sharply than I

121

should have. "Please don't everyone make such a fuss. I'm hardly an invalid; I'm only wet!"

Charles's face remained expressionless, and he calmly poured a cup of tea and handed it to me.

Derek's eyes studied me and there was an air of unfinished business about him. When he rose rather rigidly to leave, I did not glance up at him, but sipped the strong, sweet tea.

"We'll talk more later, Miss Stevens," he said, "after you've had time to rest."

Only then did I look up to meet his eyes, and I did not miss the glint of determination in their expressive depths.

"Really . . ." I protested. "It's not necessary . . ."

"It is," he said firmly, ". . . necessary. Allow me this one concession, if you will."

As he walked from the room with that long-legged, purposeful stride of his, I took a deep breath. I did not realize my lips were clamped stubbornly together until Charles spoke.

"What was that all about?" he asked coolly, as if he was not at all curious. "And why are you so angry with him?"

I sighed again and wiggled uncomfortably in my wet clothes. "Oh, he has this notion that he should *pay* me somehow for rescuing his daughter. Can you believe that? As if I had performed some chore for him that needed payment!"

"Then you should let him," he said quietly.

"What?" My eyes flew to his face in disbelief. But he only smiled and raised his hand to halt any further protest.

"Do you realize how much money this man has, Elizabeth? Enough to set you up for life! And believe me, you've only to ask. His daughter means more to him than anything."

"How can you even suggest such a thing?" I asked.

122

"It wouldn't be honorable."

"Ah, sweet Elizabeth," he sighed, leaning back comfortably against the sofa and spreading his long arms across the back. "You are an optimist . . . a romantic. I suppose I'm only wasting my breath in trying to get you to see the practical side of this."

"Yes," I said firmly. "You certainly are. I only did what was right. It was not something I even had time to think about. Anyone would have done the same."

He smiled wryly at me and shook his head as if he found me very amusing. "Oh, my dear girl. You have so much to learn."

"I can't believe the two of you," I said, staring at him, trying to see into his thoughts. "I'm only a housemaid here, for heaven's sake. Why should I be treated with such gratitude?"

He laughed aloud then. "You know . . . that's why I like you! You are so delightfully honest." He leaned forward then and put his long, slim fingers together. "You have no idea, do you, how men are? We're all the same, you know. No matter what their station in life, men are all fools for a beautiful woman. And my dear little Elizabeth . . . you *are* a beauty."

My face became very warm and I stared at him with skepticism. "But I'm not . . . I'll never be beautiful. I'm plain, and . . ."

He turned to me then and reached out one finger to push a strand of wet hair back from my face. Then his finger traced the outline of my face as he looked into my eyes.

"Ah, but you are anything but plain, my sweet little innocent. With your silvery gray eyes, skin as soft as the petals of a summer rose . . . and those lips. Oh yes, you are indeed a beautiful woman." His words were a mere whisper.

He laughed when I suddenly pulled away from him. I suppose my reaction convinced him of my naivety,

123

but I could not help it. He made me feel things, hope for things that I knew were impossible. I stood up and placed my teacup back on the tray.

"If you'll excuse me," I said firmly. "I'm going up to change out of these wet clothes."

I ignored his knowing smile and turned quickly to leave the room.

What on earth was happening to me? I had not expected my life to become so complicated here in this beautiful house. I'd hoped only for a quiet place to live and a job that I might enjoy. And now I found myself involved with a family that I did not understand, one I was not even sure I could trust.

And now there were two men whose attentions confused me and made me wonder just how well I really knew myself.

Chapter Thirteen

I tried not to think about anything as I changed from my clothes before dinner. Anything except Derek and his cousin Charles. But as I twisted my still damp hair back into a chignon, I found myself gazing at my reflection in the mirror.

Without my glasses, I supposed my eyes were not quite so bad. But I hardly would give their gray color such a flattering name as silver. My hair was too straight and fine, but it was shiny and healthy, I admitted, and as Miss Olivia said, there was a golden color to it if the light was exactly right.

I touched my face lightly, recalling Charles's poetic description of my skin.

"Oh, this is ridiculous," I said, turning from the mirror. "I should be spending my time wondering how I shall afford a new pair of glasses."

But if I thought to put the events of the afternoon from my mind, I was mistaken. For as soon as I entered the servants' dining hall, it was the immediate topic of conversation.

Dottie was as excited as a child as she plopped herself into the chair next to mine at the table. "Oh, and you're a hero, Elizabeth Stevens!" she cried, reaching out to hug me.

I looked down at my plate, aware of all the faces gathered about the long dining table. They were curious to hear every detail of what happened.

"No, I'm not a hero," I muttered, wishing everyone would just go on with their meal.

"Sure you are," Frederick joined in. "Johnny's brother works belowstairs. He's already told us all about it, how Mr. Simmons and his lordship was fussin' over you in the library."

I looked around at Johnny, who sat grinning next to Dottie. Of course. His brother was the one who had brought tea to Mrs. Vanderworth and me that day, the boy who had smiled at me in such a friendly manner. I could see the resemblance now. He must have been among the house servants who ran outside when Amy fell into the pool.

"Well, aren't you gonna tell us about it?" Dottie exclaimed, her green eyes wide with curiosity.

"It . . . it all happened so quickly. Really, I hardly remember any of it, except seeing Amy fall into the water. Next thing I knew, I was in the water myself, trying to find her."

"And you did!" Frederick said with pride.

Everyone at the table was grinning at me. It was as if my being the focus of attention had somehow brought accolades to them as well. I suppose that thought made me happier than anything, for I felt as if now I truly belonged somewhere. The warmth of their approval wrapped around me like an embrace, and I felt welcome as I'd never felt in my own home.

"Yes, thank goodness," I said. "I was lucky enough to find her. And she's going to be all right." I smiled at all of them.

My explanation seemed to satisfy them, and we all began to eat. I had not realized how hungry I was until the large bowls of steaming vegetables and platters of fried chicken were passed.

Later some of us were still sitting at the table talking when Mrs. Pennebaker stepped into the room from the kitchen area. She jingled the ring of keys at her waist nervously as her eyes scanned the people still at the table.

"Oh, there you are, Elizabeth," she said, looking straight at me. "You've been asked to come to the Palm Court just as soon as you've finished your dinner."

I looked at her for a moment, wondering who wanted to see me and why. But as was her nature, Mrs. Pennebaker bustled out of the room before I could ask.

Dottie made a grimacing face and rolled her eyes as she nudged me with an elbow. "Oh, my! What do you think that's all about?" she asked with exuberance.

"I have no idea," I said. But all the while my thoughts were swirling about in my head. What indeed, was it all about? More of Mrs. Hunt's disapproval? Or further attempts by Derek Vanderworth to pay me for saving his daughter? I sincerely hoped that was not the case.

I left the dining hall after promising to tell them later everything that happened.

It was late as I made my way up from the basement to the first floor. The house was so immense that it was impossible to light every corner, and I felt a tingle of apprehension travel across my shoulders as I walked up the narrow, dark stairway.

I entered the first floor just beneath the grand stairway. Here all the lights were aglow with the gigantic chandelier that hung in the middle of the stairway, the brightest of them all.

I glanced toward the Palm Court and noted the glow of purple from the sunset that lit the domed skylight.

The man waiting for me there paced restlessly back and forth, head bowed as if he was in deep thought. He looked up at my footsteps and came forward to take my hand and lead me down the few steps into the room. I thought Derek Vanderworth had never looked so handsome as he did that evening and I found my breathing a little troubled as I faced the prospect of being alone with him.

"Sit here," he said, motioning to a rattan chair near a clump of potted greenery.

The chairs assembled for the Sunday services had been removed, and the court was clean and spacious. Derek did not sit, but rather continued to pace as his lean, dark fingers rubbed at his chin.

"Amy's governess has left," he said, still not looking at me. "She was overcome with remorse about the accident today. I'm not so concerned at the moment with Amy's education as I am with her emotional well-being. I'd like you to become her companion."

His words, with no preliminary warning, took me completely by surprise. I must have gasped, for he turned on his heel to gaze down at me.

"I . . . I don't know what to say," I stammered.

"Say yes," he said with a shrug of his broad shoulders, as if he saw no reason on earth why I would refuse.

"But I . . . I've never done anything like this. I . . ."

"You are accustomed to being around children, are you not? Brothers, sisters . . . ?"

"Well, yes, of course. But . . . what exactly would I do . . . as companion?" I asked, suddenly aware of the difference he had made in the title.

"You will have no duties as such. I just feel my daughter would benefit by spending time with a young woman . . . with you. It's obvious she was taken with you from the first moment you two met."

There was such a wealth of emotion in his voice and in the depths of his catlike eyes, and much that the actual words did not relay. But I could not be sure exactly what it was about him that bothered me so.

"But I have no experience with a child who cannot speak. Perhaps she needs a professional . . . someone who . . ."

"No!" he said. "I have tried professional help, a doctor from New York who supposedly dealt with children like Amy. She was terrified of him and experienced nightmares for weeks. It took months for Grandmother and

me to bring her back to normal. So don't speak to me of professionals." He was so angry that he sounded breathless.

"Did you pick me because you think I should be repaid for this afternoon?" I asked tentatively.

He stood looking down at me and his eyes were shadowed in the waning light. I tried to hide the shiver that traveled down my body. Was he always so serious . . . so stern?

"Partly," he said. He surprised me with his honesty. "If you won't accept a gift from me, perhaps you will at least accept a better position here in my home."

"I suppose it would be foolish for me to refuse."

There was the slightest flicker of a smile across his lips. "Unless you prefer dusting and cleaning to spending time with a spirited four-year-old child."

I smiled at him then, the tension I'd felt earlier already gone. "No," I said. "I much prefer the child."

"Good," he said, still looking steadily at me. "Tomorrow morning we will move you to another room on the second floor, closer to Amy. As her companion, you will, of course, be considered a member of the family."

His remark surprised me.

"You will have the run of the house and an allowance that should permit you to live as independently as you wish. In addition, I will establish a trust fund in your name . . . yours to use whenever you like. Anything you request in my home will be done."

I was speechless, stunned by his generosity.

"There will be a new wardrobe for you, one which I think will make you the envy of any young woman of society." To his credit, he did not look down his nose at my worn dress as he spoke.

"But . . . really, this is far too much. I can't . . ."

"Where are your glasses?" he asked abruptly, disregarding my feeble protests.

"I . . . they fell off as I ran to help Amy."

He frowned at me for a moment. "I hope you're all

right without them." His voice was immediately changed from his haughty recital of before. Now it was all concern and caring.

"Of course I am," I said. Actually, though I didn't say so to him, I'd hardly missed them. "It isn't as if I'm blind," I added hastily.

He laughed aloud at that. "I'll see to new ones tomorrow."

As in the library earlier, he did not embarrass me by telling me I looked better without them. Even kind Charles had made that common remark to me. But his cousin now seemed only concerned with my being able to see properly.

"Are there any questions?" he asked.

"Well . . . no. Actually, this has happened so fast I'm at a loss for words."

"We'll give you plenty of time to become accustomed," he said with a smile. "I've already spoken to Mrs. Hunt, so don't worry about that."

"You have? But what did she say?"

He grinned broadly then. "I don't think you really want to know what Mrs. Hunt had to say about it."

"No," I said sheepishly. "I guess I don't."

He smiled and held his arm toward me. "I'll walk you upstairs."

He had not mentioned my work in the library. I did not think I could bear never to go there again, never to delve into the many volumes of books. I hesitated.

Two small lines appeared between his eyebrows as I waited. "What is it?" he asked. "If there is anything else you require, you've only to name it."

He was such an enigma to me. And although I did think he placed too much importance on money, he was extremely generous. And he was not at all the way some people had portrayed him.

"It's just . . . well, I was wondering about the library."

"The library?" he asked, looking at me with a puzzled frown. "You mean your work there? Let me assure you

130

that you will not need to perform any more boring tasks there . . ."

"But I want to!" I said quickly. "I love it . . . it has meant so much to me. Of course, I don't wish to take any time away from Amy."

His frown turned into a slow, easy grin as he shook his head. His amber eyes twinkled as he looked down at me. He looked so different when he smiled that way.

"Your enthusiasm is very refreshing. Has anyone ever told you that?"

I shrugged, not knowing what to say.

"Of course you may continue to work in the library. I am delighted that you wish to. Amy usually naps immediately after lunch, so any afternoon will be fine. And please, feel free to *use* the library, not just work there. As I said, I'd like you to consider this your home now, and not a place of employment."

"I can't believe how kind you are . . . how generous." I spoke the words before I thought.

The warm smile immediately left his face. "Oh? Don't believe everything Charles tells you about me, Miss Stevens," he said. His lips twisted in an angry grimace.

Without another word he offered me his arm. He seemed thoughtful as we went upstairs. He escorted me all the way to my room with nothing more than a curt goodnight.

That night I could hardly sleep for thinking of what he had said to me. What exactly did he expect? He mentioned a wardrobe and spoke of treating me like a member of the family. And those ideas frightened more than delighted me, for I was certain I did not know how to behave properly as a member of a wealthy household.

Early the next morning, Frederick and another young man came to my room. I felt rather foolish, for there was only one small bag to carry. Nevertheless both of them went with me down to the second floor, making me feel rather like a princess being escorted by two soldiers.

Frederick whispered to me along the way. "I can hardly believe this is happening to you, Elizabeth. The servants' quarters are abuzz with the news. Imagine, one of our own being put in such a high position! We're awfully proud of you; it couldn't have happened to a nicer girl. And Dottie says to tell you not to go getting a swelled head!" We laughed together and I felt as if I was in a wonderful dream from which I would soon awaken.

The room Frederick took me to was the first one at the top of the stairs, just off the large sitting hall. Mrs. Vanderworth's room would be immediately above mine.

It's hard to believe now, but I had thought little about the room I would occupy. Oh, I had imagined how nice it would be and how much more pleasant than my tiny room upstairs. But I had been so busy with other thoughts that such details had not entered my mind.

Now, as Frederick pushed open the door, I could only stare in amazement, for I felt as if I had entered a fairy-tale world. This feeling was only heightened when Mrs. Vanderworth rose from a chair and came across the room to greet me, her arms outstretched.

"Welcome, my dear. I am your fairy godmother!" Her words were said with a teasing chuckle.

I hardly noticed the departure of Frederick and the other servant. I stumbled into the room, mouth agape, unable to say all the things that raced through my thoughts.

"It . . . it's the most beautiful room I've ever seen," I finally managed to stammer.

"This is all Louis XVI," she said, waving her arm about the opulent room.

The room was oval-shaped, with white woodwork and elegant molding rounded to fit its curvature. Panels between white woodwork were covered in rich red damask and a swag of the same material made a half canopy over the large, lacy bed. All the furniture was elegant and feminine, from a plush chaise longue to the diminutive carved desk by the lace-curtained windows. A large arched mirror over the fireplace reflected the beauty of the room and the crystal vases of freshly cut red and white roses.

"Derek wanted you to have the best," she said proudly. "After all, if it were not for you, our precious Amy might no longer be with us."

"Oh, it frightens me even to think of it," I said, feeling my heart race a little.

"It is our wish that you be happy and that you live here with us for as long as you like. I suppose my grandson also told you of the trust fund he is opening for you?"

"Yes," I said, shaking my head. "I could hardly believe his generosity."

"He is a good man," she said quietly. "A generous man. If he sometimes emphasizes material possessions, it's only because he has never known what true love is all about. I hope someday soon he will."

I said nothing, trying to hide my curiosity about her words. I thought it an odd thing for her to say. Surely he had loved his beautiful wife, had he not?

"Well, enough of that," she said briskly. "I just wanted to welcome you, make you comfortable. I think Derek has a full agenda scheduled for you the next few days. Amy will be allowed to visit here with you while you're being fitted for your new wardrobe. And he has assigned a girl named Jenny to help you with Amy so that you might be free to visit the library whenever you choose. Tomorrow there will be a trip into town where you'll be fitted for your new glasses."

"My . . . my new glasses?" I asked.

"Oh, yes. Didn't Derek mention it? He has contacted a doctor in Asheville to replace the glasses you lost. We did find yours on the library terrace, but they were smashed to pieces. So . . ."

I touched my forehead shakily and sat down in one of

the red damask chairs. "I can't believe all this. Everything has changed so suddenly. I . . . I just can't seem to take it all in."

She patted my arm. "Of course you can't, darling. But you will. I'll help you. I will teach you everything you need to know about etiquette, fashion, everything. You already know so much. Much more than I did at your age, actually. But if there's anything, dear, anything at all that you have questions about, you've only to ask. I, more than anyone, understand what a change there will be in your life."

It was such a relief hearing that, for my social etiquette was sadly lacking. And I didn't think I could bear to make a fool of myself before Derek Vanderworth and his elegant houseguests.

"Thank you," I whispered, smiling at her.

"Well, I'm going to leave you and let you become acquainted with your new living quarters. I'll return shortly, just as soon as the dressmaker arrives. All right?"

She bustled out and I turned back into the beautiful room. Impulsively I threw my arms out and laughed, whirling about the room until I became slightly dizzy and fell upon the chaise. My favorite childhood fairy-tale was coming to life. I *was* Cinderella!

Chapter Fourteen

I had no idea that day how drastically my life really was to change, just as I'd had no idea when I'd raced to Amy in the pool how it would affect my future.

But even though I'd been told what would happen, what would be mine, I don't think I truly believed it.

When the dressmaker came, it seemed like some childhood game to me. She was a small, quiet woman who treated me with a gentle kindness. As she measured and pinned and turned me about, there was never a hint that I was anything other than one of her wealthy patrons.

When Jenny, the girl Mrs. Vanderworth had mentioned, brought Amy to me, the child skipped into the room. When she saw me, she ran to me as she always did and wrapped her small arms about my legs. I laughed and held her away, afraid one of the dressmaker's pins would stick her.

It was not easy talking to Amy, because she was so young. But I took one of the pins from the material and tapped it lightly to her arm. "It will stick you," I explained. Her golden brown eyes grew wide and bright. Then she laughed.

I decided then and there that if her voice had returned in her laughter and her cries, surely her speech would soon return as well. I vowed to make that my goal, not only for Amy, but also for her father, who had been so generous to me.

After a while Amy settled into playing, seeming happy and content to be with us in the bright, airy room. It was a peaceful, contented morning and one we all enjoyed.

The dressmaker stayed so long that Mrs. Vanderworth had lunch sent up to us. It was great fun, with Mrs. Vanderworth, my fairy godmother, as she had begun to call herself, presiding as regally as any queen. Mrs. Tillis, the dressmaker, seemed tremendously pleased to be included and chatted freely with us about news in town.

When Diana Gresham opened the door and stepped into my room, all of us at the table became quiet, waiting for her to speak. Even Amy seemed to sense the tension in the air.

"Well, so what I've heard is true. Derek has indeed taken one of the maids and placed her in a lofty position. There's even been talk of the outrageous salary he's paying you."

"Diana," Mrs. Vanderworth warned.

The petite blonde moved slowly toward us, her eyes riveted upon me. She completely ignored Mrs. Vanderworth's soft-spoken voice.

"You're the young woman that Amy ran to in the Palm Court that Sunday." Her words, though quiet, were an accusation.

"Yes," I said evenly. "That's right. My name is Elizabeth Stevens." I stood and offered her my chair, determined to make friends if I could. "Won't you sit here and join us for lunch?"

"Why not?" she said with a curl of her lovely red lips.

"You know, Grandmother Vanderworth, I'm perfectly capable of caring for Amy. There was really no reason for Derek to bring in an outsider. After all,

Amy is my niece. Surely you could have persuaded Derek of that if you'd wanted to."

Mrs. Vanderworth slowly lifted a glass to her lips. "Yes, Diana, I probably could have . . . if I'd wanted to."

Diana visibly stiffened in her chair. "So . . . you're saying that you do not trust me with Amy?"

Mrs. Vanderworth sighed. "Of course not, Diana. Why must you always be so sensitive? I had no idea you would be willing to spend all your days with Amy. You certainly gave no indication of that, either to Derek or to myself."

The young woman took a sandwich from one of the trays and her mouth pouted prettily. I was certain it was a practiced move, but it was completely lost on Mrs. Vanderworth.

"Well," Diana still pouted. "I do wish Derek had asked me before . . ."

"Oh, come now, Diana," Mrs. Vanderworth said. "You know Derek has a mind of his own. Does he ever ask us when he intends to do something?"

"Well," Diana said with a sigh.

She turned to me, apparently having exhausted her argument with the older woman. "You know, of course, what everyone is saying about you? That you have . . . designs on Derek?"

"Designs?" I frowned at her in disbelief. What on earth was she insinuating now?

"Diana, you are being ridiculous," Mrs. Vanderworth said with a frown. "And indulging in gossip is hardly becoming to someone of your position."

I had hoped to make friends with Diana, or at least hoped we would not be enemies. But I could see that she intended to make trouble for me any way she could. She seemed an extremely emotional woman, and I recalled that day in the stairwell when she had grown so angry with Derek.

"I assure you, Miss Gresham, I hardly know Mr. Vanderworth. I've only been at Stormhaven a short while." I looked straight into her devious blue eyes as I spoke.

She did not reply, but made a slight, throaty noise of disbelief. She was all posturing and posing, as if she were used to having all attention focused on her. I suppose she thought that even as she daintily ate her sandwich we were all dying of envy at her every movement. I could not resist smiling at my whimsical thoughts.

Suddenly her blue eyes flashed dangerously. "And what, may I ask, do you find so amusing about me, Miss Stevens?" she snapped.

"Nothing," I said, feeling immediately sorry. I had no wish to become enemies with this woman. After all, she was a member of the family and Amy's aunt. "I was thinking of something else," I said.

She tossed her blond locks and gazed dramatically into the air. "Poor Derek has lost the love of his life, and very tragically, I might add. It will take a special kind of woman to help him begin to live again." From the look on her face I guessed we were all to assume that woman would be her.

I glanced at Amy, who was watching her aunt with a strange expression. There was sadness in her eyes, and I was certain that regardless of her young age, she knew exactly what Diana was talking about.

"Amy," I said quietly. "Come here, sweetheart." I stretched my arms out to her and she came immediately, climbing up onto my lap and laying her head against me. "Are you all right?" I asked, smoothing her riotous curls back from her face.

She shook her head but did not look up at me. She didn't look at any of us around the table. But I felt her small sigh and the slight relaxing of her body as I held her. I was surprised at the tenderness she evoked in me. I'd never thought to feel that way about anyone other than my little sister Angelina. But I could not deny it, I felt such a forceful welling of protectiveness inside, and I wanted to make sure that nothing ever hurt this little girl again.

It was growing late, and Amy was almost asleep. Mrs. Vanderworth said good-bye to Mrs. Tillis, then turned back toward me where I still sat at the table.

"Mrs. Tillis brought two ready-made dresses with her. I'll have one pressed and brought to your room before dinner, Elizabeth."

"I'm going to take Amy to her room. I'll probably stay with her until she wakes," I said, giving way to my intuition that something had disturbed the child and that I should not leave her alone.

"The dress will be on your bed," she said, smiling at me and touching Amy's shining hair as she walked by.

Diana's blue eyes were bright as she watched me stand and cradle Amy's small body in my arms. Only when we were completely alone did her true nature begin to reveal itself.

"I know what you're up to, you know," she said with a cold glint in her eyes. "You think to wheedle your way into Derek's life through his daughter."

"That is not true," I said, turning to leave the room. I was determined not to let her goad me into an argument.

"Oh, yes, it is true! You know you certainly have nothing else to offer," she said with a snort of disdain. "But I can tell you right now that Derek is not the sort of man to settle for a mouse like you. Some motherly little creature who creeps quietly through the house, who looks at him with great adoring eyes. Oh, no. He needs a real woman, one with blood in her veins. Someone who can match him passion for passion!" Her eyes were bright and a bit glazed as she began to rant. Her pale skin had become red and splotched.

139

"And I assume that *real* woman is you?" I asked coldly.

"Well, at least you're perceptive," she said with a leering smile as she placed her hands at her small waist.

"I'm leaving now," I said calmly. "I must take Amy to her room. I cannot help what you think, Diana. And I don't intend to waste my time trying to convince you you're wrong about me."

I turned then and hurriedly left the room, hoping that Amy was sleeping soundly and had not heard Diana's hateful words.

"That's right. Run, you little mouse! You can't give him excitement! Love! I'm the one he will turn to. Me! Do you understand? I won't let some little nobody like you spoil everything! Do you hear me?"

I kept walking. Diana seemed completely out of control as she continued to shout her ugly accusations at me.

I closed the door, shutting off her voice. She sounded like a madwoman, and something in that thought sent shivers down my spine. I found myself hurrying across the corner of the sitting hall and down toward Amy's bedroom. I only hoped that, without an audience, Diana would soon leave my room.

I placed Amy on her bed and covered her with a small quilt. Then I stood for a moment looking down at her. She seemed so tiny and fragile. Something had hurt her badly, so badly that she had lost the will to speak. Something was bottled up deep inside her, perhaps something she had forgotten herself. Did I dare risk finding out what that something was? Or might I only hurt her in the process?

I pulled a rocking chair nearer to the bed and sat watching her, thinking about what I should do. I was so lost in thought that I did not hear anyone enter the room, until suddenly I sensed someone behind me.

I turned to find Derek watching me quietly. The room was darkened for Amy's nap, and I could not see his face clearly, or the expression in his eyes. He stood near a doorway, one I had not noticed earlier. Apparently it led to one of the other bedrooms. His?

"How is she?" he asked quietly, his eyes intent upon the small figure on the bed.

"She's well," I said, watching him, remembering how stern and cold he'd been the day I'd come here and found Amy sobbing.

He walked to the bed and pulled a small stool closer so he could sit beside his daughter. I think for the first time I saw him as an ordinary man. Not the incredibly wealthy Earl of Chesham, or the debonair owner of the estate who raced with the hounds and filled his house constantly with guests. That man needed diversion, needed the comfort of never being alone. This man was different. This man who watched his daughter with such tenderness, such concern, was simply a daddy. And it touched my heart and dredged up feelings of my own insecurities about my father. Just for a moment I envied Amy, for I thought I'd never seen such love as I saw reflected in his eyes as he looked at his daughter.

He turned to see me watching him. I smiled, perhaps displaying some of the thoughts I'd just been experiencing.

"You have a nice smile," he said. "I think you'll be good for her."

"I hope so," I said, looking away from his piercing gaze. I told myself he meant his words in an objective way. He was speaking to me as Amy's companion, not as a woman.

"Do you like your room?" he asked, the expression on his face becoming more external, hiding the emotion I'd seen just minutes before.

"Oh, yes," I said. "It's lovely. I don't think I'll ever

become accustomed to the beauty of Stormhaven."

He turned his head to one side and studied me with an odd glint in his eyes. "Oh, yes," he said matter-of-factly. "You will grow used to it. In time you will probably take it for granted, just as the rest of us do. By then you will no doubt be the belle of Asheville and will rival Diana in her many social pursuits."

"I . . . I don't think so," I said stiffly.

Did he really believe that? That every woman was like Diana, interested only in new clothes, in spending each night gossiping and flirting, whiling her life away in self-indulgences? I was insulted and I was hurt that he thought I could ever be like her.

I got up and walked to the window that faced the mountains. I pushed back the heavy curtains and gazed out at the magnificent sight.

"What's wrong?" he asked with a touch of annoyance. "Did I offend you with my comment?"

"No," I lied. "Of course not. You are entitled to your opinion."

"I *did* offend you," he said, rising to come and stand behind me.

"The mountains are beautiful at this time of day," I said, hoping to change the course of our conversation.

"Yes," he said, following my gaze toward the lush green forests of the Pisgah. "I own them." There was pride in his voice. But there was something else as well. Weariness . . . boredom?

I turned to stare incredulously at him, studying the firmly clenched jaw, the hooded catlike eyes.

"You own . . . all that?" I could hardly believe it. There must have been thousands of acres before us.

"Ummm," he murmured.

"You sound as if owning all this is nothing," I said quietly.

He made a small noise in his throat and his mouth quirked upward at one corner. He seemed to change before my very eyes as he stepped closer, challenging me with his eyes, provoking me with his nearness.

"Less than nothing," he drawled. "Your eyes are so bright, so innocent when they look at everything in this house, Elizabeth. Everything you see seems to delight you. Why is that? Don't you ever feel bitter . . . angry?"

"Bitter?" I asked, frowning at him. I refused to step away from him, and I could sense that he meant to intimidate me with his closeness. "Why should I be bitter?"

He looked perplexed with me, annoyingly so. "Your life has hardly been pleasant, I presume. And it certainly has not been filled with ease. When you see all this, don't you feel resentful, angry that you had nothing, while someone like me . . . ?"

"No," I said quickly, shaking my head at him. "No, I don't feel that way at all. And I could never resent you . . ." I bit my lip, afraid I'd said too much.

He frowned and stepped away from me. "Then you're a fool," he said, going back to stand at the bed.

"Am I?" I asked, becoming bold, now that we were alone. "Has your wealth made you so happy, then?"

His eyes darted to mine, and in them I saw such frustration, such pain-filled anger, that I could hardly believe it.

"Yes, damn it!" he said, his voice a hoarse whisper in the quiet room. "Money is everything. It's the only thing I need."

"How can you say that?" I said, becoming angry myself. "Even as you stand here looking down at this child . . . could money have brought her back to you? She needs *you,* not your money. You're all she has to hold on to. And no matter what you say, Derek Vanderworth, I think you need her just as much."

His jaw was clenched as he stared at me. "My, but you've become so *wise* with your new position here,

143

haven't you? One day a maid; the next an insightful adviser." His voice was cruel, sarcastic.

And just as he'd intended, the words went straight to my heart, hitting me with such force I thought I would have to sit down. He struck at the very thing that hurt me most, the fact that I would never really belong here. And I knew now that was exactly what I did want, to live here and more than that to be accepted as an equal by him.

I took a deep breath, but I could not disguise the shudder that ran through me, nor the tears that filled my eyes. "I . . . I'm sorry if I've overstepped my bounds."

I hated myself when my voice trembled and kept me from saying more. "Excuse me," I muttered as I turned and ran from the room.

I ran from his hateful words and from his disturbing amber eyes that always seemed shuttered and closed. For I wanted so much to see into them and into his heart. But he would not let me, and I could not help wondering if he would ever let anyone in.

Jenny was in the sitting room as I ran lightly past the stair railing and toward my room. She looked up and smiled at me.

"Afternoon, Elizabeth," she said shyly.

I asked her if she would check on Amy from time to time while she napped and tell me when she woke. Then I hurried to my room, lest she come closer and see the tears that still stung my eyes.

I barely glanced at the new white dress that lay on my bed. I was too intent on the numbing pain that gripped my heart. Why was I feeling this way? My life had changed drastically and I now had a future that would allow me some freedom and pleasure. I would even be able to help my family. It was not my nature to let something eat at me this way.

But it was not *something*, I told myself. It was someone . . . Derek Vanderworth . . . who had hurt me, a man I'd hoped to know better. And now that seemed impossible.

I had time for a long, leisurely bath before dressing for my first dinner with the family. I wanted to look my best, with none of these negative feelings to drag me down. It would be difficult enough as it was to spend an evening with Derek, not to mention Diana, who seemed to hate me. I could not let myself feel unworthy in the process.

After a slow, relaxing bath, I sat at the window for a moment and looked out over the front lawn. I would miss my own view of the mountains, I thought wistfully. Unbidden, Derek Vanderworth's words came back to me. The mountains were his. How easily he said it, as if anything he wanted was his for the asking.

I turned to the dress on the bed, the one Mrs. Vanderworth had sent up. I was a bit surprised when I looked at it more closely. Not that it wasn't beautiful with its layers of sheer white silk. But it seemed far too sophisticated, too exquisite for me.

I ran my hands across the lovely material, touching the iridescent beading that covered the bodice. Suddenly I could wait no longer to put it on, to feel the silk against my skin.

The fit was perfect, as if it had been made for me. An attached beaded collar sparkled at my throat, and below it the delicate lace netting exposed the warmer color of skin beneath it. The opaque silk curved across my breasts and nipped in tightly at the waist. The yards of filmy material in the skirt were of different lengths and layers, each of them edged in iridescent beading.

I turned slowly, holding the skirt out from me as I danced about the room. I stopped before the arched mirror over the fireplace and gazed at the girl in the reflection. But it was not a girl who faced me. It was a woman, no longer the skinny and shapeless child I'd once been. My eyes grew wide as I continued to stare at myself and noted how the dress emphasized the swell of my breasts and hips. I could hardly believe the transformation. I smiled at myself, forgetting the way I'd felt before, forgetting how Derek had spoken to me.

This was what any girl would want, I told myself, what I'd always dreamed of. To live in a beautiful house and dress in clothes that made one feel beautiful.

Quickly I turned to find a brush and comb, determined to do something different with my hair. Moments later, when I'd finished the last of the braids and looped them behind my head into an elegant knot, I smiled.

"Cinderella, my little drudge," I whispered with a smile to the girl in the mirror. "At last, you are going to the ball!"

Chapter Fifteen

Before going downstairs I walked back to Amy's room and quietly opened the door. I was surprised to see that she was awake and sitting at a table near the windows. Jenny was with her.

"Did you have a nice nap?" I asked.

She jumped down from her chair and ran across to me. Her eyes were bright with excitement as she reached out to touch the shimmering white dress I wore. I knelt down and put one arm around her.

"It's pretty, isn't it, Amy?" I asked.

She nodded and made a little noise with her indrawn breath as she ran her fingers across the beadwork. I laughed. She was so delightful and seemed always so cheerful.

I looked across at the dark-haired girl sitting quietly watching us. There was a smile on her face, and it was obvious she adored little Amy as much as everyone else in the house did.

"Are you going to stay with her for a while?" I asked.

"Yes, we're going to have our supper together."

"Well, that's wonderful," I said. "I suppose it will take a day or two to settle into a routine with Amy. And I appreciate any help you can give me."

"Happy to oblige," she said almost shyly.

"Goodnight, then," I said.

"You . . . you look beautiful Eliz . . . Miss Stevens. All of us in the quarters are real happy for you. Gives us hope, I guess, that we might one day do better." It was as if the dress had transformed me in Jenny's eyes as well.

"Thank you, Jenny," I said. "But I'm still the same as before, and I hope you'll still call me Elizabeth."

Before I left, I noticed the flash of lightning in the windows of Amy's room. The sky seemed terribly dark for early evening. But spring in the mountains often brought evening storms.

As I made my way down the grand staircase, the lightning flashed closer. It outshone the lights along the stairs and made my head reel dizzily as it flickered and then darkened again.

I walked around the corridor of the Palm Court and watched the lightning as it made a spectacular show through the glass-domed roof. As I grew nearer the family dining room I could hear voices, and I hoped I was not the last person to arrive for dinner.

I smoothed the skirt of my silk dress before I entered the room. There was a small group tonight, as most of the guests had gone. They had not yet sat down, but stood talking in the small, elegant room.

As they turned to greet me, I saw the smiles on their faces change suddenly to ones of shock and dismay. Derek Vanderworth's eyes glittered with fury as he looked at me from head to toe as if he couldn't believe his eyes.

I stopped still, wondering what blunder I could have committed already. But the moment passed and everyone made an effort to hide their discomfort by seating themselves at the oval table.

Mrs. Vanderworth came forward quickly and put a comforting arm about my waist, urging me into the room. She whispered into my ear, only loud enough for me to hear.

148

"Where did you get this dress?"

As we moved slowly into the room I could see Charles and Derek still staring at me. Diana Gresham was grinning broadly, her blue eyes sparkling with mischief.

"It . . . it was on my bed, just as you said," I whispered to Mrs. Vanderworth.

"This was not the dress I sent to your room!" Then, with a little murmur of understanding, she turned toward Diana.

She was still watching us, and her face was as serene and innocent as a babe's.

"Ah," Mrs. Vanderworth said. "I think I begin to see what happened."

"But what?" I asked. "What have I done?"

"You've done nothing, child," she said firmly. "I'll explain later. Just smile and pretend you're not disturbed at all by this."

As she pointed to my seat at the table, she raised her voice so everyone would hear. "Sit here, darling, beside me."

She took her place at the end of the oval table and I sat beside her. Derek sat at the other end. I had not noticed the Reverend Webster until now as he nodded to me from the other side of the table.

The family dining room was much smaller than the other rooms in the house, and I supposed it was planned that way, since it was considered a private room. As the servants began to serve the meal, I glanced about the room. The walls were covered in something that looked like tooled Spanish leather. It was a rich wine color that contrasted beautifully with the elaborately carved white ceiling and wide molding. There was a small, neat fireplace with lovely blue tilework around it. Even the pictures here seemed less formal and were undoubtedly those of family members.

149

My entrance seemed to have caused an awkwardness in the room, and I was very curious to know what was wrong. I knew from what Mrs. Vanderworth said that it had something to do with the dress, but I could not imagine what.

As we ate, I hardly noticed the food, for I was concentrating so hard on following Mrs. Vanderworth's use of the silverware. But she made it easy for me and smiled at me from time to time in encouragement.

"Well, Miss Stevens," the Reverend Webster said. "I understand you've become quite a heroine since I saw you last."

"I . . . it was nothing," I stammered, not really wanting to talk about it again. I glanced toward the head of the table and saw Derek's eyes on me.

His knife was poised above his plate, and the look he flashed my way was cool and amused; he was waiting, it seemed, for me to make a mistake. I had not forgotten how cruel he could be.

"Elizabeth is being . . . modest," he said, his eyes mocking me.

I lowered my eyes to my plate, but I could not hide the flush of anger that rose to my cheeks. I could not believe he had rewarded me with this position only to ridicule me each time he saw me. Perhaps I didn't know him as well as I thought I did.

"And how is little Amy?" the Reverend Webster asked.

"She's quite well," I said, smiling at him and trying to ignore Derek's knowing looks.

"We're delighted to have Elizabeth with us," Mrs. Vanderworth said with a pointed look toward Derek.

"Yes," he drawled. "Delighted. She's brought quite a refreshing bit of spring to Stormhaven with her honesty and candor."

I almost choked on the bread I was eating. My eyes flew to him, and he lifted his wineglass toward me in a little salute. "We thank you, sweet Elizabeth," he said.

I frowned at him, wondering at his odd manner. Then I noted the look of smug satisfaction on Charles's face as he glanced down at his cousin. Then it became clear to me. Derek was drunk! Or at least well on his way. And when I looked at his plate, I could see he had hardly touched his food; while his wineglass had been filled several times.

I glanced uneasily toward Mrs. Vanderworth. Her eyes met mine and she gave a little shake of her head, as if I were simply to ignore Derek.

I became anxious for the meal to end, not knowing what Derek might say next. And I was growing quite tired of Diana's little looks of triumph. I was certain now that whatever was wrong with the dress I wore, it had been her doing.

When everyone took their coffee to the morning salon in the next room, I excused myself, pleading tiredness.

"Oh, stay, Elizabeth . . . the evening is young!" Once again Derek lifted his glass my way. He was the only one not drinking coffee.

When I left without answering him, I could hear his laughter ringing down the hallway even as I fled. I went immediately to the library for some books, then made my way quickly upstairs. The storm had intensified, and I always loved reading on rainy nights.

It was such a relief to be away from the Vanderworths. I could not imagine how I was going to adjust to these people, was not even sure I wanted to. Perhaps I should try to find employment elsewhere, I thought. But when I went to Amy's room to check on her before I went to bed, all those thoughts just fled my mind.

She was a sweet child at any time, but when she was sleeping so quietly in the big bed, she looked like a beautiful little angel. I had an overwhelming urge to crawl into bed with her and hug her close, make her feel safe and wanted. But instead, I tucked the sheet around her and slowly ruffled her blond curls with my hand.

I left a small lamp burning near the window and went across the hall to my own room.

I undressed and slipped into my faded and worn cotton nightgown. It was too bad I had nothing new to wear to match my elegant new room. I laughed at the thought, enjoying nonetheless every moment in it. I took the beautiful white silk dress and hung it in the closet next to my old gray suit. To my surprise, I saw there were other dresses there, two new ones which would be suitable during the day, probably the ones Mrs. Vanderworth had mentioned.

I stood back a moment and gazed at the white dress. It seemed to shimmer with a glow of its own there in the dark closet. Who had put it on my bed? Diana? But why? Obviously it had shocked or displeased everyone at dinner, and I was burning with curiosity to know why.

I closed the door thoughtfully, reluctant to put the lovely dress out of my sight. I'd never worn anything as beautiful, and it had given me a confidence that quickly faded after what happened at dinner.

Just then the little gold ormolu clock on the mantel chimed loudly and a low rumble of thunder shook the windows of the house. I glanced into the mirror above the fireplace and grimaced at the wisps of hair that were coming loose from my elegant coiffure.

"So much for Cinderella," I said with a laugh.

I unbraided my hair and brushed it until it lay in fine, shining strands across my shoulders and down my back. Then, as the sound of thunder ripped through the house, I ran and jumped quickly into the big, fluffy bed.

I looked at the small stack of books I'd brought from

the library, among them a selection of Tennyson's best works. Longfellow's sad, grieving poems or James Russell Lowe's zealous political words could not hold my attention, and finally I reached for *Jane Eyre*. I had read it many times, usually hiding it from my mother. She felt the romantic novels were too silly and sentimental and certainly unsuitable for a young girl.

But now, here in the privacy of my own beautiful room, I could read it to my heart's content and relish every word of it.

I scooted down into the bed and began to read, oblivious to the storm outside, or indeed of anything except Jane Eyre and her beloved Edward.

I don't know how long I'd been reading when I heard the noise. It wasn't the storm, I was certain of it. It was the sound I'd heard before, the sound of someone crying. And it was nearby.

I held the book perfectly still and listened. There was a heavy thump, and this time I was certain it came from the sitting hall just outside my door.

I sat quietly for a moment just listening and trying not to let the storm and the big house prey on my imagination. Then I heard it again, a high-pitched, shrill scream that rang and echoed so clearly that there was no mistaking it this time.

Quickly I ran to the door and threw it open. I gave little thought to the fact that I was clad only in my nightgown. Indeed, I thought of nothing except finding out what had caused the cries.

The scream came again, and this time I was sure of its direction. It came from Amy's room!

Before I could turn to grab my robe from the foot of the bed, I saw a flash of white across the stair rail just at the entrance to the hallway. I blinked and looked again. Was it only the lightning that made my eyes see things that were not there?

The ghostly figure in white ran directly toward me.

I gasped, the sound of my breath clearly audible in the room. The person stopped and stared straight at me and I thought my heart would pound from my chest.

It was a woman, that much I could see in the gloom. Her hair, a pale silver, stood out about her face and fell down her back in a tangled mass of curls. She was thin, her pale, bony hands clearly visible in the light coming up from the stairway. I could not see her eyes, could not see her face at all. It was hidden in the shadows of the sitting hall. We stood staring at each other for only a few short seconds, but it seemed like forever. I could not move, could not utter a word, and I had no idea exactly who, or *what*, I was seeing.

Then she turned and with a silent grace ran swiftly across the sitting hall and toward the other wing of the house. I clutched the front of my gown, gripping the material until my fingers were almost numb. For as the wraithlike woman ran away, I saw more clearly the dress she wore. It was white, and the skirt was made from yards of iridescent material that flew out gracefully as she ran. There were several layers, several different lengths of the skirt. *It was amazingly like the one I'd worn to dinner tonight.*

I ran quickly across the hall toward Amy's room. Had the woman come from there? Fear churned within me, for I was almost certain she had.

Amy's door was open, and just as I stepped into the room, Derek Vanderworth reached the bed and took the small blond child in his arms. The shaft of light from the doorway of his room was our only illumination.

It cast a soft, golden glow upon the bed and across the silky royal blue robe that encased Derek's broad, muscular shoulders.

"What's wrong?" I said breathlessly as I came to the foot of the bed. I had to make sure for myself that

Amy was all right, that she was safe.

Derek turned to look at me and the sound of his voice was slow and studied.

"It was only a nightmare. You may go back to bed, Miss Stevens."

But Amy had other ideas. I could see her great, luminous eyes in the light from the doorway. They looked at me with pleading appeal as she lifted small, chubby arms toward me. She was terrified, and tears shone brightly in her eyes.

"Mommy!" she screamed. "Mommy!"

Her words stunned me so that I stopped immediately and stood staring at her. Derek's head turned slowly to his daughter. I could glimpse only the side of his face, but it was quite enough for me to see his shocked expression. The child's first words in a year were for her dead mother.

Amy's hands reached for me, her fingers clasping and unclasping as she began to cry. "Mommy?" Her word grew weaker as her childish tears began to overtake her.

I walked to her. Derek seemed too stunned to react, and I bent to take Amy in my arms.

"It's all right," I said quickly. "She's had a bad dream and thinks I'm her mother. Let me . . ."

"No!" he said, whirling to look at me. "Look at her eyes! She isn't looking at you, she's staring at the door to the hallway."

I turned on the lamp beside the table. He was right. Amy's eyes were riveted upon the open doorway; she was trembling, and tears ran down her frightened little face.

"Hold her," I said. "She's frightened."

It was odd that he needed someone to tell him that. But as he took her in his arms, I could see it was not a natural thing for him. It was achingly painful; he could not hide that fact from me.

But as he continued to hold her and she wrapped her small arms about his strong forearms, I could see a transformation take place almost before my very eyes.

I sat down in the nearby rocking chair and watched, unable to take my eyes from him. The sight of them there together filled me with such incredible longing that I thought I would have to run from the room. It was something that I did not understand about myself.

With one hand he held her head against his chest while the other quietly caressed her soft blond curls. I watched those hands, so strong and yet so gentle. They mesmerized and fascinated me. He spoke softly to her and began to rock her in a slow, rhythmic motion. All his awkwardness was gone, as was the fierceness that always seemed to be a part of him. I thought then that no woman, no mother could have been sweeter or more tender than he was to his child.

Soon Amy was asleep again and he laid her carefully back upon her pillow. When I rose from my chair and reached to turn out the lamp, he motioned that I should leave it on.

"Come into the sitting room," he whispered, nodding toward the shaft of light from the open doorway.

The passageway to the next room was like a short arched tunnel. The structure was completely paneled in dark, elaborately carved wood. It was an unusual and beautiful touch.

As soon as I entered the long, brightly lit sitting room, I remembered how little I was wearing. I stopped immediately and clutched at the bosom of my high-necked gown, holding it against my body.

Derek turned as if sensing that I was no longer behind him. From across the room he looked at me, his strangely colored eyes raking me from head to foot and back again. When his lids lifted to my face, they revealed shining eyes that slowly scanned my features. The look in his eyes made me feel warm and strange, and I was at a complete loss to understand exactly why.

"I . . . I forgot my robe," I finally stammered. "I heard Amy scream, and I . . ."

His lashes dropped and raised again slowly. A smile flickered across his handsome face and he took a step toward me. I knew instinctively what his look meant, knew it as if I'd been born knowing. I know now it's a knowledge all women possess, even in their purest innocence, that knowledge of a man's desire. But I was shocked at my first recognition of it. Not so much that I was seeing it in this particular man's eyes . . . but that it was directed at me, and that even through my fright, it thrilled me to my very soul.

"My, my," he drawled. His deep voice sent shivers along my spine. "You certainly seem to have a way of showing up in the most amazing state of dress."

Chapter Sixteen

I took a step backward until I was standing in the shadows of the paneled archway. He began to walk toward me, his eyes never leaving my face. I felt spellbound, unable to move or to speak. And all the while I knew I should run from him. He was a strange, unpredictable man, a dangerous man who frightened me even as he fascinated me.

I turned then, but I wasn't quick enough. I felt the grip of his strong fingers on my arm and stopped, too surprised to struggle, too proud to beg him to let me go.

I turned slowly, intending to reason with him. As I glanced up into his eyes, I saw them dancing with mischief as he released my arm. Slowly he lifted his hand and pushed a garment of some kind toward me.

"I only wanted to give you a robe to wear. Whatever did you think?" His lips quirked crookedly as he placed the silky material in my hand.

"I . . . I was just going to get my own," I stammered.

He knew I was lying. If he had not seen my confusion and my fear, he most certainly saw the flush that now covered my neck and face.

"I'm sorry," he said, his voice mocking. "I simply could not resist seeing you run like a frightened kitten."

But I was still smarting from embarrassment and from the fact that he knew why he had so alarmed me.

"Do you enjoy frightening women?" I asked with a touch of annoyance.

"Sometimes," he drawled, giving me another flash of his heavy-lidded eyes. "But at this moment I think I'm more interested in what you saw earlier . . . before you came to Amy's room."

I was more than happy to change the subject, and as I draped his large silk dressing gown around me, I sat in a chair opposite him. I shivered as I recalled that strange, unearthly figure I'd seen earlier.

"There was a woman," I said, thinking. "She ran from Amy's room just as I opened my door. When she saw me, she stopped and looked straight at me."

His eyes had grown hard and cold, and they studied me now as if I were an animal he had captured.

"What did she look like?"

"I . . . I couldn't see her face. But she was slender . . . very thin. And . . ." I looked up at him, wondering if he was thinking the same thoughts as I.

"And what?" he asked coldly.

"And she had very pale hair," I said quietly. "A mass of silver hair that fell about her shoulders. And . . . and she was wearing a white dress like . . . like . . ."

"Like the one you wore tonight?" he said with a sarcastic twist of his lips.

My mouth flew open, and I could only stare at him. He *was* thinking the same thoughts, and I was almost afraid to hear his next words.

"I suppose you thought it was very clever to appear at dinner in that dress, Miss Stevens. And now you've concocted this elaborate story to go with it." He waited, letting me squirm as he watched me.

"I'm afraid I don't understand any of this," I said. "I have no idea what significance that dress has or . . . or who it belongs to."

"Oh," he scoffed. "You might have convinced me,

159

had you not added that last breathless little phrase. I think you know exactly who it belonged to. What I don't understand is why you did it. Was it to shock me, to repay me for my rudeness to you earlier? Or is it something far more simple . . . perhaps a little game between yourself and Charles?"

I gasped and shook my head. "Charles? Of course not. Really, Mr. Vanderworth," I began. "I have no idea . . ."

As quickly as a cat he'd moved from his seat and taken my arms, pulling me so strongly from the chair that my feet almost left the floor. He held me against him, my arms pinned against his chest as he shook me firmly. I could smell the masculine scent of him, of tobacco and spice and the faint but distinct smell of liquor.

"Mr. Vanderworth," he mocked. "Don't look at me with that big innocent gaze, Elizabeth," he said angrily. "Just tell me why you wore the dress!"

"You're . . . you're still drunk!" I said, feeling the shock of my words even as I spoke them. I felt a twinge of fear then as I realized how very little I knew about this unpredictable man. I remembered too late the violence that always seemed a part of him.

He laughed. "That frightens you, doesn't it? Then let me assure you, my dear, I never drink enough to affect my mind, or my body."

His grip on my arms loosened, and he turned his head to one side as he sometimes did when he was thinking. He looked at me quizzically for a moment, then frowned.

"That's it, isn't it? You really *are* afraid of me," he whispered.

I tried to pull away, but his fingers tightened, only pulling me closer again.

His eyes burned into mine, would not release me from their strange spell.

"Answer me," he said quietly, shaking me slightly as

160

"I suppose it's no secret that my wife always wore white." He stopped and gazed at me pointedly.

"I didn't know that, but . . ."

"But . . . ?"

". . . There are some here who say that her spirit still wanders the halls, especially on a windy, stormy night." The words came rushing from me.

"Ah," he said with a wry lift of his brows. "And so now I'm to assume that this . . . thing you saw tonight was my wife's spirit, then?" His voice had grown hard and sarcastic. "And tell me . . . do you suppose she came to torment me, or her daughter?"

I could only imagine the anguish he was feeling. Of course, he did not believe in ghosts . . . any more than I did. But it was clear that Desiree's spirit still haunted him nonetheless.

And I didn't know if it was because his wife had loved Charles instead of him or for some other, unknown reason. Was his pain the result of his bruised pride, as Charles implied, or, as I suspected, a broken heart?

"Neither," I said. "I don't think for a moment that your wife's spirit was here. And I don't think you do, either."

He looked at me for a long while, his gaze sharp and probing. Then he took a deep breath and lowered his chin to his chest. He stood for a moment with his hands at his hips before looking up at me again.

"Why don't you just go back to bed, Elizabeth?" he said quietly, as if he were defeated.

"I want to tell you about the dress," I began. "To . . . to explain that . . ."

"Don't," he said tiredly, rubbing his hand across his eyes. "I don't care about the dress, or how you came to wear it."

"But . . ."

"Elizabeth, what I said earlier today, about your being only a servant . . . I shouldn't have said it. And I

163

hope you will overlook my bad temper and remain here as Amy's companion." He looked at me then and his eyes were so weary, so uncaring.

Where was the fierce man who had just kissed me, who had warned me about his intentions? It hurt so badly to think that the mere mention of his wife could cause such a look in his eyes, could change him so quickly to this cold, defensive man.

"Of course I'll stay," I said quietly, waiting, hoping he would take me in his arms again.

He straightened his shoulders and looked straight into my eyes. "Good. Then I'll say goodnight."

"Derek . . ." I began, unwilling to have it end this way. I stepped toward him.

He closed his eyes and expelled the air slowly from his lungs. "Elizabeth, I'm only going to say this once. I don't want to hurt you." His eyes came open and I was thrilled to see the spark of desire there. But this time he was trying to hide it with his cool words, trying to pretend it was not there.

"You are a sweet, innocent girl, one whose eyes see only the beauty around her. You never seem to see the ugliness underneath, while I'm never able to see anything else. And I . . . I don't ever want to look into those eyes and know the pain there was caused by me. Do you understand?"

"No," I whispered, almost in tears. "I don't understand. You would never hurt me. You . . . you couldn't."

"Yes!" he said through clenched teeth. "I could and I probably would. Tonight was a mistake. You were right, I *was* drunk and I didn't know what I was doing."

"No . . ."

He came to me in two quick strides. He took my arm and turned me roughly toward the arched entrance to Amy's room.

"Get out of here! Now! And don't ever come

164

through this doorway again unless you're prepared to give me what I want. Don't you know what a man like me is really after? Or are you so naive that you think it's love that I want from you?"

His cruel words did what he intended. They hit me like a fist, threatening to knock me to my knees. I ran through Amy's room so quickly that I hardly realized it until I was almost in my own bedroom.

I ran inside and closed my door, leaning against it and letting the tears come. He didn't mean it; he couldn't. I would never believe that what he'd felt for me tonight was meaningless . . . never! But the fact that he wanted me to think that and that he could be so cruel in the process hurt. It hurt deeply.

I fell into bed as the last remnants of the storm moved away from the great chateau. I looked down at the silk robe I still wore and the dark tearstained splotches on the front. Then I hugged it tightly around me and slept.

When I woke next morning the sun was already shining brightly, making cool, spidery patterns on the walls through the lace curtains. I realized that a light tapping at the door had awakened me.

"Come in," I said, sitting up in bed and pulling the sheet up to hide Derek's robe.

It was Jenny, and she carried a tray with a small silver pot and a linen-covered basket.

"Breakfast, Elizabeth," she said in her quiet, shy voice as she placed the tray on the table before the window.

"Heavens," I said, stretching my arms toward the ceiling. "What time is it? I should already have seen to Amy."

"Mr. Vanderworth said to let you sleep this mornin'." She looked at me speculatively, as if that had some special meaning.

"Oh, well . . . how . . . kind of him." His changing moods puzzled me.

"One of the other girls is dressing little Miss Amy. Mr. Vanderworth wishes to remind you of your trip into town today . . . to see the doctor about your glasses. You're to come out to the sitting hall whenever you're ready."

My trip! I'd already forgotten the trip. But I wished now that I never had to wear those glasses again. Of course my eyes burned terribly after reading last night without them. I'd had to squint to see the small print. But other than that, it hardly bothered me at all.

There was something else I'd forgotten in my encounter with Derek last night: Amy had actually uttered her first words.

I hurriedly ate breakfast, wanting more than anything to see her and find out if all her speech had returned.

I took one of the new dresses from the closet. I wanted to look bright and happy, so I chose one of pale yellow. After I had it on, I turned about before the mirror, pleased with the result. It was simply made, and I thought it made me look less like a child than my own worn clothes. The stiffly starched bustle behind trailed away to a short flounce that swished as I walked across the soft carpet.

Before leaving my room, I hung Derek's robe on the inside of the closet door, hoping Jenny would not notice it when she came to tidy my room. For a moment my eyes watered as I recalled Derek's hateful words of warning.

As I stepped out into the sitting hall, I felt a surge of both relief and disappointment to find only Mrs. Vanderworth and Amy. I wanted to see Derek, and yet I dreaded so much looking into his eyes and seeing that cold indifference. For what had happened between us could never be meaningless to me.

Mrs. Vanderworth rose from one of the couches.

166

"Oh my, Elizabeth," she said softly as she walked toward me. "You look absolutely lovely. Yellow is a wonderful color for you."

"Thank you," I murmured. I was not accustomed to such praise, certainly not where my looks were concerned. I wondered if she knew that and was trying to make me feel better about myself.

Amy ran to me, her usual exuberant self. If the events of last night still lingered in her mind, there was certainly no indication of it.

"Good morning, Amy," I said purposefully. But she only clung to my skirt and looked up at me with those big amber eyes. She said nothing.

I put my hand on her shoulder and led her back toward her great-grandmother. "How is she?" I asked, assuming that Mrs. Vanderworth already knew about last night.

"She seems fine. Derek said she slept soundly the rest of the night after . . ." She hesitated and looked toward the girl. "He told me what happened, but I'm not sure she even remembers it."

"Amy," I said. "Come here, darling." She did as I asked and climbed up beside me in the overstuffed chair. I put my arm around her as I spoke.

"Did you have a bad dream last night?"

Her eyes grew huge as she gazed up at me. She shook her head excitedly but still did not speak. Had she forgotten calling for her mother last night?

"Do you remember what it was?" I asked carefully.

Again she shook her head yes.

"Can you tell me about it?"

Suddenly her small face crumpled and with a little sob she hid her face against my side. As I glanced up I saw Derek standing near the stair railing. He stood perfectly still, listening to my question. From his expression I could see he had also noted Amy's silence. I stared into his eyes, hoping to see a hint of what had been there last night. But he straightened his shoulders and looked away from me before moving into the sitting hall.

"I've had Higgins bring the carriage around to the north portico, Grandmother, assuming you did not wish to ride in the new automobile." His words were light and teasing as he came to stand with us.

I smiled as she lifted her chin and flashed her eyes up at him. "I certainly do not!" she said. "I'd just as soon walk as ride in that noisy contraption!"

He laughed and the sound of his deep voice rang merrily through the hall. I liked hearing him laugh, seeing him smile. And that morning I could hardly take my eyes from him. It was as if he had never warned me away from him during the stormy morning hours. I forgot everything but his smile and his voice.

He seemed to tower above us all with his trim, athletic build. His clothes always fit him to perfection, and there was an air of confidence about him that seemed to draw one's attention naturally to him. But as I looked at him I thought of last night and the way he had been.

Something ate at him, tortured him, and I was beginning to see that his confidence was only a carefully erected facade. I had only to look into the depths of his smoky amber eyes to see that.

He swung Amy up into his arms; his act of affection seemed easier for him today. She laughed and wrapped her small arms about his neck, and as he smiled at her I thought my heart would melt.

I decided that as soon as we returned I would speak to Amy alone. I wanted to find out what she remembered about last night and if she thought the ghostly figure was her mother. I was determined to learn what had happened to frighten the child so badly that she could no longer speak.

"Your great-grandmother does not like my automobile!" he said with mock surprise. "But you do, don't you, Amy?" He tickled her gently and she giggled again. This time she nodded vigorously in answer to his question.

"Good," he said. "Then you and I will take a ride together one day this week." I could see he was pleased with Amy's happier response to him today.

Amy turned in his arms and held her plump hand toward me. As she had learned to do when she wanted something, she wiggled her fingers frantically.

Derek's lids came up slowly and although there was still a smile on his face, I could almost feel the coolness of his gaze.

"You want Elizabeth to go?" he asked.

Amy nodded and clapped her hands together in reply.

I did not give him a chance to rebuff me. I have no idea where my boldness came from after his treatment of the previous night, but suddenly I spoke up.

"I'd love to go, Mr. Vanderworth," I said innocently, emphasizing his name ever so slightly. "Anytime."

He glared at me but said nothing. His eyes were hard as they met mine and told me he was not in the mood for games.

"Shall we go?" he asked, turning and carrying Amy toward the stairway.

Mrs. Vanderworth came quickly to my side and took my arm. "What was that all about?" she whispered.

I shrugged my shoulders and gave her an innocent smile.

As Derek carried his daughter downstairs ahead of us, Mrs. Vanderworth put her arm about my waist. She gave me a little shake and whispered in my ear. "You are a little minx. And something tells me this household will never be the same again, now that you're here!"

Chapter Seventeen

As we approached the carriage, I saw Mr. Higgins waiting for us. His round face was open and friendly as he nodded to us and helped Mrs. Vanderworth into the two-seated conveyance. There was only a fringed top to keep the sun off; the sides were open to allow the breeze to flow freely as we rode.

Derek was behind me as he waited for Mr. Higgins to help me into the carriage. The jolly Englishman who had driven me here that first day was grinning broadly as he placed a gloved hand beneath my elbow.

"Well, Miss Stevens, if you ain't turned into the very picture of loveliness," he said smoothly beneath his breath.

"Why, thank you, Mr. Higgins," I said with the same light tone. I placed my hand upon his arm and stepped up the coach steps.

I did not realize the coachman stood watching me until I heard Derek's impatient groan. "Higgins," he said, not unkindly, in a deep, reminding tone of voice.

Mr. Higgins immediately stepped back to allow his employer into the carriage. "Beggin' your pardon, sir. I . . . I was just admirin' the, uh, the weather."

With a flip of his coattails Derek took a seat across from me beside his grandmother. His look was irritable as he nodded to the flustered coachman.

"So I see, Higgins," he said wryly, letting his gaze wander ever so briefly over me.

Mr. Higgins' cheeks were a bright red as he closed the door of the coach. With a look of chagrin he tipped his hat to me and hurried to the front of the coach to climb up into the driver's seat. Amy slid from the seat between her father and her great-grandmother and moved across to sit beside me. As she did, she smiled at me and pushed herself as close as she could.

I smiled and brushed her shining hair from her eyes. I thought she was the most loving child I'd ever met.

Mrs. Vanderworth was watching us with a note of appreciation. "You seem to have a way about you, Elizabeth," she said with a touch of admiration. "I've never seen Higgins so disconcerted, and Amy seems to positively adore you."

I said nothing, but without thinking I glanced quickly at Derek. He acted as if he had not heard his grandmother. He looked every bit the highborn English nobleman as he tightened his square jaw and focused a cool gaze out the side of the coach.

The drive into town was even more beautiful than I remembered. The trees now were completely green and full, and although the azaleas no longer bloomed, there were numerous lilacs and mock orange which took their place. The breeze was light and fragrant, and I could feel it nipping at my cheeks as we rode.

Derek ignored me almost completely. Except for an occasional glance, I might just as well not have been there. Mrs. Vanderworth sensed the tension between us, I think, and did her best to keep up a running conversation with me.

Derek's behavior disturbed me, I could not deny it. And being so close to him, able to look at his handsome features whenever I wished, was distracting. But

171

the weather was perfect, I was free to enjoy the beautiful scenery, free to do almost anything I pleased. How could I be anything but happy? And strangely enough, my obvious happiness seemed to irritate my employer even more.

The doctor's house was a tall white structure located on the side of a hill overlooking the city. There was a white picket fence over which cascaded hundreds of flowers in every color imaginable. The grass needed trimming, and there were several cats roaming about or sitting on the wide front porch.

I smiled as Amy ran toward the cats and attempted to catch them. One, a yellow tabby with bright green eyes, wanted to be friendly with her. It was almost as big as she, but allowed itself to be handled, hanging across Amy's chubby arms like a limp shawl.

"Dr. Turner is somewhat eccentric," Derek said, seeing my wondering expression.

"But he's an excellent doctor," Mrs. Vanderworth added quickly. "And very respected in all the southeast."

I nodded. I really did not question his ability. I just found it odd that Derek would choose a man with such simple tastes.

Mrs. Vanderworth waited in the outside room with Amy as Derek, to my surprise, went with me to the examining room.

Dr. Turner was as charming as his home. He was a little snippet of a man, not much taller than I. His thinning hair was gray, and he had sharp black eyes which peered at me across the spectacles perched atop his nose.

I was seated in a chair as the doctor focused a small light into my eyes. As he reached forward to turn my face further toward the light I noted his thin, delicate hands. They seemed the youngest part about him and were very soft and gentle.

172

Derek sat quietly behind us in the darkness as the doctor examined my eyes and had me read various eye charts. I found I did not feel at all uncomfortable with Derek there. In fact, the whole affair was rather pleasant.

"You have lovely eyes," Dr. Turner murmured as he gazed into them from every angle. "It's a shame to cover them with spectacles."

I had hoped by some miraculous occurrence that he would tell me I no longer needed glasses. But by the shake of his head I could see that was not the case.

"Do you have the glasses you've been wearing?" he asked.

I started to tell him I did not when Derek pulled something from his jacket pocket. He reached forward and handed it to the doctor. I was surprised to see my broken glasses, for I had no idea he had brought them with us.

"Hummm," the doctor muttered, holding them up to the light. "Tell me, young lady . . . do you often have headaches?"

"Why, yes," I said, looking at him skeptically. "I do, although I don't think I've had one recently."

"Not since you broke your glasses, I'll wager."

"Well . . ." I said, trying to think.

"And did you wear your spectacles at all times?"

"Oh, yes," I said. "I was careful to do that."

"Ah," he said, turning to open a small cabinet door.

"Is anything wrong, Dr. Turner?" Derek said quietly from behind me.

"No, no. Nothing that can't be corrected. Miss Stevens needs reading glasses very badly. These . . ." he held my broken ones in the air before tossing them into a waste bin ". . . are not reading glasses."

He turned back to me and placed a pair of glasses over my nose. "There!" he said softly, turning me around to a mirror on a small table. "Wear these only when you read. There is no need to wear them at other times. If you do, your headaches will likely return."

I opened my mouth as I saw my reflection in the mirror. I doubted I would ever like glasses, but these looked so much better with their dark tortoiseshell rims instead of the thin gold ones I'd had. Besides, I thought they made me look rather like someone's maiden aunt.

Dr. Turner laughed softly at my expression and turned to shake hands with Derek.

"I think she likes them," he said with a nod toward me. "Good to see you again, my boy. Take good care of this lovely little lady."

I could hardly stop looking at the mirror, amazed at the difference I saw. Derek came to stand beside the chair and I glanced up at him. Suddenly I felt very shy with him; he had been present during a most private moment.

I saw his reflection as he watched me in the mirror. His eyes were warm and expressive and he smiled wryly at me.

"You look surprised," he said.

"I am . . . I mean . . . You can't imagine what this means to me," I said. How could I explain to this man who had everything just how pleased I was and how lucky I felt to be given so much? "Thank you" seemed somehow inadequate.

"It's nothing," he said, regarding me with that puzzled look I was growing used to. "After what you've done for our family, believe me, this is nothing."

We ate lunch in a quaint little restaurant just down the street from the doctor's house. We sat outside on a shaded balcony that overlooked the city and gave us a splendid view of the mountains beyond.

We spent the rest of the day shopping and strolling

along cool shaded streets until Amy finally grew tired and sleepy. It was a perfect day, and I suppose that was evident to anyone who looked at me. I could see it in Derek's wry expression every time he looked at me, or whenever I exclaimed over some new sight.

"I hope Mrs. Tillis has Elizabeth's new gowns ready before the weekend," Mrs. Vanderworth mused as we looked into a dress shop.

"Why not buy her one today?" Derek suggested quietly, glancing down at me. He allowed his eyes to wander briefly down the length of my new yellow gown. "Then you will have no anxieties about it."

His grandmother brightened immediately, always happy to discuss clothes. "Well, I suppose we could do that. What do you think, Elizabeth? Are you too tired to try on a gown or two?"

"No . . . but what about Amy? She's tired and . . ."

"Don't worry about Amy," Derek said with a soft look. "I'll buy her some lemonade and we'll rest here in the shade until you're ready to go."

I frowned at him. How could he have changed so since last night? There was absolutely no hint now of that anger I'd seen so often. He actually seemed to be enjoying the quiet, easy day.

As it happened, he did not have to wait long, for I chose almost the first dress I saw. Mrs. Vanderworth teased that I simply looked good in anything. But I was more inclined to believe that I was very easy to please. I'd had so little in life that the simplest things gave me great pleasure.

Amy slept quietly as we drove back toward the chateau. It was dark in the dense forest; the sun was long past the tops of the huge trees. The air had grown chilly, and Derek removed his jacket to spread across his sleeping child.

As he caught me watching him, he seemed ill at ease. There were shadows in his beautiful eyes, shadows so deep that I had no inkling of what they recalled.

"You mentioned this weekend, Mrs. Vanderworth," I said, turning away from Derek's disconcerting eyes. "Is there a special reason I will need the dress?"

She laughed and shook her head. "Oh, my dear, with all the excitement, I had not even thought to tell you. We're having a spring ball. Many of our guests will be returning, and it seemed the perfect time. The weather should be lovely, so everyone can wander in the gardens. It is so beautiful with lanterns strung about in the trees."

I felt a great excitement rising in me. My first ball! And it would be spent in the magnificent chateau of Stormhaven. And as impossible as it was to believe, I would not be in attendance as a servant, but as a member of the Vanderworth household.

Mrs. Vanderworth continued to chatter while Derek beside her showed little interest.

"And it is time, after all. We have a ball every year in early summer. And now that the anniversary has passed . . ." She stopped and looked apologetically at her grandson.

Derek only looked at her, his face expressionless except for a small twinge in his muscled jaw.

I had not thought of that . . . the first anniversary of Desiree's tragic death. When I first came, someone speculated that Desiree's ghost would walk the halls on the night of the ball's anniversary. And yet it had passed with hardly a mention. I looked at Derek. Surely that passage would have upset him.

"When . . . when was . . ."

"Last night," he said, turning his potent gaze on me. *"My wife died a year ago last night."*

A chill ran quickly up my arms. I was certain he had been waiting for me to ask, if only to throw those words at me and let me wonder. Last night I had seen

176

for myself the specter in white. And last night Amy had cried for her mother.

I had been surprised by Derek's drinking; he did not seem the type. And now I was beginning to understand the reason.

A long shudder ran over me and I felt the chilliness of the late afternoon shadows upon my face. Automatically my hands chafed at my arms as I tried to warm myself again.

Derek smiled slowly, a cool, knowing smile, as if he enjoyed shocking me. He saw the recognition on my face and I'd have thought he was pleased if not for the dark flicker of pain in his amber eyes.

"I . . . I see," I stammered. "And last night was when I saw the . . . the . . ." What was I to call the woman I'd seen?

"Ghost?" he asked quietly, looking at me with a sarcastic smile. "Don't be shy about using the word, Elizabeth. I'm sure you've heard all the rumors . . . about how my wife is now a ghostly spirit who wanders the halls of Stormhaven, resplendent in one of her infamous white gowns."

"Derek, don't . . ." Mrs. Vanderworth warned, concern for him evident in her pale blue eyes.

"No, no, Grandmother . . . Elizabeth saw Desiree herself last night. Now, isn't that true, Elizabeth? I daresay it was probably my wife's ghost that placed her dress in your room for you to wear . . . to frighten all of us, no doubt. Did you speak to her, did she tell you how I pushed her from the upstairs balcony because she had betrayed me with my own cousin?"

His face was dark, and even though his words were said in a fiercely quiet tone, he was more furious than I'd ever seen him. It was as if all the venom he'd been holding inside just suddenly spilled forth against his will.

"Derek," Mrs. Vanderworth said, glancing down at

the sleeping child. "Darling, don't do this . . ."

"Why not, Grandmother?" he asked through clenched teeth, as his eyes blazed. "Do you think if we don't talk about it, it will go away? Besides, I'm certain Elizabeth has heard all of this before."

He turned his angry eyes on me then. "I'm sure cousin Charles has told her all about it, isn't that right, Elizabeth? And perhaps he's right, you know . . . perhaps even you are not safe here."

His look said much more than his last sentence implied. I knew he was speaking of last night and the fire that had ignited between us. And when he spoke of my safety, he meant so much more.

Strangely, his words did not frighten me. They only made me feel a sad, longing ache inside. I wanted to hold him and comfort him. I wanted to tell him that I could never believe the rumors about him, that I knew he had not harmed anyone. And I felt another pain knowing that this agony of his must stem from the fact that he loved Desiree so much. For surely a man with such hurt in his eyes a year after her death must truly have adored her.

As we pulled into the shadowy dimness of the portico, there were tears in my eyes. And I did not try to hide them from him.

Mrs. Vanderworth picked Amy up in her arms and handed her to one of the maids who waited on the steps. Derek looked into my eyes for one long moment before he stepped from the carriage and walked quickly toward the stables.

Mr. Higgins stood waiting for me, but I was in a quandary. What was I to do? Dared I stay when my presence seemed only to antagonize Derek so much? I seemed to be the catalyst for his anger. And the last thing I ever wanted was to hurt him more than he'd already been hurt.

"Miss?" Higgins said.

I'd forgotten he was there. I slipped my hand into his and let him help me from the carriage. Of course he had heard all of Derek's words. How could he not have?

"Don't think harshly toward his lordship, Miss Elizabeth," he said quietly. "Not all of us feel the same as Charles Simmons." There was a noticeable sneer on his face when he mentioned Charles.

"I wish I could understand him," I said. "But I don't . . . he won't let me."

"Aye, he's a hard man to know, that's for sure. But just don't you give up on him, miss," he said with a sheepish grin. "Your cheery smile is just what his lordship needs. I'd stake me best horse on it."

"Now, that *is* a compliment," I said, returning his smile.

I walked slowly up the steps and into the hallway where Dottie and I had entered that first day. It seemed so long ago. My small world had turned upside down since then, and in spite of Mr. Higgins' encouraging words, I had no idea what I was to do about my growing attraction to Derek Vanderworth or my inability to help him.

Chapter Eighteen

I did not see Derek for the next few days except from a distance. He did not appear even for dinner, and I could see that Mrs. Vanderworth was worried about him. I spent almost all my time with Amy. We played together, and went for long walks. I read to her and took almost all my meals with her. She seemed happy and so was I, except for the estrangement between myself and her father.

One evening after putting Amy to bed I declined dinner with the family so that I might go downstairs to the servants' hall. It was time I learned more about Desiree Vanderworth and her tragic death. I wanted to know everything before I broached the subject of her mother to Amy.

Everyone in the dining hall seemed happy to see me. Some of them exclaimed over my new appearance and my beautiful new attire. A few hung back shyly, as if I were indeed a member of the Vanderworth family rather than only a maid who had chanced upon good fortune.

It was funny how much more I enjoyed the meal there than in the elegant private dining room upstairs. But here I felt little pressure; I felt as if I was among friends.

After supper we went to the sitting room where Dottie and I, along with Frederick and Johnny, sat together at a table in the back of the room.

"I can't believe it's really you," Dottie said, plucking at the sleeve of my dress. "Are you happy . . . do you like takin' care of the little one?"

"I love Amy," I said truthfully. "She is the sweetest, most delightful child. I only wish there were something I could do to help her regain her speech."

Frederick sat forward in his chair. "His lordship had the best doctors come to see her, but none of them seemed to make a difference. It was a very sad time here, it was, what with the mistress being dead, and then to find out his little daughter could no longer speak. Well, most men would just have gone out of their minds!"

It was obvious that Frederick and Johnny were loyal to Derek. And I knew both of them had been here last summer during the ball and the tragedy.

"Did you work upstairs during the ball last year?" I asked. "Does either of you remember anything about that night?"

"Oh, I remember everything quite well," Frederick said. "Just as if it happened yesterday. I did work upstairs, but Johnny, here, he helped Mr. Higgins with the horses and the carriages."

"Did either of you see Desiree Vanderworth that night?"

"Oh, sure," Frederick said. "Though Johnny could probably tell you more about her than I could."

I looked at Johnny, who remained silent. His eyes could not quite meet mine, and he looked blankly above my head.

"Go ahead," prompted Frederick. "You know we can trust 'Lizabeth."

Still Johnny hesitated.

"I won't repeat anything you tell me, Johnny, I promise."

181

He nodded and began to speak. "Well, I saw the mistress outside, late in the evenin'. It was about the time everyone inside began to miss her. She wasn't at the stables long, though, but no one saw her after that."

"Then she must have gone directly up to the fourth floor from the stables. Is that what you think, Johnny?" I asked.

"Well, I don't know that for sure, but yeah, I did think about it."

"But was she with anyone?" I asked.

Johnny glanced uneasily at Frederick.

"Go ahead, Johnny, tell her."

"You have to promise you won't tell nobody, 'Lizabeth," Johnny whispered.

"Of course I promise," I said, curiosity making me want to hurry him along.

"Well, it were his lordship she was with, and they had a terrible quarrel right in the courtyard outside the stables. I was just comin' around a corner. It was dark and they didn't see me."

"Could you hear what they argued about?"

"Just bits and pieces," Johnny said, still whispering. I could understand his not wanting others in the room to hear this story.

I nodded, urging him to continue.

"He told her he knew about her . . . uh, that she had a new lover. He said he'd find out who it was if it was the last thing he did. But she only laughed. He swore at her then and said he hated the day he married her, that he'd been a fool. He said she weren't a fit mother for little Amy. And . . ." He stopped, his face ashen as he looked away from me and about the room.

"And what, Johnny?" I asked quickly. "What else did Derek Vanderworth say to his wife that night?"

182

"He said, Lord forgive me . . . he said she would pay for what she'd done. That's exactly what he said. That he'd see she paid for what she'd done."

"He threatened her," I whispered, almost to myself.

Was this why Derek was so burdened by bitterness, why his eyes were filled with such agony when he spoke of his wife? Was it guilt he felt . . . guilt because he had something to do with her death?

"But I don't understand," I said. "The authorities dropped their investigation of him. If they knew he was the last person to see Desiree alive . . ."

"That's just it, Lizzie," Frederick hissed, urging me to keep my voice down. "They don't know it!"

"But why?"

"Cause he had an alibi . . . that's why! He said he was with someone else that night, and that person swore to the authorities that it was true. So Johnny kept his mouth shut about what he saw."

I frowned at them and shook my head in disbelief. "But who?"

The two young men exchanged glances again. Then Johnny bent closer to me and whispered. "Diana Gresham."

I don't know why I should have been shocked. But I was, and I felt as if I'd just been kicked in the pit of my stomach. This was not what I wanted to hear, and it was not what I wanted to believe. But I knew Johnny had no reason to lie. If anything, he was protecting his employer by keeping quiet about what he knew.

"But . . . but why would he lie? He couldn't have been with her all night if . . ."

"He weren't guilty, 'Lizabeth, if that's what you're thinkin'," Frederick declared with determination. "I'd bet my life on that. His lordship ain't no murderer!"

183

I didn't know what to think.

"I think he done it to protect Miss Diana," Frederick said. "I think it was her what needed an alibi, and he simply went along with it to help her."

I was more confused than ever and shook my head wearily, trying to put it all together.

"You see . . . Diana really hated her sister," Frederick said. "They quarreled all the time, and neither of them seemed to care who heard them. Once they got into a regular catfight after Miss Desiree accused Diana of trying to steal his lordship from her. Diana called her a real bad name and said she didn't deserve a man like Derek Vanderworth."

"Oh, my," I said. My head was aching and this time it was not from the glasses. It was because of all the thoughts that raced around inside my head and confused me so badly I could hardly find anything that made sense.

"Does either of you know where Amy was that night?"

"No," they said in unison.

"I was real busy most of the night and never went above the first floor. So I wouldn't have seen her."

"When was the child told about her mother?"

"Oh, the next morning sometime, I think. They say when his wife's body was found at dawn Mr. Derek went straight to Amy. But she wasn't in her room. He found her sleeping in the sitting room on one of the couches. She ain't spoke a word since."

How horrible it must have been for Amy that early spring morning. After the storm it would probably have been cool; mists and fogs must have covered the house like a shroud. I shuddered at the thought.

One of the women in the sitting room turned out a lamp and gave us a pointed look. It was getting

184

late and we had hardly noticed that everyone was leaving except us.

Dottie had listened intently through the whole thing, her green eyes glowing with curiosity. And now she looked about with a glint of fear in her eyes. "You boys give me the creeps with all this talk of death and alibis and who was where. I ain't so sure I'd have come here if I'd knowed all this!"

"There ain't nothin' to be afraid of, Dottie," Frederick said solemnly. "Rich folks have funny ways. They like to give parties and drink and they don't think anything about going off in the gardens with each other's wives and husbands. But that don't mean they're murderers. His lordship wasn't doin' anything that night that everybody else wasn't doin', his wife included. Can't accuse the man of murder because of that."

"Then who do you think killed Desiree?" I asked.

"She did!" he declared. "She was a moody one at that, and the prospects of being kicked out of this palace was probably more'n she could stand. Yessir, I think she killed her own self. Wouldn't be surprised if she done it out of spite!"

"Freddie!" Dottie scolded. "What a horrible thing to say."

"And how about you, Johnny?" I asked. "What do *you* think happened?"

His pale blue eyes grew dark as he looked around the room. "I ain't so sure Freddy here ain't right. But if I ever decided that it wasn't suicide . . . that someone else was there . . . well, then I'd bet my money on Charles Simmons. I think he had his eye on the Vanderworth money, thinkin' when Miss Desiree left the earl, he'd go along with her. Something went wrong that night. I ain't sayin' it was murder, mind you. But I think Simmons was there

185

and I think if anyone in this house knows what happened, it was Charles Simmons."

I left the servants' hall more confused than ever. I had doubts that I would ever learn what had happened in this house on that stormy spring night last year.

I decided to use the back staircase the way I often did when I was working upstairs. I decided to go up to the third floor and speak to Ruthie before she went to bed. Ruthie seemed to always know everything that went on in the mansion. Perhaps with the knowledge I already had I could begin to piece things together.

I'd forgotten how dark and quiet the back stairway was. Dottie was not the only one disturbed by the evening's conversation. It had left me feeling uneasy and jumpy. For a moment I considered going back, perhaps even using the elevator to go upstairs. Then I heard voices above me in the dark cavity of the stairwell. I was nearing the third floor landing, the same place where I had hidden the day I saw Derek and Diana together.

I stopped. I did not want to blunder into another embarrassing situation. I listened for a moment to see if I recognized the voices. Perhaps it was only Ruthie and Miss Olivia or one of the other servants.

I heard a woman's voice. I was certain it was Ruthie.

"Well, I don't want to get meself in trouble," she said in her soft nasal tone.

"You won't, love," the man's voice whispered. "Besides, all I want you to do is keep those big blue eyes open. Find out what the girl knows. She's been asking an awful lot of questions."

The man's voice was deep and his words were well spoken. He was not one of the servants, I was quite sure. But because of my distance from them and the echoes of his whispered words, I could not recognize exactly who he was.

"She's concerned for the wee one, that's all. She only wants to help the child," Ruthie said.

"Help her what? Why should she want to help her do anything? The child is nothing to her!" His husky voice sounded impatient and angry.

"Well, how should I know? It's her job, ain't it? Besides, she's a very nice girl, she is."

They were talking about me! But why?

"She's too inquisitive for her own good," the man said. "If she finds out . . ."

"What?" Ruthie asked quickly. "That you was with the missus up there that night? There ain't nothin' wrong with that. You had a perfect right to be there with her. Besides, I already told you, I won't say nothin' to nobody about seein' you there."

"I know that, love," he whispered. There was a note of intimacy in his voice now, and I heard her answered giggle.

There was silence, then the sound of material that rustled and whispered in the quietness. My face grew warm as I realized what was happening. I did not have to see them to know that he was kissing her, caressing her. I heard her sigh, then give a soft little groan. I had to get away, but I was afraid to move. I would be humiliated if they knew I'd heard their conversation, not to mention what was happening now.

I could hear his whispering voice. The words he used as he murmured to her shocked me. He was using the most primitive of languages, some phrases that I had not even heard before. But Ruthie only giggled all the more.

"Why, sir," she said. "You surprise me, you do.

187

Who'd have thought a man like you would say such things to a poor, innocent girl like me."

"Come upstairs with me and I'll show you exactly what I mean," he whispered.

"But . . . but the ghostie," she said.

"You don't really believe in such nonsense, do you, sweetheart?" he cajoled. I could hear him murmuring to her, but I could not understand any of his words.

He must have convinced her, for I heard them going up the landing to the upper floor. I stood back against the wall, waiting until I was sure they were gone. Then I hurriedly ran up the remaining stairs and through the door away from the stairs. I did not want to take a chance on being seen now.

Since talking to Ruthie tonight was out of the question, I decided to walk the length of the third floor and use the grand stairway. I could not make myself go back down the dark, cold rear corridor. I was anxious to be in my room and away from the seductive whispered words that still seemed to linger in the stairway.

I hurried through the dimly lit narrow hallway and past the strange, grotesque collection of art that lined the walls.

As I reached the sitting hall, I was walking so fast I hardly saw the person coming around the corner.

Mrs. Vanderworth gasped and reached toward me to steady herself. I had frightened her as much as she had me.

"Elizabeth!" she cried. "What on earth are you doing up here at this time of night?"

I glanced behind me, afraid that somehow Ruthie and the man she was with had followed me.

"What's wrong?" Mrs. Vanderworth said sharply. "You look as if you've seen a ghost."

I laughed uneasily. "Nothing . . . nothing is wrong," I stammered. "And of course, I haven't seen a ghost. I've been downstairs talking with some of my friends, and I decided to take the back stairway."

She frowned as if she did not quite believe me.

"Then why are you on *this* floor?"

"Oh, I . . . I was going to say hello to Ruthie, that's all. But I think she's asleep."

Her pale blue eyes seemed illuminated in the lamplight as she studied me. Suddenly she stepped closer and grasped my arm. I was surprised at the strength of her fingers through the material of my dress.

"You haven't been on the fourth floor, have you?" she asked. Her words sounded almost desperate, and I could see the accompanying fear in her eyes.

"Why, no . . ."

"You must not go up there! Do you hear me? Promise me you will never go up there."

I placed my hands on hers. She was trembling.

"Mrs. Vanderworth," I said. "What is it? Why are you so upset?"

She seemed to realize how excited she sounded and made an effort to compose herself. She stepped back and straightened her shoulders. Then she smiled almost politely and began to speak, more slowly this time.

"Oh, my dear," she said. "You must think I'm an old fool. Of course nothing is wrong. It's just that I have had a terrible feeling about the top floor ever since Desiree's death. You do understand, don't you?"

"Yes, of course I do," I assured her.

"Then indulge me, child, and promise me you will never go above this floor."

"All right," I agreed reluctantly as I watched the

189

worried flicker in her eyes. I'd never seen her this distraught.

She left me then, saying she was going to visit Olivia. She waved her hand airily at me, as if to dismiss any doubts I might still have about our conversation.

"Go to bed, dear," she said.

I had not, of course, considered going to the fourth floor of the huge house. But now the thought nagged at me and pulled at my imagination. What was up there? Was there still evidence of Desiree Vanderworth's last night on earth and how it was spent? And who was the man I'd heard tonight with Ruthie . . . the man who admitted he was there with Desiree the night she died?

I was certain it was not one of the servants. The man had spoken with an educated voice. It could have been Charles. And as much as I hated to admit it, even in the privacy of my own thoughts, it could very well have been Derek Vanderworth. I blushed, remembering the things he had said to me that night in his sitting room. But was he the kind of man to use the vulgar language I'd heard tonight?

Johnny said Derek had quarreled with his wife near the stables. Could he have followed her upstairs expecting to catch her in a secret assignation? And had he? I shivered at the thought of his cold, angry eyes, the eyes of a panther stalking its victim.

I practically ran through the empty sitting hall and down the turning of the grand staircase. When I let myself into my room, I was gasping for air and my knees were trembling so badly I could hardly stand.

Too much was happening in this house. I could feel the tension building around me. There were too many secrets, and even through my newfound fear I felt a burning curiosity to know why. And if Mrs. Vanderworth had known me better, she would have known that her warning about the fourth floor only whetted my appetite and made me more inquisitive than ever.

Everything I'd heard that night brought me to one conclusion. Amy's loss of speech definitely had something to do with her mother's death. And I had the feeling the child might have seen or heard something so upsetting that it had swept everything from her memory.

But if I wanted to find out what had happened, I would need to start on the top floor of the chateau. The place, as Ruthie said, where the ghostie lived . . . and the place that was forbidden to me.

Chapter Nineteen

The next morning was cool and clear, a perfect day for getting out of the house for a while. I could not think clearly in the troubled confines of the house. I needed the space of the outdoors, the peace that would come from being away from the watchful eyes of Stormhaven.

Mrs. Vanderworth had mentioned that Amy had a pony which she loved dearly. What better way to spend a quiet morning than out riding across the lush green estate that surrounded the house.

Amy's golden eyes lit with joy when I told her my plans. Her enthusiasm was contagious, and soon we were laughing as I helped her dress.

I was hardly prepared to see Derek as he quietly opened the door from his sitting room and entered Amy's bedroom. His cool gaze scanned me briefly, taking in my emerald riding suit, one of Mrs. Tillis's newest creations. Only when his gaze traveled to his daughter did he smile.

"Well, kitten," he said warmly to her. "I'm pleased to see you're going riding."

Amy's excitement had quieted and she stood at my side with her body partially hidden behind me. I put my hand on her hair and looked down into her face. Her father's appearance always seemed to change her, and I wondered why. There was a little frown between her eyes, but I did not think it was fear I saw.

What was it that troubled her? At that moment I would have given almost anything to hear her speak.

I looked up into Derek's steady gaze. He was as aware of Amy's mood change as I. And if I was correct, he had no more idea about the reason than I did. And it hurt him. It was clearly visible in the shadowed depths of his eyes.

"Why don't you come with us?" I asked, more to banish those shadows than anything else.

His smile was skeptical as he shook his head slowly. "I think you will enjoy yourselves more without me," he said, glancing briefly at Amy.

I wanted to deny it as my look met his, wished that Amy did not still cling to me so strongly. But as he nodded and turned to go, I had to admit he was probably right. And if I ever hoped to learn what had happened to this little girl, I knew it would require many long, quiet hours alone with her.

Mr. Higgins seemed very pleased to see us. He already had Amy's pony ready and also had a small black mare with white stockinged feet waiting for me.

"Oh, Mr. Higgins," I exclaimed upon seeing the sprightly little mare. "She's beautiful."

"I knew you'd like her, Miss Elizabeth," he said with a wide grin across his broad face. "Her name's Stormy, although her disposition is as calm and sweet as any you'd ever wish to ride."

"Good," I said. I was not the most accomplished horsewoman, and Mr. Higgins's assurance did a great deal to put my mind at ease.

I noticed that one of the young stableboys was upon a horse and sat waiting for us.

I looked questioningly toward Mr. Higgins.

"It's not necessary for someone to accompany us," I said.

"Oh, but I'm afraid it is, miss. His lordship's orders."

193

"But . . . but I only just saw him upstairs a few moments ago," I said. "When did he . . . ?"

"Left only a few minutes before you came, he did. Came to pick out a mount for you." Mr. Higgins' words always seemed to carry a note of pride when he spoke of his employer.

"He personally came down to pick out the horse I am to ride today?" I asked.

"Oh, not just today, Miss Elizabeth. Stormy is yours to keep, compliments of the earl."

I was so surprised that I hardly remembered anything Mr. Higgins said afterward. I thought the mare was the most beautiful little horse I'd ever seen. And that she now belonged to me was almost too wonderful to be true. Just when I thought I knew Derek Vanderworth's mind, he did something like this . . . something quite generous and kind.

Amy and I rode slowly out of the cobblestone courtyard and toward the back of the chateau. I wanted to ride across the rolling grassy glen behind the house. It was a view I had often looked on with pleasure from my little maid's room high in the big house.

Amy was not at all afraid of riding and often urged her small pony into a trot. But she was also quiet and obedient and when I would caution her, she always slowed and came back beside me. The stableboy rode a distance behind, allowing us our privacy.

We took a long, winding route to the hilly rim that overlooked the glen. From there we could see the shining river and the miles of rich bottomland along its path. The mountains beyond were so clear that they seemed to tower directly above us, shining blue-green against the brilliant sky.

We had ridden almost an hour and had come back toward the house. I found a perfect spot atop a small rise where we could sit beneath the huge old trees and rest.

After we dismounted and found a cool place upon the long, soft grass, the stableboy took the reins. He led the horses over the other side of the hill to a small stream for water.

As we sat there I studied the house in the distance. It looked quite different from the back and seemed even larger than I thought. My eyes wandered time and again to the top floor and my heart skipped a beat at the long distance from the balconies to the ground below.

I turned to Amy, who sat very still beside me. I hardly knew how to approach the subject with her.

"Did you ride often with your mother, Amy?" I asked.

Her huge eyes looked up at me as she shook her head no.

"I saw her picture in the house. She was very pretty." The girl gave no response at all.

"You look very much like her, you know."

With a sweet gesture, she took a strand of her blond hair between plump fingers and held it out from her head. With a bright smile she seemed to be pointing out the reason for her resemblance to her mother.

"Yes," I said laughing. "Your hair is exactly like your mother's."

She nodded exuberantly and bent to pull blades of grass from the ground around us. Then she scattered them silently from her fingers.

"I'm sure your father misses her very much," I said, watching her closely. I did not want to upset her.

She shrugged her small shoulders. I was not sure she understood what I meant.

"Do you remember the ball last year?" I asked.

Suddenly her head lifted. Her amber eyes were large with fright, and her lips trembled slightly. Just as suddenly she turned toward the house and pointed. She was making little murmuring noises like a child just learning to speak. She seemed terribly agitated and upset.

Quickly I put a comforting arm around her, but still she pointed. I followed the direction of her finger.

"What is it?" I asked.

Her eyes were filled with such terror. I wanted to help her, wanted to understand what she was trying to say.

"The house?"

Yes, she nodded, still pointing and gesturing. It was then that I realized exactly where she motioned. It was toward one of the balconies on the fourth floor.

"The balcony?" I asked in a whisper.

She shook her head almost frantically. Then she buried her face against me and wrapped her small arms about me. I held her close as a shudder coursed through her.

I had no idea which balcony Desiree Vanderworth had fallen from. But in that moment I knew without a doubt that it was the one to which Amy pointed.

But how on earth could she have known?

I held her and stroked her trembling shoulders. What terrible thing had this child seen or heard that night?

"It's all right, darling," I murmured. "I'm here. I won't let anything happen to you."

Soon her trembling stopped and she lay against me, making a small hiccuping sound from time to time. My heart ached for her. Would the child ever be able to live a normal life again? I wanted with all my heart to see that she did.

Her head slid downward until it rested upon my lap. I sat stroking her back until she finally fell asleep.

When I heard footsteps behind us, I did not turn to see who was there. I assumed it was the stableboy returning.

"May I join you?" the polite English voice asked.

"Charles," I said, looking around in surprise. "Of course you may," I replied, smiling up at him. It was good to see a friend.

He sat beside me and propped his arms across his bent knees. He wore riding pants and knee boots, and I thought he looked quite dashing and handsome with his rumpled fair hair and clear, inquisitive eyes.

"How is the child?" he said with a gesture toward Amy.

"She's frightened about something," I said. "And I'm almost certain it has to do with the night her mother died."

"Pity," he said. His gaze took in the house and he became distant and thoughtful. "Amy was such a bright, happy child before Desiree's death."

"She still seems that way at times," I said. "It's as if the thing that troubles her is far beneath the surface, like a dream."

"Well, I'm sure it's only because she lost her mother. What else could it be?" he offered.

"I don't know," I murmured.

I looked at the balcony at which Amy had pointed. I wanted to tell Charles about my suspicions. But some instinct told me I shouldn't. What if Derek *had* followed his wife upstairs that night? And what if the man he had found with her was Charles? Was it possible that both of them were keeping a secret about what had happened to Desiree Vanderworth that night? I could not seem to make my heart believe it and yet I did not feel confident enough to broach the subject with Charles.

"How are you getting on with Amy's father?" Charles asked suddenly, bringing me back to reality.

"I hardly ever see him," I said thoughtfully. "And I'm afraid I don't understand him any better than I did before." I remembered the generous gift of the mare.

Charles snorted disdainfully. "Who does?"

"But surely you know him well. After all, you *are* cousins."

"We've never been particularly close in our adult years. Before I came to Stormhaven, it had been ages since I'd even seen him." He twirled a piece of grass between his slender fingers. "As a boy he was clever, always fun to be with, although sometimes a bit too full of mischief to suit our mothers." Charles smiled as he recalled their youth.

I watched him. He did not seem to hate Derek so bitterly as he recalled their childhood.

"What happened?" I coaxed.

"Oh, the usual boyish pranks, I suppose. Although I thought no one could think of so many keen ideas as Derek," Charles laughed. "We once tied a long string to Grandmother's doorknob in the middle of the night. We would rattle the door on its hinges and make what we thought were frighteningly ghoulish noises."

"Oh, you didn't!" But I smiled, imagining the two boys together, one dark, the other fair. "And I suppose you almost frightened poor Mrs. Vanderworth out of her wits."

"Oh, no," he said with a chuckle. "She knew immediately who it was. She stormed out of her room like an avenging angel and snapped the string like a twig. When she quickly reeled it in, we were too dumbfounded to let go and she caught us quite easily."

I laughed at the story. How very much like Mrs. Vanderworth that sounded. She was very much a no-nonsense kind of woman.

"We still laugh about that escapade," he said. His eyes clouded and he grew quiet. "Or at least, we did." He looked away from me, and for the first time I realized how much he missed his cousin's friendship.

"So, you and Derek have not always been enemies?"

"Oh, no," he said, his voice soft and quiet. "We were once the greatest of chums, until . . ."

"Until what?" I asked, urging him to continue.

Charles laughed, a short bark with not much humor in it. "Until I met Desiree," he said with a touch of bitterness.

"Was she married then?"

"Oh, yes," he said, looking over at me. "She was married to my cousin. And the rest of the story you already know."

"I'm sorry," I said. "I did not mean to pry."

He took a deep breath and looked up at the sky. "No, it's quite all right," he said thoughtfully. "I'm just beginning to realize that. I think when Desiree was alive I was so completely absorbed in her that I could see nothing else. And . . ." He hesitated and threw the grass on the ground, as if in disgust.

"And . . . ?"

"And now, a year later, I still miss her and the way she made me feel. But as hard as it is to admit, I think Desiree used people. And she probably used Derek most of all. And you know something? I think I miss my cousin's friendship as much as I miss Desiree."

"Why, Charles," I said with surprise. I was pleased at his words and hoped it meant he and Derek might reconcile one day. For I was more certain than ever that they needed each other. "I think that's wonderful."

He smiled at me and his gray eyes twinkled. "And do you know what I think is wonderful?" he asked.

"No, what?"

"You are, Elizabeth Stevens." He pulled a daisy from the grass and leaned toward me. "Your brightness and optimism, your obvious pleasure in everything around you, have opened more eyes than mine, I think. And somehow, since you came, Desiree seems far away, someone from another life. And I have you to thank for that."

199

I was flattered, and I smiled up into his face as he reached forward and tucked the stem of the flower into my hair. I felt none of the overwhelming emotions I felt when I was with Derek. But it was a pleasant, companionable moment. And even though I did not know Charles that well, I did not feel awkward or afraid in his presence. He was not the sort of aggressive man to push his attentions on a woman.

The flower fell forward onto my face and we laughed. Both of us reached for it at the same time and his hand covered mine.

From across the wide meadow I heard the whicker of a horse and turned to look. Charles's gaze followed mine. On a grassy knoll stood a regal black horse and a man sitting tall upon its back who was looking toward us. I was certain he had been coming our way. Even at this distance I knew it was Derek, and even though I could not see his face clearly, I could feel the stab of his tiger eyes upon us.

Time seemed to stand still, and I realized I was holding my breath as we gazed at each other. Then suddenly his hand tugged at the reins and he wheeled the great horse about. Like a short, brilliant flash of lightning they were gone over the crest of the hill.

"Oh," I said, more a sigh of disappointment than anything.

"Well," Charles drawled. "It seems my dear cousin is angry once again."

"But . . . but I don't know why," I said, turning to him with a frown.

Charles laughed and bent toward me. He placed a light kiss upon my lips.

"No, my little Elizabeth, I'm sure you don't. I'm sure you don't." He smiled at me and shook his head. "And that, my dear, is what makes you so totally enchanting."

Chapter Twenty

Charles rode with us back to the house and we did not see Derek again. Amy was still asleep, so I took her up to her room to finish her nap.

Once inside her room, I gave her her favorite raggedy bear, the one she'd asked for that first day. She cuddled up on her bed and I lay beside her, taking the opportunity to rest and to think about Derek and Charles.

I only hoped that the antagonism they felt toward one another would not erupt at the ball on Saturday night. But I had a terrible feeling that the problems of Stormhaven were coming closer and closer to the surface.

Without realizing it I fell asleep and woke to the movement of the bed. Amy was awake and sat bouncing on the bed, tossing her bear into the air and catching it. She seemed so normal and happy.

"Well," I said. "I believe your nap has done wonders for you, little miss."

I stayed with her the rest of the morning and into the afternoon, playing and reading to her. There were moments when I could have sworn she was on the verge of speaking to me. Her enthusiasm was sometimes almost too great to be contained.

After Jenny brought my tea and some milk and cookies for Amy, it gave me an opportunity to speak to the child further.

"Where did you get your bear, Amy?" I asked, hoping the familiar object might help her to speak.

She looked at me and held the bear proudly up for me to see as she nibbled at a cookie.

"Yes, I see. What is the bear's name?"

But she only smiled shyly and ran her hand back and forth across the bear's scruffy tummy.

"I know," I said. "I'll bet the bear's name is Amy Vanderworth."

Amy laughed and grabbed the bear to her chest, hugging it hard against her. She shook her head at me as her eyes sparkled with glee.

"No? Then let me see. Perhaps its name is . . . Elizabeth! Yes, I'll bet that's it," I said, tickling Amy's fingers. "Elizabeth bear is what I shall call it."

She shook her head even harder, and I could see she was thoroughly enjoying the teasing game.

"Well, I suppose you're not going to tell me the bear's name," I said with an exaggerated sigh.

I sat quietly watching her. She tried to appear unconcerned, but I sensed she wanted to please me, wanted so badly to speak for me. My heart almost broke for her.

I saw the door open quietly from the hallway. Amy did not see her father as he stepped softly into the room behind her. I touched my fingers to my lips and he stopped, waiting silently by the door.

"Bo," Amy said hesitantly, still looking down at the bear in her hands.

The sound of her voice in the room seemed to hang in the air. Even though I had been coaxing her, I still felt a jolt of surprise at hearing her first spoken word in more than a year.

"Bo?" I whispered, almost afraid I would frighten her.

I looked up at Derek's startled eyes. I had not missed the soft intake of his breath when he heard

202

Amy speak. And now he stood in the shadows, anxiously waiting to see what would happen next.

Amy shook her head and with a grin handed the bear to me. She was so sweet and so quietly yearning for approval. I took the bear and held it so she could see its face.

"Hello, Bo bear," I said in a silly childish voice. "My name is Elizabeth. And this is . . . what was your name, little girl?" I asked Amy as I jostled the bear in a little dance.

Amy looked up at me trustingly, her amber eyes large and excited. Her mouth was pursed to speak, and the expression in her eyes was wondrous to see.

"Amy!" she burst with a giggle.

"Yes, of course," I said, trying to still the excited pounding of my heart. "Amy Vanderworth."

I heard a noise from the shadows where Derek stood. He could contain himself no longer. With a sound of choked surprise and pleasure, he stepped across the room to us. He bent on one knee and scooped Amy up into his strong arms.

"Oh, Amy, sweetheart," he murmured. His face was pressed against her neck and his words were muffled.

His long, dark lashes were closed, and I found myself longing for them to open so that I might see the joy in his beautiful eyes.

Amy's little arms crept up around his neck. Then I saw one plump hand pat her father's shoulders, the consoling action of an adult. And I could not stop the tears that filled my eyes.

When Derek looked up at me, I saw my tears mirrored in his own eyes. I was stunned and pleased, and it seemed to wrench the heart right from my chest.

He looked into my eyes for a long moment and I saw his gratitude and a certain relief there as well. Then he held his daughter away from him and looked into her face.

"Daddy's so proud of you, sweetheart," he said.

She placed one finger in her mouth and looked down, as if not able to meet his eyes. And she said nothing.

"Can you tell your daddy about the bear, Amy?" I asked.

Still she did not speak. I saw the glint of disappointment in Derek's eyes. And I knew exactly what he was feeling. That moment made us both wonder if we had actually heard Amy's voice or if we had only imagined it.

"It's all right," I assured him softly. "It will take time. We mustn't expect everything to happen at once."

He nodded, but he looked down at the little girl with a frown of concern, then hugged her once more. His face changed and I could see that he was trying to recover his usual cool and noncommittal manner. He did not want to frighten her or push her too hard.

When Jenny came back a few moments later to take our tea tray, she asked if Amy might come with her to the kitchen. The staff downstairs loved the little girl and delighted in having her play at one of the tables in the big, bright kitchen as they worked.

After they left, Derek looked across the table at me. "How can I thank you?" he asked quietly.

"It's not necessary to thank me," I said. "I love Amy and I want to help her if I can."

What else could I say to him? I could hardly throw myself into his arms and tell him what it meant to see him smile, that seeing the unfamiliar joy fill his eyes was thanks enough for me.

"I just want her to be normal and happy again," he said, looking down at his hands as if the moment was awkward for him.

"She will be," I said. "Today makes me feel very hopeful about that."

Should I tell him about my suspicions that she had been upstairs when her mother fell from the balcony? I opened my mouth to speak, then hesitated.

"What is it? What were you going to say?" he asked.

"I . . . nothing. I only wanted to thank you for the mare. I never thought to have a horse of my own. She's beautiful."

"It's nothing," he said with a wave of his hand.

We seemed so awkward with one another that day, so unable to express anything beyond polite stilted conversation.

"Derek . . ." "Elizabeth . . ." we both spoke at the same time. And now we both laughed.

Finally he spoke. "I should not have been so harsh with you the other day in the carriage. I apologize."

"There is no need . . ."

"Yes," he interrupted quietly but firmly. "I had no reason to vent my frustrations or speak to you that way. Not to you . . ." He turned and walked to the long window and looked out toward the mountains.

"I understand . . ."

"Do you?" he asked abruptly, turning back to face me. "How can you say you understand when you hardly know me? Why were you so kind to my daughter when you barely knew her? And in such a way that makes me feel you are also being kind to me?"

I knew his doubts were directed toward himself and not me. Was he so unused to kindness? Or did he think his only worth to others was because of his wealth?

"Do you think you don't deserve kindness, Derek?" I asked, stepping closer to him. I looked up into his face, intently studying the expressions that moved across his handsome features. "Won't you tell me what has happened to make you think that about yourself?

He frowned and shook his head almost imperceptibly.

205

"Elizabeth . . . you have such a straightforward, open way of seeing everything. Life is not always black or white."

"I suppose I do," I said. "And I know I'm too naive about things, but . . ."

Suddenly he was close to me, so close that our bodies were almost touching. I could feel the warmth of him through my clothes. His hand moved to my face and I shivered as his fingers trailed lightly down my cheek.

"I'm not saying you should change, Elizabeth," he murmured. "Don't change; stay exactly as you are. Sweet, naive, hopeful . . . whatever you wish to call it. You are the first person in years who has made me feel good inside, who has given me hope that . . ." He hesitated and his hand fell away.

"What?" I urged. "Don't shut me out again, Derek."

He tilted his head back and closed his eyes as a sigh lifted his chest. And when he looked back at me, there was such regret on his face.

"Elizabeth, don't you know? Can't you see that I've hurt everyone who ever cared about me? Desiree is dead because of me; my little girl can't speak. And even Charles . . ."

He started to turn away again, but I put my hand on his arm and pulled him back.

"None of this is your fault!" I said. "Why are you blaming yourself?"

Once more he reached out and caressed my cheek, his fingers moving softly to brush the tears from my eyes.

"That day in the carriage . . . you cried for me then, too. I don't think anyone has ever cried for me before," he said tenderly, his voice tinged with awe.

Slowly he lowered his head and kissed my eyes, then my cheeks. And when his mouth reached mine I turned to meet his kiss. I was hungry for him, for the taste and feel of his lips on mine. And the feeling he evoked in me that day had little to do with goodness and naivety. I felt the tears streaming from my eyes at the depth of my emotion. But my feelings for him were confused. I wanted him as a woman, in every way, but I felt his pain as if it were mine and I understood why he was afraid to trust what was between us.

When he pulled slowly away from me there was a look of disbelief in his eyes. And I myself felt stunned by the power of his kisses and the fire that surged between us.

"This is wrong," he said, his voice shaky. "You're much too young and sweet to be mixed up with someone like me."

"No," I said, moving to him again. "I'm not. Can't you see how I feel?" But I hardly knew how to express myself, how to speak to him of the new emotions he made me feel.

"You don't know what you're doing," he said. "If you did, you would leave this place and never come back." His strong hands gripped my arms as he spoke.

"If you really believe that, Derek, then why don't you send me away? I will go if you ask me to." I was willing to challenge him, daring to see how far he would go to stop what was happening between us.

He frowned down at me and a shudder coursed through his body. His amber eyes grew dark and shadowed as he struggled with his own desire. I smiled at him as I saw his eyes dart to my lips. I knew he was losing his will to fight me.

He pulled me almost roughly into his arms, and this time he held nothing back as he kissed me passionately.

I clung to him and his arms tightened about me so that my feet barely touched the floor. I felt weak and dizzy with gladness and I forgot everything else except the feel of him and of being held firmly against his strong body.

I began to feel heavy and warm, as if I would fall if he let me go. He had only to lead me to the archway toward his rooms. For by then I would not have protested; I would have followed him anywhere.

But slowly and with a puzzled reluctance he pulled away and looked down into my face. He took a long slow breath and moved back one step.

"I'm going to hate myself for this tomorrow," he murmured with a wry smile.

I didn't say anything, although I wanted to with all my heart. But as much as I wanted him, I could not seem to find the words to tell him.

He cupped my chin in his warm hand and gazed down into my eyes. His look was no longer cold, and I was overjoyed to see the spark there that I'd so often longed for.

"We'll talk about Amy later . . . and about us. Preferably in the presence of a great many people," he added with a grin.

I smiled, more at the look on his face than the things he had said. Could I really be the reason for the happy bewilderment in his eyes? I could hardly believe he had even kissed me, a kiss that said he could not get enough of me. And now he was saying he feared being alone with me.

"I'll see you at dinner," he whispered, moving away from me.

I watched him as he went across the room, watched the lithe, graceful strides he took and the powerful way he carried himself. I thought no other man could be as beautiful as he. He turned at the doorway and looked back at me. I could feel the heat of that look all the way to my toes and I felt a little catch at my throat. Then he was gone and I gave in to the weakness he'd made me feel.

I sank slowly onto the bed, thinking about every detail of what had just happened. I touched my lips, still warm and sensitive from his kisses. I threw my arms out exuberantly and fell backward onto the bed, laughing out loud into the empty room.

"Oh, Derek," I whispered. "I love you. How very much I love you."

It was with a little tingle of shock that I heard my own words. I *was* in love . . . helplessly, headlong in love. His long, passionate kisses had rendered me practically senseless, with a yearning I could only attribute to love. And in that sweet moment I forgot everything except seeing him again and being kissed by him again.

In that moment I forgot that he had been suspected somehow in his wife's death, that his actions had caused a rift with his cousin and dearest friend Charles. I even forgot that he had been cold at first to sweet little Amy.

Indeed I forgot my very own instincts as I reveled in these new, exciting feelings that swept over me. My mind had room only for Derek and the way he made me feel. And I pushed everything else aside.

Chapter Twenty-one

I sat for a long while in the quiet of Amy's bedroom. I could not seem to rouse myself into moving. I felt exhausted, as if I'd run a long distance. And I could not seem to rid myself of the feeling, nor the vision in my mind's eye, of Derek's dark head lowering to mine, his lips parted to kiss me.

I needed to keep busy, I told myself. And I wondered what I would do to occupy myself while Amy was gone.

Suddenly I sat up. The library! Of course, I would go to the library. I had not had the chance to go there for any considerable amount of time since Amy had fallen into the pool. Going there always made me feel happy and content. And I loved the new feeling of freedom, of being able to go anywhere I wished in the beautiful chateau.

I ran quickly to my own room to fetch my reading glasses. Then I walked down the stairway and through the tapestry gallery to the library.

As I stood for a moment looking at the muraled ceiling and taking in the beauty of the room, I sighed with pleasure. The smell of leatherbound books mingled with the lovely scent of fresh flowers, and I thought I would never grow tired of being there.

I went immediately to work, soon becoming so deeply engrossed that I completely lost track of the time. I already had one entire shelf of books removed and ready for listing. I looked up in surprise to see how far the sun had fallen toward the west.

It cast a bright stream of light through the French windows across the rich wood floor. I stood up and stretched, looking up toward the balcony of the room. I had never gone up there, and suddenly I felt an urgency to explore.

I climbed the elaborately carved spiral staircase and sighed with contentment once I reached the narrow walkway that lead around the room.

I became lost in the books, walking slowly and scanning the leather covers, reading the various titles. Then, with a little jolt of delight, I noticed that the narrow corridor ran behind the fireplace as well. It made a little tunnel behind the huge wood carving above the mantel.

Inside the small passageway was a bench covered in soft green velvet. There was a small reading table and on the wall hung a candle-shaped sconce, its dim light glowing softly on the wood-paneled walls. There were two books on the table.

I picked up one of the books and stared curiously at its odd title. Sitting slowly on the bench I turned the book over in my hand.

"*Non Compos Mentis,*" I read, my interest growing. Below the title were the words "Caring for the Demented Patient." I shrugged and picked up the other book. Its title was even more puzzling. "*Psychology and the Aspects of Psychopathic Behavior.*"

I stared at the words for a moment. Psychology was not a word with which I was familiar, and I opened the cover of the book to read the introduction in the front.

It read, "Psychology, the study of the human mind and human behavior, can be traced to the beginnings of the written word. Even Plato and Aristotle attempted to describe the instincts, and social motives that unite human beings in their day-to-day efforts to relate to one another. This book is an attempt to further that study."

"Man's relation to one another," I repeated aloud. "How interesting." It was a subject I'd always been interested in, even before I knew there was a proper word for it. The relationship between humans and what makes us behave as we do was a fascinating idea.

It was growing near dinnertime and I hardly had time to read more than a few paragraphs. I flipped through the book quickly and my eyes were caught by various lines drawn beneath certain passages. One in particular caught my eye. It was called simply "Abnormal Psychology."

I looked at the other book with dawning realization.

"Of course," I murmured, beginning to make a connection. "Demented patient . . . abnormal psychology." It seemed that someone was interested in finding out about insanity and the reasons behind it.

Who had been reading the book? I had to think it was Derek. After all, this was his private domain and I knew of no one else in the house who seemed so interested in books besides Derek or myself.

I noticed a small slip of paper between the pages of the psychology book. When I opened the book at the marker, I saw another underlined passage. This section dealt with psychopathic behavior. The underlined words fairly leapt from the page at me.

". . . the psychopath appears charming and competent. His intelligence is above average . . ." I skipped to other descriptions. ". . . outward action often conceals a complete lack of morality in all his personal relationships." I closed the book not wanting to read any more.

Suddenly I felt bitterly cold, shaking with some unknown fear that gripped me. The slip of paper fell from the pages. I opened it and read what appeared to be a list of reference books. The fear within me grew as I read the titles. The paper began to tremble in my fingers as I tried to steady it.

The list was of more books on the subject of psychology. I read them aloud with a growing feeling of dread.

"Outlines of Psychology, Wilhelm Wundt; *Physiological Optics,* Hermann von Helmholtz; *Leviathan,* Thomas Hobbes; and *Origin of Species,* Charles Darwin."

With my curiosity growing, I placed the slip of paper back in the book. And despite the fear in my heart, I could not resist reading further about what the book described as "psychopathic behavior."

". . . often abandons his family in pursuit of casual pleasures. His sexual life is shallow, impersonal, and promiscuous. He may cheat, steal, or even kill . . ."

My breath caught painfully in my throat. The passage was underlined not once but twice.

I read on. ". . . incapable of understanding his own behavior or profiting from experience. Yet he suffers no anxieties and usually appears outwardly normal."

"Oh, my God," I murmured aloud. The sound of my own voice in the small enclosure seemed to surround me and echo, reverberating eerily back into my ears.

It could not be. Surely Derek could not think himself to be a person of this description. And yet even as I sat denying it, the words of others came back to haunt me as they described Derek Vanderworth. "Cold," I'd heard more than once. "Interested only in obtaining possessions," Charles said about him. And Derek himself had warned me twice that I should not become involved with a man like himself.

I knew how indifferent he could be, how cold he was sometimes, even to his own daughter. And he was so changeable, kind one moment and almost violently angry the next. But I was jumping to conclusions, I told myself. Perhaps Derek had not been the one studying these books.

And did I really believe that the man who had kissed me so tenderly today was capable of these behaviors? For if he was, couldn't he have simply dragged me into his room, or even have taken me right there on the bed in Amy's room? He had been the one to gain control and pull away, the one to smile at himself as he teasingly admitted we would be safer surrounded by other people. But was he only afraid of his own violence?

"No," I whispered vehemently. No, I could never believe that about him, not until he himself told me it was true.

I had always been one to trust my own heart, and this time would be no exception. I wanted to trust him, wanted to believe that the man I was in love with was none of these frightening things I'd just read. There had to be some other explanation.

"Yes," I said firmly. "That's it. There must be another reason."

I placed the books back on the table and took off my glasses, laying them atop the books. My eyes were tired, and I was beginning to feel the dull throbbing of a headache coming on. As I sat for a moment with my eyes closed, I heard the quiet murmurings of voices as someone entered the library below.

I stood up to go back out onto the balcony, intending to make my presence known.

But the words I heard stopped me. That and the agitated voice of Diana Gresham.

"I don't want to talk about it, Derek," she said. "It's too soon."

"Too soon?" he exploded angrily. "It's been over a year. I should already have done something."

"Let's not talk about that, darling," she cooed. "I'd

214

much rather talk about us."

I could hear his footsteps ringing across the wood floors. "There *is* no *us,* Diana. I've told you that before." His voice was flat and emotionless.

"Well, there might have been if you had not put that . . . that nothing of a girl in my place."

"What does that mean?" he asked, his words quiet and clipped.

"I mean . . . I was just beginning to win Amy over to me. You know, I could have taken care of her just as well . . . better than that girl! Why, she's nothing more than a maid for all her glorified airs and her attempts to convince everyone she is so intelligent."

"Jealousy does not become you, Diana," he said quietly.

"I have every reason to be jealous! I loved you long before Desiree died! You know I did. And now, just when I thought there might be a chance for me in your life again, this Elizabeth appears from out of nowhere and spoils everything between us!"

"Diana . . ." he began with a sigh of exasperation.

"No, hear me out! You never listen to me. Just once, let me tell you how I feel."

"All right," he said with a soft grunt of acquiescence. "Speak your mind. You will anyhow."

"I know I was always considered the dumb one; Desiree was smart as well as beautiful. But I'm not so dumb that I can't see what's going on between you and that girl, Derek."

"And what exactly do you think is *going on,* as you so delicately put it?" His voice had grown very soft and there was a dangerous note, an angry rasping quality to the sound of it.

"Don't pull your lordly tone of voice on me, Derek. I know you . . . remember? It was me you came to when Desiree turned her back on you in favor of some other man. That first time . . . you'd hardly been married six months. You were so hurt and I comforted you. I know you haven't forgotten it."

"No, Diana, I haven't forgotten," he said quietly.

"It was my arms you wanted then, my lips . . . and the night of the ball, have you forgotten? God, I was almost ecstatic that after all those years you came to me again and . . ."

"Get to the point," he said angrily.

"That *is* the point. Can't you see? I love you! Oh, I know you probably only used me. But I don't care, Derek! I wanted you to because I couldn't bear seeing what that bitch had done to you. And yet you still turn your back on me. Why? I have to believe it's only because someone new has come along, a young, innocent new challenge."

"That's not true."

"It is true. I see the way you look at her. And heaven knows she can hardly keep her eyes off you. It's truly pathetic. She looks at you as if you're some kind of god. Does she know about all the other women, darling? About the drinking and carrying on that has taken precedence in your life these past few years? I hardly think so."

I blushed as I listened to her accusations about me. I knew it was only too true. Whenever Derek was near me, I could not stop myself from staring, from taking in every inch of him with my eyes.

"There is nothing between Elizabeth and me, Diana. And there never can be. She's young and innocent, as you say, and infatuated, that's all. But there will never be anything between you and me, either. I'm sorry."

"No, Derek . . ."

"I'm sorry if I've hurt you. Coming to you was unforgivable of me, but I had no idea it was love you expected from me. I'm not sure I'll ever be able to give that to anyone again." He must have turned from her,

216

for his voice grew more muffled. "I've told you before, Diana, it was a mistake; I was angry and hurt. And you, if you recall, were more than willing." His words seemed to come by rote, as if he had used them all before.

He sounded so cold, so uncaring, that I almost felt sorry for her.

"But Derek . . . I loved you. Your lovemaking still haunts me; it's all I think about!"

"Hell," he muttered disdainfully.

I could hear her muffled sobs through the fireplace and up into the shadowy little tunnel where I sat, stunned and embarrassed. Her dress rustled as she must have moved nearer to him.

"I'm sorry, Diana. Even your tears won't work this time."

I slipped from the bench and peeked around the passageway. They stood below me, just in front of the fireplace, and he was holding her, soothing her, as he might do Amy. And she was clinging to him as if he were her very life.

It tore at my heart to see his arms about her, to see the way his hand slowly caressed her long blond hair. Even his words of rejection to her did little to ease the ache inside of me. For he had also seemed to reject me.

And her conversation had done one thing: it had made me doubt. For the first time I doubted the wisdom of my own heart. And it made me wonder if my fate was to be the same as Diana's.

When they moved apart I stepped back into my secret hiding place before they could look up and see me.

"I still intend to go through with my plan," Derek said. "I just wanted you to know."

"Even though I don't agree?" she asked.

"Yes," he said tersely. "Even though you don't. I

can't let her stay here any longer after what happened the other night. It's too dangerous . . . for all of us. Surely you can't disagree with that?"

"I don't know," she said, her reply muffled and unsteady. "I know you are afraid she was involved the night of the ball. But how could she have been? Her room is always locked; I made certain of that."

"It's the only explanation. Somehow she overheard my argument with Desiree. I hate to think of what might happen if anyone else finds out."

Diana sighed heavily. "All right then. If you think it's the only way. I know you've done your best, but if you think she should be sent away, then I won't argue with you about it any further."

"I do," he said. "Believe me, it's for her own good, Diana."

"I suppose," she said rather dejectedly.

"Go upstairs, angel," he said softly, his voice now more tender and intimate. "Wear your loveliest gown to dinner tonight. It always makes you feel better to dress up."

I heard their footsteps cross the floor and then the muffled ring of their voices as they moved beyond the library into the tapestry gallery.

I sat back heavily against the panels. I was gripping my hands together so tightly they felt numb, and I could feel the tears stinging my eyes.

What on earth were they talking about? And who was it they intended to send away? Surely not Amy, my heart cried. Had she overheard her parents quarreling, just as I had suspected, and if so, had she witnessed something else . . . her mother's death?

"Dear Lord," I whispered softly. "That poor child."

And if that were true, then I had to face the possibility that Derek was sending away his only child just to protect himself. For now that he'd heard her speak for the first time in over a year, he must realize she would soon tell what she had seen and heard that dreadful night.

What was I to do? I knew I had to find out where Derek intended to send the little girl. And I had to decide who in the huge household I could trust with this information.

Chapter Twenty-two

I waited in the hidden compartment behind the fireplace until I was certain that Derek and Diana were no longer nearby. Then I hurried upstairs. I had an overwhelming compulsion to see Amy and to assure myself that she was well.

When I opened the door to look into her room I was startled to see Derek again. He stood at the long windows looking out toward the mountains. Amy had not yet returned.

I stepped back and started to pull the door shut when he spun around and saw me. I had no idea what I would say to him or how I would hide the confusion that was threatening to pull me apart.

"Elizabeth?" he said.

He smiled at me as he waited for me to come in. And as I studied his face, I searched for something, some clue that would assure me he was the same man I had decided I loved only a few hours ago.

"What is it?" he asked, frowning at me as I stood motionless. "Is something wrong with Amy?" He seemed alarmed as he took a step toward me.

"No," I said quickly. "No, Amy is fine. I believe she's still downstairs in the kitchen. I only wanted to make sure she was safe."

"Safe?" he said, still frowning at me. "What an odd choice of words."

I shook my head, feeling my confusion growing even stronger. *He* was confusing me, with his steady tigerlike eyes upon me and the hint of a frown between his dark brows.

"Yes, wasn't it?" I said, laughing shakily. "What I meant was, I was afraid she might be here alone. I don't want her to be alone."

He walked slowly toward me, his eyes studying my face as he came. "Jenny has orders never to leave Amy alone when you're not here. You know that." He reached forward and took my hands in his, pulling me toward him into the light from the window.

"You're trembling," he said. "Tell me what's wrong." His voice was a warm, husky command, and listening to it, I almost gave in to the emotions he made me feel.

For one brief moment the words were on the tip of my tongue. I wanted to tell him exactly what I'd heard and what I suspected, even if my interpretation was right and he intended to send Amy away. What would he do if I told him I heard? Would he deny it, or explain it away? The prospects were too frightening even to think about. For if he was not the decent, honorable man I thought he was . . . if he had lied about his wife's death for more than a year, I did not think I could bear it. Not on the heels of my admission of love for him, if only to myself.

But I was certain now that no matter how Desiree had died, Derek had been on the fourth floor with her that night.

I looked up into his eyes as he stood waiting for an answer. I smiled, pushing back my thoughts and the words that threatened to tumble from my lips. I pulled away from his warm hands and stepped backward, exactly as Mrs. Vanderworth had taught me

221

to do in the company of a gentleman.

I could see a flicker of concern in his eyes even as I moved away from him.

"I'm only tired, that's all," I murmured. "If you will excuse me, I must get dressed for dinner."

Without heeding his softly muttered entreaty, I turned and hurried down the hallway. I practically ran around the stair railing and let myself into my room. And I was grateful that he made no attempt to follow me.

I locked the door behind me and stood for a moment, wondering if I had made a mistake.

I loved him. Dear God, but I thought I loved him even more. And yet I could not let myself give in to that love until I knew for certain exactly what part he had played in his wife's death. And what he intended to do with Amy.

I had to think. But I found that difficult to do when I was in his compelling presence. If I could somehow coax Amy into talking again, I thought I could help her remember exactly what she had seen that night. And it was a plan I could tell no one.

Jenny had laid a dress on the bed for me to wear to dinner, and I was grateful for her help. I was almost late as it was. How strange that generally I would be excited about wearing one of my new gowns, but that night I hardly took notice of it as I quickly pulled it on.

Later, when I stood before the mirror arranging my hair, I did notice the dress. I could hardly believe it was my reflection staring back at me. I looked older, and the unhappiness I felt was stamped upon my features. With my hair up my face appeared thinner, my eyes dark and almost haunted.

I pinched my cheeks to add a bit of color and even added a touch of colored balm to my pale lips. Then I stepped back and ran trembling hands down the beautiful rose-colored dress. It was exactly the color Miss Olivia said I should wear, and I had to admit she was right.

The silky material shimmered and glistened beneath the lights as I moved. The neckline was low and flattering to my fair skin and shoulders. The straight skirt gathered perfectly at the hips before falling to a soft flare at the hemline. I wore no jewelry except the tiny gold ruby earrings that Mrs. Vanderworth had given me when she saw the dress.

I should have felt like a princess, like my legendary Cinderella. But for once my optimism seemed to have vanished, and I walked slowly down the steps as if to a funeral.

I was late. The family and a few guests who had arrived early for Saturday's ball sat at the table, chatting and sipping from their fragile wineglasses. At my appearance there was a hushed gasp and the room grew quiet and still. The men at the table rose, staring at me silently. With a start I recalled that other night when my appearance had caused a similar stir. I had been wearing Desiree's white dress.

But I realized that the looks I saw now were not ones of shock or dismay. They were warm and admiring, eyes sparkling with approval and lips smiling flirtatiously. I had never received such attention in my life and I assumed that the rose gown, designed and fitted for me alone, made the difference.

I should have been flattered, thrilled at the attention directed my way. But that night my mind was elsewhere. I felt aloof and far removed from their actions or thoughts. And I suppose that, as much as anything, gave me the look that they seemed to admire so boldly.

"I'm sorry I'm late," I said quietly as I stood near the head of the oval table.

223

I heard Mrs. Vanderworth and looked toward the chair where she pointed. "Sit here, dear, beside Derek."

I looked uneasily into Derek's watchful eyes. For a moment I felt as if he and I were the only two people in the room. I was oblivious to the admiring glances of the men who stood waiting patiently for me to be seated. I stared into Derek's eyes as if somehow I could see the secrets he kept hidden there.

He took my hand and pulled me gently to the chair beside him. And with a rustle of movement the men took their seats and conversation began again about the table. The spell was broken and I turned away from Derek, pulling my hand quickly from his.

From across the table Charles smiled at me and lifted his wineglass in a little salute. The Reverend Webster was also at the table, as was Mrs. Hunt, who sometimes joined the guests to even out the ratio of women to men.

James Webster smiled at me, and for the first time I thought I saw a hint of admiration in his brown eyes as well.

Being so close to Derek was disconcerting; every time I glanced up, he was watching, his look quiet and questioning. I knew he wondered about my strange behavior today.

Mrs. Vanderworth introduced me to the new guests and I made a determined effort to speak to them throughout the meal, so that I would be looking away from Derek.

But even if the guests were charming and interesting, I could hardly ignore Diana's resentful looks at me. She was directly across the table. And I often noticed her glancing from me to Derek. I could hardly wait until dinner was ended.

But after dinner, to my dismay, Mrs. Vanderworth

announced there would be music in the Palm Court. It seemed unbelievable that after all my daydreaming about this kind of evening, now I could hardly wait to leave, to be away from these people and back in the privacy of my own room.

Charles immediately came forward to claim me, placing his hand upon mine as I took his arm. I did not even look at Derek, who stood very near to us. But I could feel his disappointment as the power of his gaze rested upon me like the blaze of a winter fire.

As we were seated down in the cool, cozy Palm Court, a string quartet began to play. The music was lovely and soothing. And I could not help the enjoyment that flooded over me. It would have been a perfect evening if I had not been so distracted by what I had heard earlier in the library.

Diana took a seat beside Derek. It seemed she still would not give up on winning his attention. I watched them, studying them together and feeling a warm flush upon my skin as I remembered their earlier intimate conversation. I could hardly bear to think of her in his arms, of her soft white skin beneath his dark hands. The thought of it sent a sharp pain through me, so agonizing that I almost gasped aloud.

Derek's eyes turned suddenly toward me, his questioning gaze capturing me before I could look away.

Oh, Derek, I love you, my heart wanted to shout. Please tell me you are not going to send your daughter away. And if there is such a thing as telepathy, then my mind spoke to his at that moment.

I saw it in the darkening of his eyes and the softening of his features. His lips parted softly and he smiled, a sweet, tender smile that would have melted icicles.

I was lost. I knew at that moment that I was lost

forever. For it did not seem to matter what this man had done — I could not help loving him. I could not control it; it was already done and I was powerless to stop it, even if I'd wanted to.

Charles nudged me, giving me a warning glance. Of course he had seen Derek's look toward me. He could hardly have kept from it.

"You two are causing quite a scene, my dear," he cautioned beneath his breath.

I looked down at my hands in my lap and did not look toward Derek again until the musicale was concluded.

Afterward, as everyone stood around talking, the Reverend Webster walked toward us. He took my hand in his and bent in a courtly fashion that took me completely by surprise. I felt the rough tickle of his beard as his lips touched my hand. His upward glance at me held a look that caught me quite off guard.

His manner and the look in his eyes were not at all what one would expect of a clergyman. But then, I told myself quickly, he was a minister, not a monk. Of course he would be interested in women, just as any man would. And he was quite an attractive man at that, once the usual stiff formality of his profession was taken away. In fact, I found him rather charming.

"Miss Stevens," he murmured gallantly. "You are the most stunning creature I've ever seen."

Charles coughed softly and looked away. I knew it was his way of expressing his disbelief at the change in the Reverend Webster.

"Why thank you, Reverend Webster," I said, blushing slightly at his continued gaze.

"Please, call me James," he said. "The word Reverend makes me sound so old. After all, I'm not much older than you, I would imagine."

I glanced up at Charles, who stood rocking quietly back and forth on his heels. His irritation with the minister was obvious. And it was also obvious that James Webster intended to ignore him.

"Miss Stevens," the pastor continued, "might I call on you one day? I'd greatly enjoy taking you for a carriage ride."

"Well, I . . . I suppose so," I said, hardly knowing how to deny him.

"Wonderful," he said warmly. "Saturday morning, perhaps?"

"Won't you be busy Saturday, Elizabeth?" Charles drawled in his most English accent. "Getting ready for the ball?"

"Well, I . . . yes, I guess so."

"I can hardly believe you will need all day to make yourself beautiful for the dance, Miss Stevens," Reverend Webster chided. "It could not take more than seconds, as natural as your beauty is."

I laughed then. I'd always read and dreamed of the lovely, ridiculous things a man might say to a woman. But I'd hardly expected my first experience to be this. And besides, I thought there was the slightest hint of teasing in his deep voice.

"Thank you," I said with a smile. "And no, it will hardly take all day." I glanced at Charles who lifted one eyebrow at me with disapproval.

"Saturday morning it is, then," Reverend Webster murmured. He bowed again and smiled, then walked away to speak with the other guests.

"Elizabeth Stevens!" Charles whispered in my ear. "I can hardly believe you just did that. First you can hardly take your eyes off my cousin, and now you've agreed to go riding with the minister! I had hardly considered you the fickle kind of girl."

"I'm not!" I said with indignation. "Besides, James is only being kind and friendly. It isn't the same

227

thing as . . . as . . ." I glanced toward Derek, who stood with his dark head lowered as he bent to catch the words of one of the women.

Charles took a deep, exaggerated breath of air. "Ah, so that's the way it is." He followed my look, then turned to take my arm lightly.

"Listen to me, my girl," he said. "I want you to be *careful,* do you hear? You're much too sweet and much too innocent to become involved with either Derek or Reverend Webster."

I grinned at him in response and laughed when he actually blushed beneath my look.

"Yes," he said nodding. "I probably *am* jealous. But I care about you a great deal, and if you were not already in love with my cousin, I would court you as gallantly as even the Reverend Webster."

We both laughed then, thinking of how ridiculous that would be. I liked Charles, but we both knew he was right. I could never be interested in any other man after meeting Derek Vanderworth. And I hardly thought Charles's feelings for me were serious.

"I'll be careful," I said. "I promise."

"And if anyone dares to be impertinent to you, you come directly to me. Do you hear?" His words were fiercely teasing, but this time I knew he was serious.

"You're a good friend, Charles," I said. "Of course I would come to you immediately, if need be."

"Good," he said softly.

Charles glanced toward Mrs. Hunt, who had been looking our way all evening. Tonight she wore a soft, silk dress, the color of turquoise. I thought it heightened her dark exotic good looks to perfection.

I was surprised to see her lower her lashes now as if to disguise the direction of her glances. I would not have thought her capable of such coy behavior.

But she really was quite lovely, and I thought with a laugh that she would be a wonderful, spirited match for Charles.

But I had mentioned it before and as was Charles's nature, I knew his mind would only go in the opposite direction if I mentioned it again. But I saw now she had captured his full attention and I could not resist pointing it out.

"She looks quite lovely this evening, doesn't she?"

"Who?" he asked innocently, turning to me with an unconvincing frown.

"You know perfectly well who," I said with a smile. "Mrs. Hunt, the dragon lady, as you call her."

His gray eyes moved again to her just as she glanced his way. I was right. There was a definite spark in the air between the two. And if I wasn't mistaken, they both recognized it tonight, perhaps for the first time.

I saw Charles's puzzled frown, and heard his swift intake of air. Then he quickly took a drink from a nearby tray and turned toward me as he sipped it nonchalantly.

"Why are you looking at me that way, Elizabeth?" he asked with impatience.

"Why, Charles, I do believe you're blushing."

"Has anyone ever told you what an impertinent child you are?" he asked.

"Why, yes," I replied. "I believe it was you." I could not resist laughing at his stricken expression. "Why not just give in and go speak to her?"

"I'd just as soon approach a she-bear," he said gruffly.

"You're afraid," I said with sudden insight.

"Elizabeth, let it be," he warned.

"You are! Why, Charles Simmons . . . who would have thought a man with your reputation would be . . ."

229

"Elizabeth . . ." he said between clenched teeth. "I'll swear, I'm going to strangle you if you say another word."

Just then I heard Mrs. Vanderworth tell Derek that she was going upstairs. I thought it would be a perfect opportunity for me to leave gracefully without having to speak to Derek.

"I'll walk up with you, Mrs. Vanderworth," I said. Then, turning to Charles, I whispered, "Think about what I said."

Derek's head came up and he looked at me. I could see he wanted to speak to me; I could feel it in his potent gaze. But I was not ready to talk to him. For despite his tender looks, I was still uncertain about what I should do.

As Mrs. Vanderworth and I said goodnight, Reverend Webster made a point of coming forward to bid me goodnight and remind me of our riding engagement. And I did not miss the glances of admiration as the other gentlemen present also told me goodnight.

I walked slowly up the stairway, not wanting to hurry Mrs. Vanderworth. She seemed tired tonight. But as usual she was warm and friendly.

"Well, my girl, you were quite a success tonight. And I must commend Mrs. Tillis on your gown. It fits superbly and looks wonderful on you."

I held out the rose-colored skirt. It was lovely and perhaps some other time I might have admired it more.

"Your behavior was perfect," she said, glancing sideways at me as we moved to the second level.

"Thank you," I said. "Not only for the compliment, but for helping me learn about such things."

"Oh, pish," she said. "Such behavior comes naturally to some, as I suspect it does to you. You have such a way about you that no one can help but love you. Eating with the wrong fork would hardly be noticed."

We stopped outside my room and she hugged me to her. "I feel as if you're one of my own," she said. "I could not be prouder of you if you were."

"You have been so kind to me," I said. "And you'll never know how much it has meant to me."

"Well, as I said, it's easy being kind to someone as sweet and lovely as you." She turned her head to one side and looked at me evenly. "You have blossomed since you came, Elizabeth, absolutely blossomed. There was more than one admiring glance your way this evening. Why, I think you've even won over our staid Reverend Webster."

I laughed. "Well, as I told Charles, James is only being kind . . . nothing more."

"I wouldn't be so certain of that if I were you. He was quite aware of the looks of envy he received when he reminded you of your riding engagement. That sort of thing only makes a man more interested."

We chatted for a while longer and then she went on to her room.

It had been a long, tiring day and night. I looked in quickly at Amy and found her sleeping peacefully while a dim light burned beside her bed. I left the light on as Derek had requested. Then I went to my own room.

After I had undressed, I stood in the darkness gazing out the window to the front lawn. The moon was full and cast a silver light upon the lawn and its surrounding trees. I was still standing there lost in thought when I heard footsteps coming up the stairs.

I knew instinctively it was Derek. And when the footsteps paused just at the top of the stairs outside my door, I was certain of it. He stood there for a long moment while my heart began a heavy pounding in my chest.

After the long, intimate looks that had passed between us downstairs, I knew how he must be feeling. The same as I was.

My hands clung to the curtains at the window and I had to practically restrain myself from going to the door and flinging it open. The image of him there, the thought of being taken into his arms and moved into the darkened bedroom, set my limbs to trembling.

But I stood quietly until his footsteps moved away and across the hallway to his own rooms. Suddenly my tiredness was gone, replaced by a tingling awareness that I could not explain. And I knew it would be a long, restless night for both of us.

Chapter Twenty-three

It was well past midnight and still I had not slept. I paced the floor, thinking about Amy, about the things I could say to persuade her to speak again. My bare feet made a soft, rasping noise on the carpet; it seemed to be the only sound in the huge, eerily quiet house.

The stream of moonlight through the windows had moved slowly, until now only a narrow silvered strip could be seen. Soon it would be at its peak and would begin its descent on the other side of the house. I wondered if its bright beams would shine through Derek's windows and I wondered if he was still awake.

As I stood there a sudden scream rang through the silence of the night. Although it was nearby, it sounded somewhat muffled, so that for a moment I couldn't be certain of exactly what I'd heard. I went to the door and without opening it, stood listening.

When I heard voices, I quietly turned the knob and opened the door only the smallest bit. The sight that met my eyes made my blood run cold, and I was afraid my responsive gasp would give me away.

Two people were moving from the hallway near Amy's room into the dark shadows of the sitting hall. There was no mistaking the tall masculine figure. It was Derek. His hand was clamped about the arm of a woman . . . a woman with long, flowing locks of blond hair.

She was dressed in white and in the darkness seemed to float across the floor as if she glided on air. But this was no ghost.

I could hear her high-pitched voice protesting as Derek pulled her along with him toward the opposite hallway. And I could hear his voice as well. The deep timbre of it reverberated about the room in angry, muffled tones.

I knew this was my opportunity to find out more about the secrets of Stormhaven and about what Derek wanted so desperately to hide. I hesitated only a moment, then ran across to peek into Amy's room. I was so afraid of leaving her alone, especially since this ghostly figure always seemed to return here.

But Amy was sleeping soundly, and evidently the intruder had not awakened her tonight.

I ran quickly across the sitting hall, my bare feet making no sound on the floor. I peeked around the corner down the hallway, but Derek and the woman had disappeared. More cautiously now, I moved down the dimly lit hallway. As I approached the narrow stairwell I heard the sound of footsteps above me and knew they had gone up to the fourth floor.

I crept up the stairway; the darkness here was almost complete. The only light came from the third floor hallway; I could see no light anywhere else. Every sense within me screamed for me to stop, warned me not to go on. But I knew I could not stop now, and I forced myself to continue up the stairs.

Once I reached the top, I felt along the walls, uncertain which way the hallway ran or where my next step would take me. Suddenly there was the flaring of a light at the far end of the narrow hallway. There was an open doorway and from inside long shadows fell and wavered out across the corridor.

I could hear Derek's deep voice. But to my surprise it was not raised in anger, but held a quiet, soothing quality. I saw someone emerge from the room and turn to walk toward me. Quickly I stepped back and found myself in a small alcove. Now that my eyes were adjusting to the darkness, I saw there was one tiny window here. I stooped beneath it lest the person coming could see me silhouetted there against the moonlit sky.

I held my breath as the steps grew nearer. It was a tall, slender woman who turned to walk down the narrow stairway. Once she turned at the landing to go toward the third floor, I blinked in surprised recognition. It was Miss Olivia!

I did not move, but sat waiting for her to return. Something in her purposeful stride told me she would be back. My legs were trembling from the strain and I slowly eased down to the floor, where I sat huddled in the corner of the alcove with my knees drawn up to my chest.

It was only minutes before Miss Olivia appeared again. As she walked past me I could see clearly the glint of light upon the object in her hand. It was a hypodermic needle, the kind that a doctor might use to inject medicine beneath the skin of a patient.

I shivered suddenly as a cold chill passed down my neck. The sight of Miss Olivia's face in the cast of light from the hallway was frightening. She looked so stern, so completely different than the kind seamstress I'd come to know.

In a few moments I heard a sharp cry from the room at the end of the hallway. Then . . . silence. I wanted to run, wanted to crawl from my hiding place and run to the shelter of my room. But I could not seem to move; I was completely paralyzed with fear.

Minutes later, I heard a door close and two sets of footsteps began to move toward me. I huddled closer against the wall and watched as Derek and Miss Olivia passed.

"I'm sorry, Derek," Miss Olivia was saying. "She fooled me again, I'm afraid. I don't know what we're to do with her."

"Don't blame yourself, Olivia," he said in a quiet, thoughtful voice. "She's grown much worse. I should not have let it go on so long. But don't worry, by this time next week it will be over. I've decided we have no choice but to send her back to the hospital."

"I know what a hard decision that was for you, Derek," she said. "But it's the only thing you can do now."

"Yes," he said thoughtfully. "In the meantime, we must keep her sedated. And under no circumstances can we allow Amy up here, or anyone else."

They had stopped at the bottom of the steps. I heard them clearly as their voices rose toward me.

"It's a good thing you moved Elizabeth downstairs. The girl was curious . . . too curious for her own good."

My heart almost stopped. Was that the only reason Derek had moved me? Because he was afraid I'd find out what was on the fourth floor of his mansion?

Derek gave a soft grunt of laughter. "I'm afraid she's still curious. And she's too clever not to figure it out after a while. I'm not sure exactly how I should handle her."

"I'm sure you'll think of something," Olivia said in an adroit, meaningful tone of voice.

Derek laughed again, a low rumble. "Goodnight, Olivia."

Then they were gone.

I was afraid to stand, afraid my shaking legs would not hold me. I crawled from my hiding place and glanced down the hallway toward the room. I could see only a faint glow of light beneath the door. I had only to walk the length of the dark hallway and open the door to uncover part of the secret. But I couldn't

236

do it. Every instinct I had urged me to get as far away from that room as possible. Tomorrow in the daylight would be soon enough. And perhaps by then Amy could tell me more about her mother's death.

Finally I slipped down the stairs and ran silently down the hallway. I felt as if eyes followed my every step, as if the grotesque figurines in their glass cases watched me and smiled. I turned several times to look behind me, but nothing was there. Only the long, wavering shadows from the dim lights.

Finally I was safely back in my room. I closed and bolted the door. I was shaking so badly that my teeth chattered noisily. And I felt cold even in the warmth of the summer night.

I slipped into bed, huddling miserably beneath the covers until I began to grow warmer. Only then did I relax a bit and begin to grow sleepy.

When I awoke next morning I had the beginnings of a throbbing headache. At least I knew it was from lack of sleep and not from wearing my glasses too long.

My glasses! I glanced to the table beside the bed where I usually kept them. They were not there. With a sinking feeling I knew where I had left them.

I had taken them off while I was in the little tunnel-like structure behind the fireplace in the library. And I had left them there . . . left them in plain sight for Derek to see if he returned to read the psychology books.

Quickly I bathed and changed into a soft white cotton dress trimmed in streamers of blue ribbon. I decided the glasses would have to wait. Surely it would be too coincidental for Derek to go directly to the library this morning.

For now the most important thing on my mind was

Amy. I went immediately to her room and helped her dress for the day. Then together we ate breakfast in her room. I could not help glancing from time to time at the arched doorway to Derek's sitting room. The last thing I wanted was to see him this morning. There were too many things I had to think about before we talked again. And I knew I could not be objective when he was near.

After breakfast I played with Amy, reading to her and listening to her cheerful laughter. Then carefully I took her raggedy bear and set him upon the table before us.

Within minutes Amy was mesmerized. It was as if she thought the bear was real, come to life as soon as I began to speak in his quiet child's voice.

Soon Amy was giggling, fully caught up now in the game with Bo Bear. And this time when she spoke it seemed easier for her, more normal and spontaneous.

I was certain now she would recover fully.

"Amy, sweetheart," I began slowly. "You love Bo Bear very much, don't you?"

"Yes," she replied with a nod of her head.

"And you love your daddy?"

"Uh huh," she said, smiling. "And Grandma Vander."

I smiled at her shortened pronunciation. Somehow it suited Mrs. Vanderworth.

"I know you do, dear. And I know you want to tell them you can talk again don't you?"

"Yes!" she cried, clapping her hands together. "Now! Let's tell them now!"

"Let's play a little game first, shall we?"

"Game?"

"Yes, sweetie. Let's pretend just for a little while longer that you can't speak. Do you think you can do that? Then we will surprise them both. What do you think?"

"I can play a game," she said.

"Good. Now . . . I want you to help me remember something. Do you think you can?"

She nodded, her big eyes bright and expectant. She thought this was part of the game.

"Do you remember upstairs? The rooms on the top floor of the house? You pointed to them when we went riding."

She frowned and her eyes grew darker, but she nodded yes.

"Were you ever there before? Perhaps the night of the big dance?"

Again she nodded yes. "Long time ago," she said.

It must indeed seem like long ago to someone so young. Dear Lord, but I hoped what I was about to do would not traumatize her back into her shell of silence.

"Can you tell me what you remember about it?"

"Dark," she said, her eyes growing huge. "I was afraid."

"I know you were, sweetie." I pulled her into my lap and placed the bear in her arms. "But Bo Bear and I . . . we hope nothing will frighten you ever again."

She snuggled closer.

"Was anyone else there?" I asked.

"Uh huh," she said. "Mimi was there. I went to see Mimi. Daddy told me not to, but sometimes Mommy took me. Mimi was funny. I liked Mimi."

"Mimi?" Who was she I wondered. I had not heard the name from anyone else in the house, not even from curious Ruthie, who seemed to know everyone. And where was Mimi now? Could she be the person Derek kept hidden upstairs? The poor woman who had received the hypodermic shot last night from Olivia?

Last night I'd even had the nightmarish idea that the woman upstairs could somehow be Desiree. But

239

that was impossible, and I realized in the light of day that it had only been my fear and imagination working.

"Who is Mimi?" I asked Amy.

The little girl shrugged her shoulders.

"What does she look like?"

"Nice," she said. "I like Mimi."

"I know, sweetheart, but tell me how she looks. Is she old . . . young?"

"Yes," she said nodding in agreement. "Pretty like Mommy."

I was getting nowhere with this.

"Did your daddy like Mimi, too?"

"No, Daddy didn't like her," she said, shaking her head as her eyes grew big and bright.

Amy cuddled close to me and held the bear so tightly to her that it practically disappeared. I could see the memories flooding back; it was clear in the darkening of her eyes.

"What happened, sweetie?" I asked the question very gently, holding her close as I did.

"Daddy was mad at Mommy. He yelled at her and said bad things to her. He said I shouldn't be there."

"You were upstairs . . . the night of the ball?"

She nodded but said nothing.

"Then what, darling?"

"It scared me and made me cry. So me and Bo Bear ran away from Daddy."

She held the bear out now as if she were speaking to it. And she seemed calmer, now that she had begun to remember.

"And did he find you?"

"No, we hid." She danced the bear about in jumpy little movements.

"Oh, you did? And after he left, did you find your room all by yourself?"

She turned to look into my face. She was frowning,

240

and I could see she was trying hard to remember.

"No," she whispered. "I played with Bo Bear. We just hid. Mimi made Bo Bear." She held the bear up and I noticed again the uneven stitching and crooked eyes.

I did not really want to know the answer to the next question. But I had to ask it. "And did your daddy come back upstairs?"

"No," she whispered with a little shudder. "But another man came." Then with a little shudder of fear she threw herself back into my arms.

"Who was he?" I asked, surprised by her revelation.

"I couldn't see him," she said softly. Her fear was painful to see, and I thought seriously then about dropping the whole subject.

"And . . . and did something happen? To your mommy?"

Oh, how I hated to ask her that question, to see the fear and agony in her young eyes. But I knew I could not stop now.

"Yessss." Her word was a wail of misery.

"Oh, sweetheart," I said, holding and rocking her in my arms. "Oh, my little darling, I'm so sorry."

What a terrible secret this tiny little girl had kept. And whether she consciously meant to or not was not important now. She had. And I hoped that the telling of it that day would help her erase it from her mind.

"Now, listen carefully, Amy, and try to remember. What did you do next? Did the man see you?"

"I heard my Mommy scream and the sound flew away. But I was scared." She made little whimpering sounds as she tried to tell me.

I shivered at her words about the sound flying away. She couldn't have known the reason.

"It's all right, darling. Take your time."

"No one came, 'Lizabeth. I waited for a long, long time, but no one came. My daddy didn't come to help

241

me and he didn't come to help Mommy."

Like a bolt of lightning the truth hit me. Amy's face held that same little frightened look, that same resentfulness as it sometimes did when her father was near. I knew only too well how one could build up the image of a father in one's own heart and mind. And Derek was the most important man in Amy's life; she adored him. And he had let her down when he did not come to rescue her and her mommy.

Suddenly the pieces were beginning to fit, the secrets of this house, the ugly truth buried beneath all the magnificently beautiful veneer of wealth.

What agonizing guilt Derek had felt this past year. I had seen for myself how tortured he was because of it. He held himself responsible for Desiree's death and he thought this little girl, the daughter he loved more than anything, had witnessed her mother's suicide.

But it was not suicide; I was certain of that now. And if Amy had been able to speak, Derek would have known it, too. And although I could not be sure about what exactly did happen, I thought I knew who the man was that Amy heard that night.

I had to find Charles, had to confront him with what I knew. But I was torn because I did not want to leave Amy yet. I wanted to stay with her until she felt safe and happy again, until she began to forget all the painful secrets we had dredged up today.

Chapter Twenty-four

I spent almost the entire day with Amy, and I felt such joy at watching her carefree play, the way her eyes sparkled clearly as she romped about the room. I could hardly wait to tell Derek.

But I felt a certain loyalty to Charles, and I wanted to speak to him first. Give him a chance to explain what happened, then convince him he had to be the one to tell Derek. I did not believe Charles had deliberately hurt Desiree; he was too kind and gentle a man to do that. But he could at least tell us what really happened.

Finally, in mid-afternoon, Amy grew tired; Jenny came in with a small pot of hot chocolate. Soon afterward Amy curled up on her bed with Bo Bear securely snuggled in her arms.

"Will you stay with her for a while, Jenny?" I asked. "I have an errand to take care of."

"Of course," she said with a smile, taking a seat in the rocking chair beside the bed.

I went straight upstairs to the sitting room near Charles's room. Mrs. Vanderworth and two other ladies were in the sitting hall having tea. There were baskets of embroidery nearby, and I imagined they had spent the day pleasantly chatting and sewing.

"Well, Elizabeth," she said. "You're just in time for tea. Sit down, dear."

"No, I'm sorry, Mrs. Vanderworth," I said, glancing

down the hall toward Charles's rooms. "But I really don't have time. I only left Amy for a few minutes with Jenny. I was looking for Charles. Have you seen him?"

Taking a sip of tea, her eyebrows lifted curiously. "Why, yes. As a matter of fact, he was just here."

"Is he in his room, then?"

"Oh, no. He was on his way out with Mrs. Hunt. Going into the city, I believe he said. And they probably won't be home until late tonight."

"Oh," I said. My happiness that he was with Mrs. Hunt contrasted with the disappointment I felt. The longer I delayed speaking with Charles, the longer I must delay telling Derek. And this was not something I wanted to prolong.

"Is anything wrong, dear?" she asked.

"No, no," I said, forcing a smile at her and the two women, who were watching me curiously. "Nothing important. I will speak to him tomorrow."

"And of course you will have all tomorrow evening to chat with him . . . at the ball," she reminded.

"Yes, of course," I muttered.

I left them rather quickly, not bothering to explain why I needed to speak to Charles. Let them think whatever they wished.

I decided to run downstairs to the library to fetch my glasses before I returned to Amy. There was no one about as I made my way through the tapestry gallery and into the library.

The lights were on, illuminating all the beauty and warmth of the room, but no one was there. Quickly I went to the spiral stairway and climbed to the balcony.

As I turned toward the passageway behind the fireplace, I stopped, surprised and alarmed. Derek sat on the bench. Whatever was I to say to him?

His dark hair gleamed in the light of the dim lamp on the wall. He watched me, not speaking as he languidly stretched his long legs out before him.

I tried to compose myself and walked slowly toward him. "I . . . I wasn't expecting anyone to be up here," I said.

"That's obvious," he said slowly.

He still wore riding clothes, and his dark boots were covered with dust. He looked relaxed and carefree except for one thing. His eyes that continued to watch me so carefully were once again cold and hard, as if I had somehow offended him by coming here. And I knew he wondered at my standoffish behavior of late.

My eyes darted to the small reading table where I'd left my glasses. I did not trust myself in his presence and only wanted to get the glasses and go. I was afraid he had only to ask what was bothering me before I probably spoiled everything by telling him.

"Looking for these?" he asked, his voice deceptively quiet and indifferent.

He held my glasses up in the air above his chest and twirled them casually as he waited for me to speak.

"Why . . . yes," I said. "I must have left them here when I was working. Did you see how much work I've done? I'm very excited about the work." I turned around and glanced at the row of books behind me, trying to calm the heavy thudding of my heart.

"Come here, Elizabeth," he said, his voice deep and echoing in the little chamber where he sat.

I whirled about, surprised by his words and the tone of his voice. His eyelids lifted slowly as he pinpointed me with those strangely colored eyes. Then he lifted his brow questioningly.

"Well? You do trust me, don't you?" he asked. "You're the one who believes in fairy-tales, in the maxim that good always conquers evil?"

"What an odd thing to say," I said, shakily.

"Not so odd, really. Your face is so readable, Elizabeth. And we both know that your trust should allow you to reform someone like me." But his voice held a touch of sarcasm.

I went slowly to him, watching his eyes and wondering what had happened to make him so cynical again. After his kisses, I thought we had progressed beyond this. But now his eyes were as pained and cold as they had been before.

Once I was inside the enclosure, he held his hand up toward me, the glasses still between his fingers. He watched me with a little smile upon his lips as he dared me to take them from him.

I was determined not to back down from him, for I thought it was exactly what he wanted. This testing of me again. I thought he wanted to prove to me once and for all that he was not the kind of man I should love. Not the kind of man I could even be safely alone with. I shivered as I remembered that night in his chambers and all the violent passion I had sensed in him.

I moved my hand toward the glasses.

With an animal-like quickness, his own hand darted forward and curled about my wrist. In almost the same movement he came to his feet and pulled me hard against him. I gasped as I looked up into his face and saw the bitterness that marred his handsome features.

"Derek . . ." I whispered as an entreaty.

"Do you have any idea what it is that a man feels for a woman, Elizabeth?" His voice was husky and fierce. "Do you? In your sweet naivety, have you ever thought of the violence in a man when he wants a woman?"

"Derek . . . don't."

His lips stopped my words as he dragged me to him and kissed me almost cruelly. He held me so tightly I could barely breathe as his mouth took mine in a kiss so intimate, so hot, that I felt as if I were being consumed.

But if he thought to frighten me, he was wrong; for he did just the opposite. I felt a tingle as his passion ignited my own, and I wanted nothing more than to remain in his arms forever.

He felt it, knew it instantly. Knew that nothing he could do would turn me away. With a soft groan he pulled away, and still holding me in the circle of his arms, looked down at me. He frowned as he studied my face. He closed his eyes and took a deep breath. Still he did not release me.

My arms were trapped against his hard chest. Slowly I maneuvered them away and slid them around his waist and pressed myself against him.

His eyes opened and he smiled a slow, exasperated smile before he kissed me again.

This time when we parted, it was I who pulled away, as I gasped for breath. The passion, the yearning that surged between us was so sweet, so overwhelming that I could hardly bear it.

"Derek, I love you," I whispered, watching to see his reaction.

He smiled again and shook his head with a look of bemusement. "Oh, Elizabeth," he murmured softly in the quiet of our secret room. "What am I to do with you? Either you are the sweetest, most trusting woman on earth, or you are a complete fool."

I laughed, delighted with his exasperation. "I'm no fool," I said, as my eyes moved against my will to his sensual lips.

He made a small sound in his throat and gently moved me away from him.

"You shouldn't look at me that way," he warned with a wry smile.

"And why shouldn't I?" I asked, smiling at his discomfort.

"You know perfectly well why not, you little minx," he said with affection. "And there are things we need to talk about before we progress . . . any further."

Derek sat on the bench and took one of the psychology books in his hand.

"When I found your glasses here, I knew you must have seen the books . . . must have wondered about them." He looked up at me with a question in his eyes.

"Yes," I said truthfully. "I found them very interesting."

He smiled. "And with that quick, curious little mind of yours, I'm certain you knew who'd been reading them?"

"You?" I asked.

"Yes, me," he said, placing the book back on the table. The look in his eye had grown more serious. "And what did you think?"

A wisp of hair had fallen over his forehead, as it often had a tendency to do. Without thinking, I reached out and gently brushed it away. Without a word Derek took my hand and brought it down to his lips, turning my fingers and bringing the palm of my hand to his mouth.

I felt such a sharp, twisting stab of pleasure at the feel of his lips on the sensitive skin of my hand. A flood of weakness ran through me so that I had to sit on the bench beside him to steady myself. I could not take my eyes from his face.

"I . . . I didn't know what to think," I said shakily. "I wondered why you would be reading such things, such frightening descriptions."

"And I don't suppose it ever occurred to your *trusting little heart* that these might be descriptions of me?" His words were careful, almost like a young boy seeking approval.

"Truthfully?" I asked softly.

"Yes," he said fiercely. "Truthfully. I don't want you ever to lie to me about what you feel."

"No," I whispered, smiling as I saw the relief in his

amber eyes. "I knew it could never be you. But I realized almost immediately that you might have doubts about yourself. But psychopathic . . ." I motioned toward the book. "No, never."

"Actually, you're right," he said, leaning his head back against the wall. "I came here seeking answers. But the person I had in mind was not me. Yet . . . after I read some of the descriptions, I must admit I felt as if I fit some of them pretty well." I recalled some of his underlined passages.

"You don't," I said simply. "Believe me, my *trusting little heart* is never wrong." I used his words only to tease his frown away.

He smiled and shook his head, looking at me as if he would sweep me into his arms again. And even as we sat in our own intimate little world, I felt the guilt begin to nag at me.

I wanted to tell him everything, needed to tell him for his sake. But something kept me from it, and I reasoned that tomorrow would be soon enough, after I had a chance to speak to Charles. Besides, what could possibly happen in a few short hours?

He stood up and pulled me up to stand in the warmth of his arms. He kissed me softly on the lips, only a brief whisper of a kiss.

"We'd better go," he said, his voice husky and warm. "I don't trust myself alone with you here."

"And you should not trust me, either," I said, assuring him that I felt the same passionate response as he.

He hugged me tight and bent to place his lips in the crook of my neck. "Oh, my Elizabeth," he said. "There are so many things I want to say to you. So many things I need to explain."

I wondered then if he was speaking of the woman upstairs, the one he needed to send away. But I said nothing. I would let him tell me in his own good time.

It was the first time I'd ever seen him so open, so

trusting. And even though he had not admitted he loved me, I felt hopeful. Perhaps by the time this whole mystery was settled, we could come to each other in a completely honest and open way.

He held me away and looked at me with a wistful smile on his lips. "You have grown into a beautiful, graceful woman," he said. "When you first came, you had the sweet look of a pretty young girl. But last night in your rose-colored gown, you made my heart do the strangest things. You were so lovely, so perfect, that I thought I would die from looking at you."

I could hardly believe he was saying those beautiful, romantic words to me. Not this stern man who had tried so often to prove just how hard and cold he was. My eyes misted with tears as I looked at him with the love I could not hide.

"How sweet you are," I murmured.

"Don't be so sure of that," he said, grinning at me. "I also wanted to strangle Charles and James Webster for their fawning attention to you."

"Well, I would hardly call it fawning," I said with a laugh. "They were only being kind."

He shook his head and smiled gently. He wiped the tears from beneath my eyes with his thumb. "Elizabeth . . . my little Beth. I hope from now on the only tears I see in your eyes are those of joy."

"These are tears of joy," I assured him.

"Being with you is like seeing the sun come out after a storm. And I never thought I'd ever feel that way again."

Suddenly from below us, a voice broke the spell.

"Derek? Is that you up there?" called Diana.

He turned slightly and called down in her direction. "Just a minute."

Then, with a quick, conspiratorial grin, he kissed me again, a hard, passionate kiss that warmed me clear to my toes. "Until later," he whispered.

When he turned to go out to the railing, I held back, thinking he would not want Diana to see us together. But he turned with a puzzled look and motioned me toward him. He made me feel so secure, so wanted. And he made the moment perfect for me when he stood at the balcony and put his arm casually about my waist, pulling me close to his side for Diana to see.

"Yes?" he said innocently. "What is it, Diana?"

Her mouth flew open and she stood staring up at us with an incredible look of disbelief. Her face turned pale, then pink with anger. But to her credit, she did not let herself lose control.

"I . . . I wondered if you'd like to take a walk before dinner." Her look was pleading, and in that moment I actually felt sorry for her, for any woman who loved Derek Vanderworth and lost him deserved pity.

My arm was around Derek and I jostled him the slightest bit as I spoke beneath my breath. "Go ahead. I'll see you at dinner."

His amber eyes were so warm and loving as they looked into mine. And in that moment I think we both felt that nothing would ever part us again. Certainly not Diana or any of his family. Not even the events of the past that had so haunted him and frightened me.

We could hardly take our eyes from each other, regardless of Diana's looks of speculation. And as he held my hand and guided me down the spiral stairway toward his waiting sister-in-law, I felt happy.

At that moment I thought all the fairy-tales were really true. There really *could* be a happily-ever-after with a handsome prince. I thought then that nothing could ever shatter my complete happiness.

You see, I had absolutely no idea of the danger that really surrounded me.

Chapter Twenty-five

I dressed carefully that night for dinner, taking special care with my hair and gown. I kept reliving every word Derek had said in the library, every look from his beautiful eyes. And I could hardly wait to see him again.

That night was one of the happiest I'd ever spent. When Derek pulled a chair back from the table so that I could sit next to him, I felt proud and secure. I suppose my happiness wreathed me in a warm, confident glow and I had no thought of tomorrow, no thought that it could ever end.

After dinner, as we once again went to the Palm Court, Derek hardly left my side. He was warm and witty, completely charming as he monopolized my time and conversation. He was just the way I'd always hoped, always dreamed he could be.

Of course, there were knowing looks all around us since Derek was always the center of attention. And tonight I was also included in that attention. I suppose it was fuel for their fires . . . the poor little maid and the sophisticated Earl of Chesham, behaving together like two infatuated schoolchildren. But I didn't care; for once I was completely oblivious to what anyone said.

And later, when the Reverend Webster approached

to remind me of our ride the next morning, I stammered with surprise.

"Oh, why . . . no, I haven't forgotten," I told him. But the truth was, I had. I'd forgotten quite everything and everyone except Derek.

James gave me a look of teasing derision and with a lift of his brows moved very close to me to whisper in my ear. "Am I to take this sudden uncertainty to mean what I think?"

"And what is that?"

"That your affections are elsewhere and that neither I nor poor Charles has the smallest of chances with you." His smile was sweet and affectionate.

I didn't know what to say, and when I glanced toward Derek, he was watching me, smiling at me so intimately that I felt breathless.

"Ah," the Reverend Webster said, following my look. "I'm afraid your eyes give you away, my dear."

"I'm sorry," I said, blushing. "I'm afraid I'm being very rude to you and I did not intend to be."

"Well, if I were a true gentleman, as I'm supposed to be, I would gracefully bow out. I would tell you I understand and release you from your promise to me. But in truth, I'd like to think you would go anyway, if only as a salve to my poor ego."

I laughed at him, feeling giddy and young and full of life. How could I refuse him after so charming an invitation?

"A very pretty speech, sir," I said. "And yes, I will still go tomorrow for the carriage ride. In fact, I'm looking forward to it."

His brown eyes sparkled as he bent to kiss my hand. "Good, then I will see you tomorrow morning."

After James left, Derek sauntered to me casually. His teasing grin completely captivated me. "I hope you know how cruelly you've hurt me. I hardly dreamed I would be thrown over for a preacher," he whispered.

"Never," I replied, glancing up at him. "You have absolutely no competition for my affections, Your Lordship."

He recognized my teasing and we both laughed together. I could recall the time I vowed never to call him by such a title. And now I thought it fit him perfectly.

The rest of the evening passed quickly. I had hoped Charles would be back by now and that I would not have to wait until morning to convince him that he should speak with Derek. I wanted everything cleared up between them, and I hoped that one day they might again be friends. And I had told myself that Desiree's death was a tragic accident and that if Charles were indeed involved, it had not been through any fault of his own.

Once that was settled, I felt certain Derek would tell me about the woman upstairs and how she had been involved.

But Charles did not return. Later, when Derek walked with me toward the stairs, Mrs. Vanderworth fell into step beside us. I could see the glint of curiosity in her eyes as she looked at us. She, perhaps more than anyone, knew what was happening between her grandson and me.

At my door, she did turn her back discreetly while Derek kissed me goodnight. But had she not been there, the embrace would have been much more ardent.

I knew as well as Derek why she was waiting. She did not think it proper and I would not have been surprised if she had offered to spend the night with me.

Derek was smiling as he pulled away from me. "I can hardly wait to dance with you tomorrow night," he whispered. "All night."

"Me too," I whispered. I could hardly bear for him to leave. And I wondered if I would ever grow tired of looking at him and being in his presence.

"Walk me up to my room, Derek," Mrs. Vanderworth said. "Goodnight, Elizabeth, my dear."

Derek and I exchanged glances, for we both knew the questions she probably had in store for her grandson. And I wondered how he would answer her.

After my near sleepless night, I was practically asleep before my head hit the pillow.

I woke the next morning to the sound of the wind racing around the big house. It whistled and howled mournfully and I smiled, peacefully unafraid, yet understanding why the servants sometimes spoke of Stormhaven so mystically. The winds of Stormhaven, they called it. A foreboding of some great tragedy.

I reminded myself that I did not believe in superstition as I jumped from bed, anxious to be up and about.

I wanted to see Amy before James came for me, and with any luck her father would be there as well.

But as it happened, Derek had already left and Amy was alone with Jenny. I asked the girl to come back after her breakfast. Then I settled down to eat with Amy.

I hardly ate more than a bite or two, for I was so excited I had lost my appetite.

"Did you see your daddy this morning, Amy?" I asked.

"Yes," she replied happily.

"And you didn't tell him our secret, did you? You remembered our game?"

"No," she said, shaking her blond curls. "I was asleep. Daddy kissed me good-bye."

At least I'd have a little time to find Charles. By tomorrow, everything would be cleared away and I could tell Derek about Amy.

Amy's attention had already focused on something else. And I thought perhaps that was the best news of all. She was too interested in her own childish amusements to be concerned about what I was saying.

255

Jenny returned and I kissed Amy good-bye, promising to see her again before the dance.

As I came down the stairs I saw James standing near the great double doors that led outside. I was somewhat surprised to see Ruthie speaking to him in a low, almost frenzied manner.

"Ruthie," I said upon approaching them. "Is something wrong?" I had not seen the girl for days, and I wondered if anything had happened . . . perhaps something that she needed to discuss with her pastor.

She turned and stared at me. And for once there was no smile on her face. Her blue eyes flicked quickly down my body, taking in the stylish riding habit I wore. I could not believe it was my attire that irritated her, but something certainly had.

"No, everything's just ducky," she said sarcastically, with a toss of her blond curls.

Then, with a withering look at James, she turned and flounced away without another word to either of us.

I stared after her, completely at a loss to know what was wrong. James seemed not the least perturbed but came forward with a warm smile as he took my arm.

Mr. Higgins stood outside by the minister's carriage. He seemed to be checking the harnesses and the wheels. I smiled, certain he thought none but the earl's carriages were good enough for my use.

He brought the reins around and held them until James had helped me up the steps into the seat. Deftly he took the reins and climbed up onto the seat beside me.

"Thank you, Mr. Higgins," I said with a smile.

"I could go with you, if you like, Miss Elizabeth," he said.

"As I told you, Mr. Higgins," James said curtly. "That won't be necessary."

"But . . ." I thought Mr. Higgins' real concern might be my going off with someone alone.

"It's all right, Mr. Higgins," I assured him. "We shan't be gone long. Just a ride through the estate."

"As I told the Reverend, here, if I drive, you both could enjoy the ride more."

"Good day, Mr. Higgins," James said curtly as he flicked the reins across the horse's rump. Without another word he drove away, leaving the Englishman muttering in protest.

"What was that all about?" I asked, turning to look back at Mr. Higgins.

"I have no idea," James said with a quick grin. "But it does seem that all the men here are overtly protective of you, Elizabeth."

I smiled. I could not deny Mr. Higgins was certainly that. He was even more protective of me than Derek.

But soon Mr. Higgins was forgotten. It was a lovely day, even with the dark clouds that hovered low in the sky. The mists were so thick we could not see the mountains. And the darkness made the foliage and trees even more beautiful than before as they and the colorful flowers along the drive seemed aglow in the dim light.

"I'm afraid it will rain before nightfall," I said, glancing up at the swirling clouds above us.

"Yes. It's too bad. I'm afraid it might bring back painful memories to the Vanderworths."

"Were you here last year? The night Desiree fell to her death?"

"Oh, yes," he said quietly. "I was here."

He seemed so completely sympathetic and the thought crossed my mind that he would be good to talk to. But I said nothing, waiting until I was certain. I certainly did not want to impose on his kindness by telling him all my suspicions.

"Did you know her well?"

He looked at me with a quick, questioning look. "Only through my ministering to the family. We had

257

spoken privately on occasion."

"I . . . I don't suppose she confided in you, did she? About . . . about another man?"

He glanced around at me, his dark eyes skimming across my face.

I continued on hurriedly in explanation. "I realize your conversations with your parishioners are confidential, James. And I wouldn't ask such a question if not for Amy."

"Amy?" he said, his eyes narrowing suspiciously.

"Could we stop here?" I asked, pointing to a wide turnaround area in the road.

"Certainly," he said, pulling the horse to the side of the road.

This area of the estate had a look of the wilderness about it. From the road we looked down upon a quiet, meandering stream, surrounded by giant hemlocks and towering pines. The cloudy day made it dark in the shelter of the trees, almost like the end of the day. The wind, although it only touched us lightly, made a loud, whispering roar through the tops of the trees as they swayed back and forth against the gray sky.

"I can see you're concerned about the child," he said. "Is there anything I can do to help?" His concern was immediate, and it gave me the courage to speak more freely.

"James," I cautioned. "I don't want anyone to know about this. I . . . I haven't even told Amy's father yet. But I need to speak to someone . . . to be sure I'm doing the right thing."

He held up a hand to silence me. "I can promise you they will hear nothing from my lips."

"I've been working with Amy. A few days ago, she said her first words since . . . since her mother's death. And now she seems completely recovered."

His eyes grew wide with interest and surprise. "Why, Elizabeth . . . that's remarkable. You're to be commended."

"I played only a small part. She needed a bit of encouragement, that's all. I believe she was ready to speak and to tell what she knew about that night."

"That night?" he asked sharply. "What do you mean?" He sat up straighter and looked at me intently. "What could she possibly know?"

"She was there," I said, my words echoing eerily there in the darkened forest. "She was upstairs when her mother died. Don't you see, that's what scared her so . . . frightened her so badly she blocked most of it from her mind and could not even bring herself to speak."

"Well," he said, shaking his head. "That's a remarkable theory you have there. But I find it hard to believe that Desiree Vanderworth would have thrown herself over the balcony with her little girl standing there watching her."

"But she wasn't. When she heard her parents quarreling, she ran away. Apparently she hid somewhere upstairs. Later, after her father left, she heard someone else come upstairs . . . a man. He and Desiree quarreled too and then Amy heard her mother scream."

"Well, this is . . . unbelievable."

"Yes, isn't it? And after what Charles told me of his relationship with Desiree, I'm certain he was the man. But I . . ."

"Charles?" he blurted out, his dark eyes blinking at me. "How do you . . . you mean Charles told you about . . . ?"

"About him and Desiree? Yes, he did. And I believe the rift that developed between him and Derek is very painful to him and something he wants to mend."

"And is that what Amy told you? That it was Charles she heard?"

"Well, actually no. She hasn't told me who it was. I just assumed that since Desiree and Charles were . . . well, I can't imagine who else it would be."

259

"Yes, yes, of course. It must have been Charles," he said thoughtfully. "Who else?" He looked at me. "What do you intend to do about this?"

"Well, that's why I needed so desperately to speak to someone. I hardly know what to do. I had hoped to speak to Charles first, give him a chance to tell Derek what happened before he hears it from me. But I can't find Charles, and I hate to delay this much longer."

"Well, I think perhaps you're correct to delay it," he said pensively.

"You do?" I asked, surprised at his agreement.

"Yes, at least until after the ball. After all, you would not want to cause the family such undue grief on this special occasion. It might be too much a reminder of last year. And what difference could a few hours make?"

"Yes," I said. "That's exactly what I thought. I will speak to Charles at the ball, then, tomorrow . . ."

"No, don't do that," he said quickly. "Don't mention this to Charles just yet, or to anyone. Let me handle that for you."

I looked at him oddly.

"Since Charles has already confided in me . . ." he explained.

"Well . . . all right," I said slowly.

"Then, on Sunday morning, everything will be settled and you won't have been involved. You wouldn't want to do anything to jeopardize your new, fragile relationship with Derek, now, would you?"

"No . . . I suppose not."

But I wasn't so certain as he seemed to be. I *was* involved, and Derek would know sooner or later that I had helped Amy speak. He had said he never wanted me to lie to him about anything. But James seemed so certain, so sure that this was the proper thing to do.

Reluctantly I agreed to let him handle everything.

Chapter Twenty-six

As we drove back toward Stormhaven the wind began to pick up. And although it was not at storm force, it made driving hazardous as twigs and limbs scattered wildly across the road. Several times James had to slow the buggy as broken tree branches rained down about us and the frightened horse. It seemed to take a very long time to reach the curving driveway to the house.

The sight of the house silhouetted against the gray-black skies was breathtaking. I'd never thought to see such a perfect picture. But as we drew nearer and heard the roar of the wind in the huge old trees that lined the driveway, I felt a sudden chill of premonition.

For some reason I glanced up to the fourth floor. And there, at the southern end of the house, was a flutter of white at one of the windows. My breath almost stopped as I stared hard, wondering if the wind and debris in the air played tricks with my eyes. But as we grew nearer I knew I was not mistaken; there was someone at the window. And I knew it was the woman Derek kept hidden away up there.

James did not see the woman, did not even look up, and I did not point her out to him. He seemed preoccupied, and all the gaiety he'd displayed the last few days seemed to have left him.

I reasoned he was only trying to compose the words he would say to Charles. It was, after all, a grave matter and one which would require a great deal of diplomacy.

James hardly seemed aware of me as Mr. Higgins rushed to help me down from the carriage. I was surprised that James did not even make an effort to step down and come around for me. Mr. Higgins and I both looked at him oddly for a moment. But he was very distracted and sat in the carriage, looking away into the distance, apparently lost in thought. He barely acknowledged my good-bye as I walked up the steps to the house.

I spent the remainder of the day with Amy, taking her to my room to see the dress I would wear. I assured her again that after the ball we would be able to tell her father and Grandma Vander all about our surprise.

But Amy seemed more interested in the ball. I told her Jenny could bring her down to see all the pretty dresses as long as they watched from a distance and only for a few moments. I couldn't take a chance on anyone talking to Amy at this late date. The thought of hiding it made me more uncertain than ever of my decision to let James handle everything.

My hands were trembling as I pinned my hair atop my head and arranged sprigs of tiny violets in the curls. I was uncertain about what the night would bring and consequently I was more nervous than I'd ever been in my life.

My dress, the one I had picked that day in the city, was hung carefully on the closet door so that the skirt did not touch the floor. There in the lamplight the beautiful ivory satin glimmered softly. It was simply made in a classic style, with no bustle, but a wide, flaring skirt under which I would wear several layers of stiffened petticoats.

Across one shoulder of the gown and the low-cut bodice was a wide sequined sash of deep, pure violet. It dipped in at the tightly fitted waist and then flared out again in an even wider swatch of violet that draped down one side of the skirt.

As I put the dress on, the sparkle of violet sequins caught in the light and shimmered in the mirror above the fireplace. I turned slowly, enjoying the play of rainbow colors it cast upon the walls and ceiling.

I went to Amy's room to show her the gown. She came forward, carefully touching the sparkling sequins as her eyes grew wide and excited.

"I want a dress just like this when I grow up," she said spontaneously.

Jenny's eyes flew wide at hearing the little girl speak and she looked immediately to me.

"Miss Elizabeth!" she cried. "Did you hear that?"

"Yes, Jenny," I said with a smile. "I heard. She has been speaking little by little and tomorrow we had planned to surprise her father and great-grandmother with the news."

"Oh," Jenny whispered with a sparkle in her eye. "How exciting. Then I will say nothing."

"Thank you, Jenny," I said, feeling a surge of relief.

I told Amy goodnight and reminded her not to stay too long watching the dancers. Then I left and with a racing heart made my way down the grand staircase.

As I expected, Derek and Mrs. Vanderworth, along with Diana, were at the doorway, greeting guests. When I stepped onto the marble floor, Derek turned almost instinctively toward me. The look in his eyes made me feel breathless and weak. Then he came toward me as if he were drawn by some unknown force.

As Mrs. Vanderworth and Diana both watched, Derek took my hand and turned me slowly around. He watched me all the while with a slow, seductive smile. He frowned a slight, teasing frown

263

and placed his hand over his heart.

"You are so beautiful, my love," he whispered, "that you fairly stop my heart."

I laughed at his foolishness, feeling as carefree and happy as a child. "Why, Your Lordship, I had no idea the English were so romantic."

He laughed, too, and with a gleam in his eye, continued to tease me. "Tell me, my little bookworm, how is your Latin?" He bent close to my ear as he spoke.

"Quite good, actually," I said with a grin.

"Then interpret this . . . *mirabile visu.*" His gaze held mine in a dark, sparkling intensity that made me feel as if I had just been kissed.

"Wonderful . . . to behold," I said in a whisper as I felt myself grow weak under his intimate gaze.

"Very good," he said in a low, husky voice. "And you certainly are wonderful to behold. Shall we join the party?"

He led me down the hallway, completely ignoring Mrs. Vanderworth, who still greeted the guests. "Derek . . ." she called. "Derek . . . where . . . where are you going? Our guests . . ."

He waved his hand back at her, still smiling down at me as he pulled me close and took me along with him. "Later, Grandmother."

I glanced back over my shoulder toward the doorway. I could feel the heat of Diana's glaring looks. It was almost as if she hated me, and I could not suppress a shiver of apprehension that ran through me, like the odd, uneasy feeling I had earlier today. I so hoped Diana was not going to spoil the evening for us all.

But as soon as we entered the ballroom, my worries vanished completely. It was one of the rooms I'd never been in, and I could never have imagined the grandeur of it. The ceiling rose two stories above us with great, round chandeliers that hung suspended from

264

heavy chains much like the one in the grand stairwell. Huge, cavernous fireplaces at each end of the room looked as if they could each hold a small tree trunk. I'd never seen anything like it, not even in all the travel books I had devoured.

In the windows high above the dance floor, I could see the flicker of lightning. Another stormy night, it seemed, was in store. I tried not to think of the last ball here in this room or of the last storm.

There must have been over two hundred people milling about and dancing. The music was so lovely it was impossible to feel melancholy, and I soon found myself laughing and dancing. In Derek's arms I forgot everything except the moment and the night with him.

We both danced with other people, I with the Reverend Webster and some of the guests I had become acquainted with over the past few weeks.

Later I saw Derek dancing with Diana, and then with his grandmother. I also noted that many of the young women present could hardly keep their eyes away from his tall, masculine form as he swung various partners about the room.

I saw Charles enter arm-in-arm with Mrs. Hunt. She looked beautiful! And she was clinging to Charles and smiling up at him as if he were the only person with her in the room.

Charles saw me and waved gaily, motioning with his eyes that I should take note of his companion. As I started to go to him, he took her in his arms and began to swing her about the floor. Oh, well, I could afford to give them a few moments' privacy.

The evening was passing so quickly and I could not seem to get Charles alone. Finally, as I danced with one of the guests, I passed close to Charles and Mrs. Hunt. She smiled at me as if we had always been the best of friends.

"Charles . . ." I shouted above the noise. "Charles, I

need to speak to you for a moment."

"Next dance, love," he said breezily as he whirled her away. "Next dance."

I nodded and continued to dance.

The storm had grown progressively worse, and the small electric bulbs in the chandeliers flickered sporadically. Even in the huge depths of the room we could hear the loud boom of the thunder as the storm raged about the house.

The servants began to carry in large standing candelabra in case the electricity should be lost during the storm. It even seemed to make the evening more exciting as everyone laughed, feeling secure inside the great chateau.

It was nearing midnight. If I wanted to speak to Charles, I needed to do it before the evening ended. I managed to catch his eye and motion him toward the door. Then I walked out into the hallway around the Palm Court for a breath of fresh air as I waited for him.

I strolled casually around the railed court when suddenly I heard voices, muffled and sounding a bit frantic. I stopped, looking about. They came from within the Palm Court in the shadows of a towering palm. Puzzled at the tone of the voices, I moved closer only to see Reverend Webster and Ruthie.

I recalled this morning and the last time I'd seen her. She'd been speaking to James then. And now it struck me as very odd that they were together again and she was just as agitated as before.

I could not hear their words and did not even want to, so I walked back toward the ballroom. Just at that moment, Charles came out and caught my arm.

His exuberance was contagious and it made me happy to see him in such high spirits for once. I was certain the exotic Mrs. Hunt, who had been in his arms most of the evening, was the reason.

"Now, love," he said gaily. "What is it you wish to speak to me about?"

I pulled him down the hallway, away from the noise of the dance. We sat on a long marble bench in a quiet, sheltered alcove.

When I told him Amy could speak, his first response was elation. But as I began to relate what she had told me about the night her mother had died, his face turned pale and he looked at me with an incredible expression.

"Wait a minute, now," he said slowly. "What are you saying? Are you saying Amy told you that *I* was the man with Desiree when she died?"

"Well, no . . . she wasn't certain who it was. But I assumed, after what you told me about you and Desiree . . ."

"Oh, my God," he said suddenly, glancing around us. "Where's Derek? We must find Derek right away."

Just as we stood up there was a crash of thunder that seemed to shake the very foundation of the house. The lights in the hallway flickered and faded away. I could not stop the cry that escaped my throat. It was completely dark except for the occasional flash of lightning through the glass dome of the Palm Court. And the intermittent flickering only made everything look strange and unearthly. It certainly was not good enough to see by.

We could hear the chorus of voices from the ballroom, most of them good spirited. There were little shrieks mingled with the muffled bass voices of the men. Then there was laughter as the candles were lit and the orchestra began to play again.

The shadow of a woman rushed past us. She seemed frightened as she ran into the ballroom. In the flickering candlelight I saw that it was Ruthie.

"Come on," Charles said, grabbing my arm. "We have to find Derek."

"Charles, what is it? What are you talking about? Do you mean the man with Desiree that night was not you?"

"That's *exactly* what I mean, love," he said, tugging at my arm. "Elyse . . . Mrs. Hunt has made a lot of things clear to me. And I think I know now who the man was."

"Not Derek!" I cried, stopping in my tracks and holding him back.

"No! God no, not Derek." He frowned at me as he dragged me through the crowd of people. He talked as we went. "I learned only yesterday that Desiree was seeing Webster as well as me. And who knows how many other men? Have you seen him tonight?"

I stopped dead still and looked at him in disbelief. "Webster?" I whispered. "The Reverend Webster and . . . and Desiree? Oh, Charles, what have I done?"

He turned to me and took both my shoulders as he looked worriedly down into my face. "What do you mean, Elizabeth? What?"

"This morning . . . on my carriage ride with Webster I . . . I told him about Amy. He said he would take care of everything. Oh, Charles, what are we to do?"

"Hope that he's still in the ballroom," he said, pulling me through the crowded dance floor as he scanned the faces around us.

"I just saw him," I said, remembering. "Moments before you came out in the hallway. He was in the Palm Court with Ruthie."

"Ah yes, Ruthie," he muttered. "Another of Webster's conquests, and a source of information, no doubt."

"No," I said, hardly able to believe what was happening. How could I have been so blind? But of course, it explained so many things. Webster was the man I'd heard with Ruthie that night in the stairway . . . the one who'd coaxed her upstairs, the man who'd spoken so crudely. Of course, she had laughed and said something about a man like him speaking that way. Had I actually worried for a moment that it might have been Derek?

"Charles!" I said suddenly. "Webster thinks Amy can identify him. We have to go to her!"

"Exactly, as soon as we find Derek." Frantically he pushed his way through the couples as he began to shout his cousin's name.

We waded into the crowd of people, uncaring of the astonished stares around us. And they could not have been more astonished than Derek when he came to us, frowning at us as if we'd lost our minds.

But Charles gave him little time to protest. He grabbed Derek's arm and pulled him toward the door. "Come on. We'll explain on the way."

To his credit, Derek did not waste time asking questions. He seemed to know right away that the situation was serious as he followed us back into the hallway and toward the stairs.

We were all breathless by the time we reached the second floor, especially Charles, who had blurted out practically the whole story as we ran.

We paused only a second at the top of the stairs. But it was long enough for me to see Derek's expression of pained disbelief as he looked at me. Then without a word he ran toward Amy's room.

My heart sank as we gazed over Derek's shoulder into the room. Amy was not there. Her bed was empty.

"Oh, no," I said, almost crying aloud as I glanced frantically about the room.

Derek turned to me for only the briefest moment. But I will never forget the look I saw on his face. It was as if all the light had vanished from his beautiful

269

amber eyes, as if nothing but pain would ever appear there again.

"Derek . . ." I whispered helplessly as tears flooded my eyes. "I'm sorry . . . I should have told you. But I . . ."

"But you couldn't quite bring yourself to trust me. Is that it?" His words were hard and cold, meant to wound. But they could not begin to relay the guilt I was already feeling myself.

"No, darling," I cried wanting desperately for him to believe me. "No, I thought it was Charles and I . . ."

"We're wasting time," he said, turning his back on me. "If Webster has her, I think I know where they are."

As we ran through the sitting hall, the lights flickered once and went back out. Derek paused long enough to whisk one of the lighted candles from a stand in the hall, then ran down toward the back stairway.

We ran almost blindly up the stairwell to the fourth floor, none of us saying anything, but only intent on getting there as quickly as possible. When we reached the top of the stairs I saw the long, black hallway stretching before us and heard a sound that made my blood turn to ice.

Chapter Twenty-seven

"Mimi! Mimi!" The voice was Amy's, and she sounded terrified.

Thunder cracked and lightning simultaneously split the dark skies outside. Amy screamed and cried even more frightfully.

"Oh God, please . . ." Derek's pleading, whispered words sent chills down my spine.

He held the candle above him and moved to the right of the hallway, where the balconies were. I picked up the voluminous skirts of my gown and followed him.

One of the glass doors stood open; the long white curtains flew out into the hallway like some ghostly apparition. Wind and rain blew freely into the house.

The sight on the balcony stopped all three of us in our tracks. The lightning now was so constant that it provided enough light to see. Derek threw the useless candle away from him, its flame extinguished by the rain.

"Webster, so help me, if you hurt her . . ." Derek's words were a low growl as he faced the man who held Amy up near the balcony railing.

"I don't want to hurt her," James said. There was genuine panic in his voice, and the flickering lights illuminated the same emotion in his eyes. We could see the whites of his eyes clearly as they darted about frantically.

"I never intended to hurt her," he screamed above the din of the storm. "I only wanted to talk to her . . . make sure she never told what she saw that night."

"She didn't see anything, James," I said. "Please, don't hurt her."

Amy held her little ragged bear in her arms. They were both soaking wet, and her hair clung to her head in wet rivulets.

"Please, James," I pleaded. "Let us take her inside. She's going to be sick."

"No," he said, his voice muffled by the winds. "I can't do that. I have to get away from here. There's no way you'll let me go if she's not with me."

"Yes there is," Derek said calmly, his voice strong and steady. "You have my word. Just put Amy down and I promise we'll let you walk away from here."

Derek took a step forward and moved his hand slightly toward the man.

"Stay away!" James said, raising Amy higher in his arms. Amy screamed again and began to squirm.

"All right, Webster. All right," Derek said soothingly. "I won't come any closer. Just let her go."

"Daddy," Amy cried.

"It's all right, sweetheart," Derek said softly. "He's not going to hurt you, Amy." I thought his voice seemed to calm her somewhat.

"Mimi," she said, moving her hand over the edge of the balcony.

I think all of us held our breath at that little gesture. What did she mean by it? Had the woman she called Mimi already fallen to her death?

"Where, sweetheart?" Derek asked. I could hardly believe the calming patience in his voice.

Amy turned her head toward the building. When I saw the wet, bedraggled figure on the ledge away from the balcony, I actually felt faint. How she continued to cling to the wet stones of the house with the wind and rain buffeting her was beyond all understanding.

"My God," Charles murmured.

"The old woman went crazy," James said with fright. "When I tried to speak to Amy, she just went berserk. I tried to calm her, but she was uncontrollable. She climbed over the rail before I could stop her."

"She's sick, Webster," Derek said menacingly. "Let me get her. Or do you want to compound things by having another death on your hands?"

"I didn't kill Desiree, Derek, I swear it! I know how it sounds, but you must believe me! I admit I was here with her that night. But she was drunk; you know that. She tried to provoke me any way she could, taunt me about other men."

"I don't care about that now," Derek said. "Just let me . . ."

"No . . . no! You're only trying to trick me. You still don't believe me."

"Let him talk, Derek," Charles said.

Derek nodded while all of us stood in the soaking rain, hoping that the frail old woman could hold on for a few minutes more while James explained.

"When I confronted Desiree about her relationship with Charles, she only laughed. She said she had used Charles to get at you and that it had worked."

I glanced at Charles. A muscle twitched in his jaw, and he looked as if he could kill James Webster with his bare hands.

"She began taunting me, singing and dancing. Then she climbed up onto the rail, laughing because it frightened me so. She said I was weak . . . that all men were weak. And when . . . when she began to fall, God help me, I couldn't get to her in time." James began to weep as he bent over in despair. All the terror of that night came back to him, and he sobbed his grief into the rain-filled night.

I knew he was telling the truth.

273

He fell to his knees, a pitiful, broken man, a man who had allowed a woman to bring him crashing from his spiritual pedestal. As he fell, he released Amy from his arms and she ran straight for her daddy, flinging herself wildly at him. I heard Derek's choked laughter as he held her close and whispered her name again and again as if in prayerful gratitude.

Charles stepped forward and grasped Webster by the collar, dragging him into the hallway. Derek and I were left to focus our attention on the poor woman still on the ledge.

Derek gently placed Amy in my arms and stepped to the balcony railing, holding his hand toward the woman. She was not more than two steps away from him; he could have reached out and touched her. But when she saw him there, she began to shriek hysterically.

"No needles! No needles!" she screamed.

Derek stopped immediately and stepped back, fearful that in her agitation she might fall to her death.

"All right, Mimi, no needles," he said. "Don't worry, no one is going to hurt you."

Still she continued to scream loudly and cry as she clung to the wet stones of the house.

"Let me try," I said to Derek. He stepped aside and I moved closer with Amy still in my arms, close enough so that the woman could see the little girl. But I made no further move toward her.

"Say something to her, Amy," I said. "Show her Bo Bear and ask if she would like to come inside and play."

Immediately Amy responded, holding the bear toward the woman on the ledge. "Bo Bear?" she said to the woman. "Mimi want to play with Bo Bear?"

The woman quieted and turned her sad, drooping eyes toward us. The storm was passing and the soft flicker of lightning lit her face, showing a quiet, childish smile as she looked at Amy.

I saw then that she was old. The hair that I'd thought was blond was actually gray, and it hung now in wet strings down her shoulders. She was only a haggard old woman. Not a ghost or a frightening spirit, but merely a pathetically sick old woman.

Amy was shivering. I put her down out of the wind, just so Mimi could still see her. Tentatively I moved to the balcony. My arms were not as long as Derek's and I could not reach her over the railing. If I intended to help her, I would have to climb over the balcony.

With a sickening lurch in my chest, I looked down, seeing the glitter of the wet, grassy ground as lightning illuminated the meadow and treetops far, far below me. I moved back, feeling dizzy and sick. I took a long, deep shuddering breath and focused all my attention on the woman. Then carefully I slid up on the balcony railing, moving awkwardly because of the expansive folds of my dress. As I leaned toward the woman, I felt a quick tingle of panic race through me. I was hanging over empty space and I knew if I grabbed her and she began to fall I would go with her.

I leaned back against the wall and gasped for breath. I felt as if I were dying. I could not do it, I simply could not.

Then I felt Derek's hand reach out and grasp mine. It was solid and warm, and it felt to me like life itself. I knew then that nothing or no one would be able to pull me from his arms and I felt safe. With my other hand I reached to take Mimi's hand. And with slow shuffling steps she moved along the ledge toward me until I could help her back over the railing and onto the balcony.

If I had not been so terrified, I would have laughed as Mimi turned to Amy and took her hand. She behaved as if nothing had happened, as if what we had just witnessed was perfectly normal. I watched in as-

tonishment as she turned and led Amy down the hallway toward her room.

It was only then I noticed the lights inside the house
burning again.

With a sickening relief I turned to Derek. He
opened his arms and I practically fell into them. I did
not bother to try and explain anything or to tell him
how sorry I was. For even though he held me, I felt a
reluctance in him to talk about what he must consider
my betrayal.

I could only hope for a chance to explain later.
Charles had already taken James downstairs. Derek
and I walked down the end of the hall to Mimi's room.
We watched from the doorway as Amy played with the
old woman. Both of them were wet and cold, but it
seemed not to matter to them at all. They were lost in
their childish game.

"Amy," Derek said. "I think you need to take a warm
bath now and go to bed."

Without a word of protest, she got up and came
with a big smile to her daddy. I think she knew finally
that her father had never really abandoned her, or at
least I hoped so. But there was no doubt he had res-
cued her tonight.

Amy was in Derek's arms. I smiled at them both
and caressed Amy's wet, curly hair.

"Don't go," Mimi whined from across the room.
"Mommy's baby. Don't go, Desie."

I looked at her with a start, realizing for the first
time who the woman was and why she had looked so
familiar to me. Her features, though older, were exactly like those in the picture downstairs, the one of
Desiree Vanderworth. I turned and saw the acknowledgment in Derek's watchful eyes.

"She's Desiree's mother?" I asked breathlessly.

"Yes," he said quietly. "Desiree, for all her selfish-
ness, loved her mother dearly. The woman has been in

one institution after another for the past few years. Desiree brought her secretly to Stormhaven and hid her away up here. She even brought Olivia to take care of her. But of course I found out about it; she could never hide much from me.

"I didn't like it; didn't like the idea of keeping the poor woman locked away secretly. And then there was the business of her escaping to the floors below. It was an impossible situation. And Mimi adored Amy, and after Desiree's death, she seemed obsessed with finding her, thinking she was her own daughter."

"And so the story of the ghostly spirit that wandered the halls on stormy nights," I said with growing understanding.

"Mimi was terrified of storms," he said with a grimace. "And as you can see, storms here are not that uncommon."

He looked at Mimi, who had settled herself on the bed and was looking at the floor. "I wanted to have her put back into a sanitarium after Desiree's death. God help me, but I even wondered if she might have been somehow responsible for what happened. I was frightened for Amy to be with her, terrified that she would come for Amy some night and harm her. That was one of the things my wife and I often quarreled about, the safety of our child around Mimi." His eyes had grown dark and pain-filled, haunted by his own private memories.

"But then there was Diana," I said, finishing for him.

He glanced at me with the merest hint of surprise. "Oh yes, Diana. I could hardly take her mother away from her after she'd just lost a sister. She needed to have her family, such as it was, here with her."

"You're a very nice man, Derek Vanderworth," I said, seeing him in a new light.

He made a soft little sound of derision.

"Derek . . ." I began. "I want to explain, to tell you . . ."

"No," he said firmly, his eyes filled with hurt again. "Not tonight. I need to get Amy to bed."

We stood looking at one another for a long moment before he glanced away.

Before we left, Amy handed her ragged old bear to Mimi, who clutched it to her breasts with glee. Then she lay on the bed, cuddling the bear to her.

"I'll send Olivia up to change her wet clothes and put her to bed," Derek said as we left.

We concentrated on talking only to Amy as we went back downstairs. She was a sensitive child; her reaction to the trauma of her mother's death proved that. And I think we both wondered how this night would affect her.

Charles, Mrs. Vanderworth, and Diana were all waiting for us in the sitting hall. As Jenny took Amy to give her a warm bath, Derek and Charles faced one another.

I'm not certain who made the first movement. At first it was only a handshake, then they were clasping each other's shoulders and embracing. I wanted to laugh, to cry at the sight of them. I was certain from my conversations with Charles that he needed his cousin, and now I could see for myself that Derek also needed him.

Mrs. Vanderworth put her arms about the two of them. She was crying as she spoke, her voice only a tremulous whisper.

"My darling grandsons. I'm so sorry that all this has happened in your young lives. But the good that has come of it is that you're together again. Now we must all put it behind us."

Then she came to me. "You're trembling, child. Why don't we let the three of you go to your rooms and change. I'll have some hot coffee sent up. There will be plenty of time to talk in the morning."

Derek and I looked into each other's eyes for only a moment. His resentment was still there. Then he turned and went across to his room. Diana followed, offering her help if he needed her. I would have thought her actions laughable if I had not been so certain I had lost him.

Charles stepped to my side and embraced me quickly, whispering as he did. "Don't worry, love. He'll come around. You've done nothing wrong."

"Then why do I feel so miserable?" I asked.

"Because you're a sweet, sensitive girl who wouldn't harm a fly." Then he smiled at me and turned me toward my room. "Go . . . take a warm bath. Do you need any help, love?"

I laughed aloud then, happy in knowing that whatever happened, Charles would still be his outrageous, carefree self.

But long after my bath, even after feeling warm and exhausted, I could not sleep. Every time I closed my eyes I could see the steep walls of the house as they dropped away below me. I seemed to still hear the wind and actually smell and taste the rain. I huddled beneath the covers, wondering if I would ever be able to erase the frightening memories from my mind.

I could not stop thinking of Desiree Vanderworth, a woman I had never known, yet one who had been such a factor in my life. Derek's guilt over his dead wife, regardless of her own behavior, had caused both of us pain, and I wondered if we would ever be able to get past that.

I'd known of Charles's guilty feelings almost from the beginning. And now there was yet another man who felt guilt for her death . . . poor James Webster, the pious minister with a secret life. He'd had many women, it seemed, but this time he had chosen the wrong one. And Desiree's fatal attraction had no

279

doubt ruined his life.

And as I thought about Desiree and Mimi, I thought perhaps the daughter had inherited her mother's madness.

Finally I threw the sheets back and pulled a robe from the foot of my bed. It was almost dawn when I stepped quietly across the hall and opened Amy's door.

The lamp beside her bed burned dimly in the room, reflecting upon the soft blond curls of the sleeping child. But another sight caught my eye and completely captured my attention.

Derek was beside the bed, slumped down in an overstuffed chair. He wore a robe, and I could see the soft collar of his shirt about his tanned neck and chin. He slept quietly, peacefully, and I thought his face looked very young and sweet, serene at last. There was no coldness in him now, no attempt to appear remote and detached. I had seen the pain in his eyes last night when he thought he might lose his little girl and I had seen the overwhelming joy when she'd run to his arms. He would never be able to fool me again.

With a sigh I closed the door.

"Thank you, God," I said quietly. I loved them both so much and was so thankful they were safe.

Then I went back to my room, fell into bed, and slept peacefully until noon the next day.

Chapter Twenty-eight

As I ate a late breakfast in my room someone knocked at the door. Opening it, I was surprised to find that my first visitor of the day was Diana.

There was fire in her blue eyes that morning, and she did not mince words.

"I want you out of here, Miss Stevens."

My eyes flew open at her bluntness. "Well," I said slowly. "At least you're honest."

"Yes, and to be even more honest, I feel you've interfered quite enough with this family. You've hurt Derek and caused him to almost lose Amy. He's been through enough with my own sister, and I won't tolerate any more!"

"I know I've hurt him," I admitted. I could not keep my lips from trembling as I remembered the hurt I'd seen in his eyes. "But it's the last thing I ever intended, you must believe that. I love him, Diana."

She gave a little grunt and stared straight into my eyes. "Well, he will never love you! And if you really care about him, you can prove it by packing your things and leaving without causing him any more grief."

"Has he told you that?" I asked. "That he wants me to go?"

"Oh, Derek would never send you packing, or even ask you nicely to leave. He's much too decent, too

281

kind for that. Besides, I'm sure he feels obligated to you because of Amy."

I frowned at her. Was she right? After all, she had known him much longer than I. And so many of my feelings about him were purely instinctive . . . perhaps even wishful thinking. Maybe I had dreamed up all these fairy-tale images of us together when all he had meant was kindness.

"Perhaps you're right," I said quietly, turning to hide the tears.

"Diana," a deep voice said from the doorway. "Why don't you let Elizabeth and me make our own decisions?"

"Derek!" she exclaimed. "I . . . I thought you were still in bed."

"Obviously," he said with a wry twist of his mouth. "Now, if you'll excuse us, there are things I need to discuss with Elizabeth."

Diana hesitated, and I knew she would like to argue the point, but with a last resentful glance at me, she left.

"We need to talk," Derek said, not making a move toward me.

"Yes, I know." I could not take my eyes from his face, his handsome face with those brilliant amber eyes that could seem to look right through you.

"I know what you must think of me," I said, hoping to make a beginning. I hardly knew how I was to explain. It had all seemed so logical before.

"No, you don't. You can't possibly know what I think." But despite his words, his voice was soft and wistful, filled with a sweetness I had not heard before.

"I wish you would tell me," I said.

He smiled and reached forward to run his hand down the side of my cheek. "I think you are the kindest, most caring woman I've ever known. I've watched you these past few weeks . . . sometimes with great doubt, I admit. But I just could not believe there was someone like you on this earth."

My face grew warm at his words and his riveting gaze.

"I . . . I should have told you right away. It all sounds so feeble now. But I . . ."

"You were, as usual, trying to protect someone, trying to spare someone's feelings. The little fixer. Am I right?"

I nodded, almost breathless with disbelief at the change in him. His coldness had completely vanished. And the light in his golden eyes fascinated me and lulled me into near speechlessness.

"And was that someone me?" he asked, moving to stand only inches from me.

"Yes," I whispered. "And Charles. I had no idea that James was involved with . . . with . . ."

"With Desiree," he said firmly. "You can say it, love. Her behavior doesn't hurt me any longer."

"But I trusted James! I was so gullible. If I hadn't told him everything . . ." I turned away, unable to face the man whose daughter I had put in jeopardy. "If anything had happened to Amy . . ."

"Sweetheart, that is exactly the way I've felt this past year . . . guilt-ridden. You helped me through that. Now don't *you* do it, too."

I looked at him, frowning. He was right.

"We all make mistakes, sweetheart," he said. "God knows I've made my share and then some. I believe James and I don't think he was responsible for Desiree falling from that balcony. I know how wild and strange she could be at times, and she was drunk that night. It was only a tragic accident. And I don't think he would ever have harmed Amy."

"Please believe me, Derek, I will never keep anything from you again."

He smiled down at me and put his hands about my

waist. "Good," he said. "Now I want you to repeat what you told Diana before I came in just now."

"That she was right . . . that you were too kind to . . . ?"

"No, before that," he said softly as he pulled me close against him. "Something about love, I believe?"

I looked at him in astonishment. He had heard me declaring my love for him, not in the romantic way I had dreamed of, but like some lovestruck schoolgirl. How foolish he must think I was.

I turned away, unable to face his teasing eyes. I placed my cool hands upon my burning cheeks. Derek's hands slid beneath my elbows and he turned me back to face him.

"Tell me."

My eyes were so filled with tears that his face wavered before me. But I couldn't mistake the look on his face. There was no mockery, no censure. There was only a sweet tenderness and a questioning look in his tigerlike eyes as he waited for my reply.

"Yes," I whispered. "I do love you. I told you before."

"And nothing's changed? You still feel the same?"

"Yes," I said quickly. "Of course I do. I'll never love anyone but you, Derek."

With a soft grunt of delight he swept me up into his arms and whirled me around, finally setting me back on my feet. I was breathless with happiness.

"I can hardly believe my luck," he said with a sigh of pleasure. "That a woman like you could love someone like me."

I looked at him as if he'd lost his mind. "Don't you have that backwards?" I asked blankly.

"No," he whispered, kissing me sweetly and gently. "I have it exactly right. I love you, Elizabeth Stevens. I adore you. That first day in Amy's room when you defied me, you were practically spitting fire in defense of a little girl you didn't even know. I had never met anyone with such enthusiasm for life and living. And against all my defenses, I found myself falling in love with you at every turn."

"I . . . I don't know what to say," I said, still shocked beyond belief that this beautiful man, a man who could have had any woman on earth, was in love with me and felt himself lucky.

"Say that you love me beyond all possible understanding; say that you cannot live without me. Say you will marry me," he urged fiercely, kissing me again until I could hardly breathe.

I stood on tiptoe and placed my hands behind his neck, then pulled his head down and slowly touched my lips to his.

"I love you beyond all possible understanding," I whispered against his lips.

He groaned and bent to kiss me again.

"I cannot live without you," I whispered, repeating his words and smiling at his teasing groans of pleasure as I kept my lips near his.

"But marry you? Well hummm . . . yes, I suppose I could do that."

He laughed with delight and picked me up again, whirling me around until we were both dizzy.

"I want you to show me the world," he said as he set me down.

I frowned at him, laughing at the same time at his boyish exuberance and his obvious joy. "What?" I asked.

"I want to see everything again through your sweet, optimistic eyes. I want to see Paris, New York, the Isle of Cyprus, and the ruins of Rome. I saw it before through vision that was jaded and unappreciative, and now I want to see it with you. And I want to take you to England as Countess of Chesham to show you our home there."

I was speechless. Imagine me, the little servant girl from the mountains of Georgia, a countess! But I knew that Derek Vanderworth was my real treasure; a title and riches was nothing compared to his love.

I was crying as he gently took my face between his hands and kissed the tears away. With him, how could I ever feel lonely or unloved again?

And I realized that all those feelings of loneliness and unworthiness were not exclusive to the poor. Derek Vanderworth, the Earl of Chesham, the owner of grand Stormhaven, had been just as lonely . . . felt just as unloved as I once had.

And I vowed on that beautiful summer day that he would never feel that way again, for as long as I had one breath of life in me, I would use it to tell him I loved him.

MORE THRILLING GOTHICS FROM ZEBRA BOOKS

THE MISTRESS OF MOONTIDE MANOR   (3100, $3.95)
by Lee Karr

Penniless and alone, Joellen was grateful for the opportunity to live in the infant resort of Atlantic City and work as a "printer's devil" in her uncle's shop. *But her uncle was dead when she arrived!*

Alone once more, she encountered the handsome entreprenuer Taylor Lorillard. Danger was everywhere, and ignoring the warning signs — veiled threats, glances, innuendos — she yearned to visit Moontide Manor and dance in Taylor's arms. But someone was following as she approached the moon-drenched mansion . . .

THE LOST HEIRESS OF HAWKSCLIFFE   (2896, $3.95)
by Joyce C. Ware

When Katherine McKenzie received an invitation to catalogue the Fabulous Ramsay oriental rug collection, she was thrilled she was respected as an expert in her chosen field.

It had been seven years since Charles Ramsay's mistress and heiress had mysteriously disappeared — and now it was time to declare her legally dead, and divide the spoils. But Katherine wasn't concerned; she was there to do a job. *Until* she saw a portrait of the infamous Roxlena, and saw on the heiress' finger the very ring that she herself had inherited from her own mysterious past.

THE WHISPERING WINDS OF
BLACKBRIAR BAY   (3319, $3.95)
by Lee Karr

Anna McKenzie fulfilled her father's last request by taking her little brother away from the rough gold mining town near City. Now an orphan, Anna travelled to meet her father's sister, whom he mentioned only when he was on his deathbed.

Anna's fears grew as the schooner *Tahoe* reached the remote cove at the foot of the dark, huge house high above the cliffs. The aunt was strange, threatening. And who was the midnight visitor, who was whispering in the dark hallways? Even the attentions of the handsome Lyle Delany couldn't keep her safe. For he too was being watched . . . and stalked.

Available wherever paperbacks are sold, or order direct from the Publisher. Send cover price plus 50¢ per copy for mailing and handling to Zebra Books, Dept. 3778, 475 Park Avenue South, New York, N.Y. 10016. Residents of New York and Tennessee must include sales tax. DO NOT SEND CASH. For a free Zebra/Pinnacle catalog please write to the above address.

A Memorable Collection of Regency Romances

BY ANTHEA MALCOLM AND VALERIE KING

THE COUNTERFEIT HEART   (3425, $3.95/$4.95)
by Anthea Malcolm
Nicola Crawford was hardly surprised when her cousin's betrothed disappeared on some mysterious quest. Anyone engaged to such an unromantic, but handsome man was bound to run off sooner or later. Nicola could never entrust her heart to such a conventional, but so deucedly handsome man. . . .

THE COURTING OF PHILIPPA   (2714, $3.95/$4.95)
by Anthea Malcolm
Miss Philippa was a very successful author of romantic novels. Thus she was chagrined to be snubbed by the handsome writer Henry Ashton whose own books she admired. And when she learned he considered love stories completely beneath his notice, she vowed to teach him a thing or two about the subject of love. . . .

THE WIDOW'S GAMBIT   (2357, $3.50/$4.50)
by Anthea Malcolm
The eldest of the orphaned Neville sisters needed a chaperone for a London season. So the ever-resourceful Livia added several years to her age, invented a deceased husband, and became the respectable Widow Royce. She was certain she'd never regret abandoning her girlhood until she met dashing Nicholas Warwick. . . .

A DARING WAGER   (2558, $3.95/$4.95)
by Valerie King
Ellie Dearborne's penchant for gaming had finally led her to ruin. It seemed like such a lark, wagering her devious cousin George that she would obtain the snuffboxes of three of society's most dashing peers in one month's time. She could easily succeed, too, were it not for that exasperating Lord Ravenworth. . . .

THE WILLFUL WIDOW   (3323, $3.95/$4.95)
by Valerie King
The lovely young widow, Mrs. Henrietta Harte, was not all inclined to pursue the sort of romantic folly the persistent King Brandish had in mind. She had to concentrate on marrying off her penniless sisters and managing her spendthrift mama. Surely Mr. Brandish could fit in with her plans somehow . . .

Available wherever paperbacks are sold, or order direct from the Publisher. Send cover price plus 50¢ per copy for mailing and handling to Zebra Books, Dept. 3778, 475 Park Avenue South, New York, N.Y. 10016. Residents of New York and Tennessee must include sales tax. DO NOT SEND CASH. For a free Zebra/ Pinnacle catalog please write to the above address.